Here's what critics are saying about
Barbara Valentin's books:

"A lighthearted and endearing blend of comedy, drama, and romance. Quick-moving and thoroughly delightful."
—*Publishers Weekly,* Starred Review

"Barbara Valentin delivers love, laughter, and a happily ever after—what more could you ask for?"
—Gemma Halliday, *New York Times* bestselling author

"*False Start* was such a wonderful romantic comedy and even though there isn't an ounce of steam in it. I completely loved it! 5 stars!"
—*Boundless Book Reviews*

"I had a hard time putting (*Help Wanted)* down. That's probably why I had no trouble reading it in two days! I'll also stubbornly admit that I got a little teary-eyed towards the end, and I absolutely loved the ending. It was the perfect finish and one of my favorite endings, hands down."
—*Chick Lit Central*

BOOKS BY BARBARA VALENTIN

Assignment: Romance books:

False Start

Help Wanted

Key Change

The Plate Spinner Chronicles
(a collection of "Plate Spinner" newspaper columns)

KEY CHANGE

an Assignment: Romance novel

Barbara Valentin

For Father Ray, an undo button pusher of the best sort.

CHAPTER ONE

———

"Music is my religion."
—Jimi Hendrix

Sara Cleff, music critic at the *Chicago Gazette*, used the undo feature on her laptop to reverse a bad edit she had just made on a concert review she was drafting—and wished for the thousandth time that life came with such a feature.

If only.

She could correct every mistake she ever made—even the one she tried to undo on her own. Ever the rebel, she set out to discredit that old adage about two wrongs not making a right.

And failed miserably.

Because she knew, as did all of the other girls who got *The Talk* from Sister Marcus, their terrifying eighth grade teacher at St. Xavier elementary, that what she did, even with 12 years of parochial education to her credit, was technically classified as a mortal sin. Not only did this mean instant excommunication from the church, she was painfully aware that her chance of gaining admittance to the pearly gates was pretty much on par with one of the Kardashians being accused of having talent.

Nobody's perfect.
What's done is done.
Move on.

Doing her best to pretend it had never happened, Sara locked the terrible memory away forever, telling no one, willing it from her mind. If only her conscience would get on board—then, maybe, she'd have a fighting chance of putting it behind her forever.

If only.

* * *

After barely making a packed train headed into the city, Claire Mendez burrowed between the crowds of fellow commuters and wedged herself between two burly blue-collar types, each taking up a seat and a half in the row next to the door.

Burly guy #1 had his eyes closed, apparently asleep, with his mouth hanging open.

Very attractive.

Burly guy #2 was staring at his smartphone. Despite the earbuds he had plugged into it, a bass beat echoed from his device. Reeking of some cheap aftershave she couldn't identify, he made no attempt to give her more room. Not even a smidge.

It's gonna be a long ride.

Only twelve weeks into her fifth pregnancy, Claire's baby bump was already starting to look more like a baby basketball. Her regular clothes were no longer an option. Instead, she wore whatever she could confiscate from her six-foot-three-inch husband's side of the closet. Today, she was sporting his Chicago Blackhawks red *home* sweater that hung on her otherwise slight frame like a dress under her open winter coat.

Comfort trumps fashion. It was her new mantra.

If only she had remembered how warm the sweater was. By the time she found a seat, she was hot, out of breath, and still irritated that her OB referred to her as being of *advanced maternal age.* She could almost picture the headline on the front page of the *National Enquirer. 37-year-old pregnant! Read shocking story on page 5!*

Pulling a little notebook and pen out of her coat pocket, she ran through her to-do list.

Put load of wash in the dryer. *Check.*

Send next week's column to editor. *Check.*

Load up Crock-Pot for dinner. *Check?*

She winced, wondering if she actually turned the Crock-Pot on after filling it with raw chicken and cream of mushroom soup, and scribbled, "Have key made for Jacquie Calderon." A trusted friend and neighbor of the Mendez family, Jacquie picked up Jonah, her youngest, from kindergarten and watched him on the afternoons Claire had to be in the office.

Pick up Paul's shirts from the dry cleaners. *Damn it. I knew I forgot something.*

Oh well, he'll just have to swing by and get them himself after work.

Yanking her laptop from her backpack, the *Chicago Gazette's* newest advice columnist for harried working parents, a.k.a. the Plate Spinner, opened her email inbox and got to work. She spotted four unread messages. The subject line of the first one read: *Can't Get Kids to Unplug.*

Chuckling, the mother of four boys started typing the first thing that sprang to mind. "And you want to *why*...?"

Deciding that the topic was too involved for her caffeine-starved brain to manage that early on a Monday morning, she deleted her curt response and moved on to the next message, the subject line of which was: What Were You Thinking? Her face pulled into a grimace. Clearly, this reader had an issue with one of Claire's earlier responses or the topic of an earlier column. It wasn't her first complaint letter, and she was sure it wouldn't be her last.

I'll deal with you later.

As the train leaned into a curve in the tracks, burly guy #2, the one with the bass-booming cell phone, smushed her up against burly guy #1, who was now snoring. She wondered if Dianne would ever let her work from home full-time instead of just a couple of days a week.

Redirecting her attention to her inbox, the third unopened email piqued her interest. The subject line read: *SOS, Boyfriend Wants to Get Married.*

While part of Claire's brain thought, "Huh, usually it's the other way around, but OK," the other part had a vague recollection of hearing this complaint before. Recently. She tried for a moment to retrieve the conversation but could only recall that she heard it while with a group. And that could've been anywhere—in one of her editor's team meetings, at lunch with work friends, at church, or at one of the boys' school events.

She stared at the screen for a moment longer before giving up and cursing her pregnancy-induced fog brain.

Dear Plate Spinner—
My boyfriend and I have three things in common: our
address, the fact that he's a musician, and I write about
musicians...

"Sara! It was Sara," Claire announced triumphantly to no
one in particular before continuing.

...and that we both agree Robert Plant is, hands down,
the best lead singer in rock music ever. Otherwise, we're total
opposites. He's quiet. I'm bold. He's short. I'm tall. He's British.
I'm not. He wants to get married and have kids. I so don't. How
can I get him to see that we would never be as happy and
carefree married-with-kids as we are right now just living
together?
Signed,
Dazed and Confused

Since getting to know the *Gazette's* rock music critic,
Claire knew that the words *erratic and brooding* would be a
much better descriptor for Sara's relationship with her boyfriend
than *happy and carefree.*
Taking some solace in knowing that her friend was not
interested in marrying a guy who, in Claire's opinion, was an
insecure mess, she wasn't confident in Sara's ability to hold him
off for much longer.
With that very thought in mind, the advice columnist had
no sooner typed, *Must ditch loser boyfriend and find a place of*
your own, when the train banked into its final curve before
pulling into the station, wedging Claire, again, between her two
seat neighbors. As soon as the train righted itself, she closed her
laptop, slipped it in her backpack, and hopped out of her seat and
onto the train platform. She then made her way to the Madison
Street exit to catch the #120 bus that would get her to the Gazette
Building in no time flat.
She had no sooner made it to her cube on the Features
floor than a colleague burst in and dropped into her visitor chair.
"What took you so long? I've been waiting for hours."

Claire glanced at her friend as she hung her coat on a plastic hook jutting out of the cube wall.

As far as looks were concerned, Sara Cleff had them in spades. At nearly six feet tall with large gray eyes offset by heavy, dark makeup, a short, dyed-black bob, and a bored expression that masked her runway-worthy features and deep dimples, she was often mistaken for a model.

Which might explain why, on spotting her in the audience, musicians tended to drop notes, lose rhythms, and forget lyrics. In short, she complained to Claire, they went all amateur on her.

While Sara liked to think that it was because of her sometimes eviscerating reviews, Claire kindly suggested that it might have more to do with her appearance.

"You make the rest of us females look like mere mortals," she reminded her friend.

But on that particular morning, Claire plunked in her own chair and laughed. "Hey, cut me some slack, huh? I had to get the kids off to school. Then Luke forgot his running shoes, so I had to go back and drop them off. He's got a big track meet over at Lane Tech this afternoon."

As soon as the words left her lips, a whisper of warning fluttered over Claire, just for a split second. She stopped, tilting her head as she tried to hear what it was saying, but the thought was gone.

Oh well.

Sara was wearing her infamous *you're-boring-me-to-death* look. "Whatever. Did you get my letter?"

"Yes." The advice columnist tucked her straight blonde hair behind her ears and glanced back at her computer screen, watching as it booted up. "Tell me, why did you bother writing when you know what I'm gonna say?"

After mulling over her response, the music critic shrugged. "Who knows? Maybe there's a woman out there like me, in the same situation, who might benefit from your infinite wisdom." She hunched her shoulders up and added, "It could happen."

Claire narrowed her eyes. "You're delusional. You know that, don't you? I can safely say there are no other women out there who are clinging to a dysfunctional relationship just so they can keep living in the apartment of their dreams." She cocked her head and looked into the distance. "Geez, at least I hope not."

Sinking back in her chair, Sara muttered. "I know. I know. I shouldn't keep leading him on."

"Exactly," Claire exclaimed. "You've got to tell him how you really feel, and be prepared to deal with the consequences. Or get your own place."

Sara raised both eyebrows and held out her hands expectantly in front of her. "Yeah, but where else am I going to find a huge one-bedroom apartment with so much character in such a high-end neighborhood? I've checked everywhere, Claire. It's one of a kind—especially at the price I'm paying."

The Plate Spinner leaned forward and clasped her friend's hand. "Which, I'm afraid, one of these days you're gonna realize is more than you can afford to lose, hon."

* * *

Andrew Benet, interim music director at St. Matthias, eased behind the organ console situated in a front corner of the church near the altar. The magnificent instrument had more buttons, knobs, and switches on it than the control panel of a 747. When he pressed his fingers against the keys, the notes squeaked out of the pipes at the back of the empty church at a much higher pitch than he expected. Lifting his hands, he flipped a switch, pulled a stopper, and tried it again.

Much better.

A few measures later, he was lost in the notes of Bach's *Sinfonia from Cantata 156* and the throbbing in his head finally started to dissipate.

Surely the day couldn't get any worse than it had started.

After a few more bars, he indulged in a chuckle, thinking of how old Father Kurtz had treated the congregation in attendance for that morning's 8:00 am mass to the sound of him whizzing in the men's room. Evidently, he had prematurely turned his microphone on. Thankfully, an usher tipped him off, but by then it was too late. Every single one of the students from the parish school in attendance had heard it. Valiantly trying to suppress their giggles, each looked like they'd just taken a swig of some unsweetened cranberry juice.

He imagined his little brother Sam, a newly minted officer on the Chicago Police Department and, like Andrew, a former altar boy, would get a good laugh out of it later but still.

"Andy."

He jumped.

Marge.

Not easily spooked, the sight of the stern elderly woman peering at him over the top of her reading glasses always put him on edge. Right from where he had been trying to get away.

He looked down at the volunteer sheet music librarian he had inherited from the previous music director who, rumor had it, apparently made off with the lead soprano a year earlier.

Wearing a sweatshirt that read, *What Happens at Grandma's Stays at Grandma's,* Marge looked like she was ready to take a swing at someone. Most likely him.

"So, did you think about it?" she snapped.

Frowning, he asked, "Think about what?"

"Asking Sharon out," she very nearly shrieked. "My niece? Remember? Now, like I said, she's a widow, not much to look at, but she can cook. No kids. She'd be perfect for you."

Andrew, still playing, gave his head a quick shake. "No thanks, Marge. Not interested."

With a huff, the woman walked behind the organ bench on her way to the choir room. "Fine," he heard her sputter behind his back. "Just don't come running to me when the rumors start flying."

Only there for a few months, he was still questioning his hasty retreat from his last parish, the Basilica of Saint Mary in Minneapolis, where everyone revered him.

That is, until he proposed to Leanne Thorsteinson high atop the Stone Arch Bridge at sunset.

Had she said yes, the pair would've been feted at a surprise engagement party thrown by close friends and relatives at the nearby Nicollet Island Pavilion.

Andrew stared at the keys in front of him, his thoughts darkening as he recalled the moment when she politely declined, citing her previously undisclosed intention to join the good Sisters of St. Joseph of Carondelet in St. Paul.

As she tearfully explained how she was waiting for the right time to tell him, all he could think was what a bad idea it was to propose on top of a bridge.

Or the best idea ever, depending on how you looked at it.

After that, the good parishioners of the Basilica couldn't seem to stop talking about how their esteemed assistant music director got turned down by the pretty parish preschool teacher.

Not a day went by when someone wasn't expressing their condolences to him, saying things like, "It's for the best," or "God works in mysterious ways."

You're telling me.

With a heavy sigh, Andrew lifted his hands off the keys and turned in her direction. "Rumors about what, Marge?"

The elderly woman turned. "Are you kidding? A good-looking guy like you, single? At your age?" She cocked an eyebrow. "People are starting to wonder."

Wonder what?

After a minute, it hit him.

Oh.

He waved her off. "Let 'em wonder."

Turning back to the hymn, he mumbled to himself, "My personal life is no one's business but my own." It was his new mantra, and he was sticking with it.

He started the Bach piece again from the top. Priding himself on never missing a note during Mass, ever, he wasn't about to start now.

A few minutes later, Marge emerged, her arms full of beaten-up, black, one-inch binders that were destined for the recycling bin. "These are goners."

Andrew kept playing. "Make sure they don't have any music in them."

"Of course." She sighed as she set them down on the seat normally occupied by first soprano Lorelei Healy and started flipping through them. "What about Carol Bingley's daughter? She's pretty enough. As far as I know, she's not seeing anyone."

Ignoring her until he finished the piece, Andrew slid off the organ bench. "Tell me, Marge. Do you work on commission?"

Marge looked confused.

Grabbing the binders she had already gone through, he dropped them onto a different chair and sat beside her. "It's not that I don't appreciate your effort. It's just that, well—" His mind scrambled to come up with a way to get this well-intentioned woman to stop playing matchmaker on his behalf. "Did you ever listen to a really magnificent performance? Ya know, the kind that makes the hairs on the back of your neck stand on end?"

Nodding, she replied, "Sure. I actually cried at the symphony once."

Relieved that she bit off on his faux reasoning, Andrew's face brightened.

Flush with confidence, he concluded, "If I ever find a woman who makes me feel like that, then I'll know she's the one for me."

So impressed by his ability to impart such an absurd notion with the utmost sincerity, he barely heard Marge mutter, "Because my shoes were killing me."

"Exactly."

After a few seconds, she squinted at him over her glasses. "You'll fall in love with the woman who makes your feet hurt?"

A laugh burst out of Andrew, and it echoed through the church. "What?"

Flustered, she spat out, "All that talk about hairs standing up on your neck or thunderbolts or whatever's supposed to mean love at first sight, it's all a myth. There's no such thing. Love grows over time. You just have to be open to it. Now about my niece, can I tell her to expect a phone call from you?"

Standing up, Andrew replied, "No, Marge. You cannot."

"I don't suppose it would help to mention that Sharon lives all alone in that great big house of hers."

"No, it wouldn't," he sighed as he bent to pick up a stack of broken binders.

"I just thought you might be wearing a hole in your brother's couch."

"As eager as I am to find a place of my own, I'm not about to enter into a relationship with a stranger just so I don't have to impose on my brother anymore."

The sheet music librarian joined him as he started down the aisle toward the exit, talking to herself. "She wouldn't be a stranger once you meet her."

While his brother hadn't complained once about Andrew crashing at his apartment, Andrew knew he never would. They'd been through too much together and got along just fine. And it wasn't like he wasn't saving up for the deposit he'd need to sign a lease. It was just taking a lot longer than he expected, that was all. Housing in Chicago wasn't cheap, not in the neighborhoods he was looking anyway. As such, he wasn't in the position to move out of his brother's yet, at least not until the parish extended him a permanent position. And on a day like today, he wasn't even sure he wanted them to.

* * *

Sara's sole ambition had always been to be a reporter. Well, that wasn't entirely true. Before she started working on her high school newspaper, she wanted to be a waitress, just like her mom had been at the Bay Shore Bar and Grill, adjacent to her family's marina.

However, once she saw her first story in print—a critique of the bands that performed at her high school's variety show— she was hooked. Without a journalism degree to her credit, she often went above and beyond to earn the distinction of being not just a reporter but also a respected journalist.

To that end, she had just submitted an unsolicited piece to her editor, Mike Teegan. Her ~~target~~ ~~victim~~ *subject* was megastar Ellie Klein who had, in Sara's not-so-humble opinion, just made a disastrous foray from hard-core country to pop. If the story didn't earn her the respect of one Daryl Swerl, the *Gazette's* reigning senior music critic, she figured she might as well pack her bags and move back to William's Cove to work at the family marina. And quite frankly she'd rather be strapped to a chair and forced to listen to opera for the rest of her life.

When she wasn't working, Sara's hobbies included selectively piecing together her eclectic wardrobe by trolling clearance sales up and down the Magnificent Mile or secondhand stores in the city's many ethnic neighborhoods. But her favorite form of entertainment involved an overinflated dose of workplace rivalry, two-for-one drink specials, large crowds, good friends, the kind you could embarrass yourself in front of and not live to regret it, and live-band karaoke contests.

Why that very weekend, despite the Sports section's recent attempt to steal the crown with a rousing rendition of an old Journey classic, the Features section ultimately prevailed after Sara's colleagues shoved her onstage where she delivered a jaw-dropping performance of the schmaltzy standard, "Because You Loved Me."

Good times. Good times indeed.

The memory of it was very much on her mind the following Monday morning when their managing editor called an emergency meeting. Squished into a not-big-enough conference room, the Features section reporters speculated on the reason behind it. Rumors had been circulating for weeks.

The paper is bleeding revenue.

Griffin Media is shopping the Gazette to potential buyers.

Layoffs are imminent.

Sara shifted in her seat and glanced at Mike Teegan, the Entertainment editor who was chatting with David Morse, a veteran food critic rumored to have just purchased a small mansion of a lake house in Benton Harbor, Michigan.

No wonder he looks as nervous as I feel.

Mike, however, was being his usual animated self. That he seemed to be avoiding eye contact with Sara, though, was odd. That he hadn't said boo about the article she had just submitted was worrisome. He had been her mentor ever since he discovered her writing for the *Williams Cove Courier* straight out of community college. Her coverage of the resort town's legendary lakefront concert series that year caught his attention after the *Milwaukee Sentinel* picked it up.

He would've told me if I was losing my job, wouldn't he?

At the time, all she had by way of a college education was a few college-level classes, but that didn't faze him in the least. He was more impressed that she was funding her tuition with winnings from open-mic-night donations and karaoke contest wins at the Bay Shore Bar and Grill than he was by the grade she got in Journalism 101.

Which was an A, thank you very much.

Mike offered her an internship straight away. Eager to escape the popular resort town in southern Wisconsin where she had grown up with her father and older brother, Sara grabbed the opportunity with both hands.

A few weeks later, she moved in with Jer Caravelli, an up-and-coming studio musician, who happened to live in an amazing vintage apartment on the near north side of the city that made her living quarters at the Uptown YMCA seem like a sparsely furnished broom closet.

Besides, given that his name was starting to appear on the credits of some decent new CDs, he was a thousand times more impressive than Jimmy Mabry, a hapless gearhead/garage band drummer she used to hang with back home in William's Cove and whom her older brother Kerry had threatened with extinction on more than one occasion.

And for good reason.

Maybe if Sara had seen Jimmy for the loser that he was, she wouldn't have accepted his invitation to join him under their pier at midnight where, after chugging back some syrupy liqueur, she gave it all away—her virginity, her virtue, and, after he shared the finer details with his buddies at the garage, her reputation.

Go me.

She bit the inside of her mouth and stared out the window.

How could I have been so stupid, so...?

"So," Dianne Devane, the managing editor, started as soon as she walked into the room. Peering into their faces, she said, "I'm not going to lie to you, kiddos. We're in trouble."

Sara blinked. She could barely afford her half of the rent as it was, and she was fairly sure Jer wouldn't be willing to float her yet another extension.

"We're going to have to figure out ways to maintain our journalistic excellence while cutting costs."

Here we go.

The managing editor stopped and placed both hands palm down on the table. "Not people."

Oh, thank God.

"So, here's what I propose." Standing up straight, she started walking the circumference of the room as she continued. "Cross-functional assignments."

Excuse me?

Smiling at their puzzled faces, Dianne airily explained. "First up, 'The Long Road from Garage to Grammy.'"

Sara pulled her eyebrows into a skeptical scowl and made no effort to change it when Dianne looked directly at her and pointed. "Sara."

"Yes?"

"Stop scowling. Wrinkles at your age are so unattractive."

Clenching her jaw, she raised an eyebrow and tried once again, in vain, to catch Mike's eye.

"That's better. Now, have you heard of a band called," she paused to check her notes, "Krypto Blight?"

Sara pressed her lips together before replying as politely as possible, "Of course. They're supposed to be the hottest band to come out of the Midwest since the Smashing Pumpkins."

Dianne looked at her for a minute, a slow smile creeping across her Clinique-covered lips. "That's right. They're about to launch a tour to promote their debut album. Midwest only. Seven cities in ten days, wrapping up here at the Aragon on the 16th. I want you to document their every move—well, not their every move but backstage, dressing rooms, who gets along and why, how they met, what makes them tick, get a sense for their staying power. You wanted a big break. Here's your chance. Make it count."

Next, she turned to the assistant food editor. "Nancy. I want a review of regional dishes, local chefs, and locally grown and produced cuisine for each stop along the way. Keep it seasonal, keep it topical."

"Would you please tell her it's still February?" she hissed under her breath to Sara.

Turning yet again, Dianne addressed the visibly nervous travel writer. "And Aubrey. Guess what? You're going along for the ride to uncover hidden destinations in each city. Diamond in the rough stuff. Antique markets, Amish settlements, winter festivals, toboggan runs, ice sculpture contests. You get the idea."

Dianne paused long enough to survey her baffled staffers before asking, "Sound good?"

Sara glanced at Aubrey who had turned at least two shades paler and Nancy who looked like she was about to say something but in a rare show of restraint appeared to have thought better of it.

Before any of them could respond, Dianne announced, "You leave tomorrow. Stop by Sheri Phelps's desk before you leave tonight. She'll have your itinerary and hotel information."

She peered down at the three women like a big game hunter who had just bagged a fresh kill before delivering her parting shot. "Use your cell phones for photos. Oh, and mileage reimbursement is only 25 cents on the dollar, so I suggest you all drive together."

* * *

"Are we there yet? I can't feel my feet."

Aubrey, who had selflessly agreed to sit in the very cramped backseat of Sara's sturdy little Honda for the first leg of the Krypto Blight tour hadn't complained once. Until now. According to the GPS they were just ten minutes away from the Davenport exit.

Sara, preoccupied with trying to dispel the nagging feeling that she forgot something, was busy running through an inventory of everything she had packed for the tenth time. Coming up empty again, she asked her travel companions, "So who are you guys bringing to Mattie and Nick's wedding?"

"I have to bring a date?" Aubrey practically whimpered from the backseat before asking for the third time if Sara's car had backseat side-impact air bags.

Nancy turned to face her. "Yeah, your plus one." Quiet for a moment, she exclaimed, "Hey. Maybe you can ask what's-his-name."

Sara glanced in her rearview mirror at Aubrey. She looked carsick. "You OK, Aubs?"

Aubrey met her gaze and nodded. Then she looked at Nancy. "Oh, I couldn't. He doesn't even know I exist."

Glancing at Nancy, Sara whispered, "Who are we talking about?"

"Malcolm Darvish."

"Who?"

"That guy in accounting? The one who has that *it's good to be me* air about him?"

"I have no idea who you're talking about."

"Oh, he's so perfect." Aubrey sighed from the backseat.

Nancy grimaced. "If you say so."

Sara smiled and stole another glance at the now dreamy-eyed Aubrey. "What do you like about him?"

Leaning back in her seat, the travel writer listed off her dream date's attributes. "He's handsome, dresses impeccably—"

Nancy chortled. "Yeah, if you can look beyond his squeaky, pointy-toed shoes and his pants that always look like they're too short." Looking at Sara, she added, "Maybe he's still growing."

Ignoring the interruption, Aubrey continued. "I hear he went to Harvard, and he just bought a condo in that new building over by the river."

Changing lanes to get around a semi, Sara asked, "Is he single?"

"I think so. He doesn't wear a ring." With a quick shiver, she nearly squealed. "I'd give anything to dance cheek-to-cheek with him. Just once."

"Then you should ask him, Aubs. What have you got to lose?"

Aubrey fell silent and stared out the window.

Glancing at her bold shotgun-seat passenger, Sara asked, "How about you, Nance?"

"Oh dear lord, it's not for what three more months? I've got plenty of time to find a date. So many to choose from, ya know?" At that, the associate food editor fell silent for a moment, then asked, "How about you Sara? Think *Jer* will join you?"

Her voice was dripping with sarcasm.

Sara drew a deep breath. The last place she wanted to invite the marriage-hungry musician was to a wedding, especially since Mattie, who used to write the *Plate Spinner* column before Claire came on board, asked her to be a bridesmaid. Not sure if either of her travel companions were asked, she didn't bring it up, but still the thought of being at the church, let alone a wedding reception, with Jer made her feel carsick.

Giving her head a quick shake, she replied, "Probably not."

"Oh, how come?" the ever-hopeful Aubrey piped from the backseat.

Sara glanced in the rearview mirror. "He's just not the dancing cheek-to-cheek type."

Nancy, who had announced as soon as she got in the car back in Chicago that she had spent much of the previous night researching restaurants and noteworthy (read: hot and single) chefs at each of their destinations with very limited success, squinted out the passenger side window at the gentle slopes of dormant, snow-covered farmland. With a sigh she announced, "Daphne's Corn Dogs, here we come."

As Sara flipped on her turn signal and curved into the slow winding descent onto US Route 61 southbound, it hit her.

I forgot to leave Jer a check for rent.

* * *

The interim music director at St. Matthias was having a horrible, awful, very bad day. First up, the printer sputtered its last toner-splotched breath just as he sent the master copy of that weekend's worship sheet to the print queue. While he was trying to get a repairperson on the line, the elementary school principal stopped by and just happened to mention that she switched the school book fair to that afternoon. If she had checked with him first (as he had asked her to do at least a dozen times already), she would've discovered that he had scheduled a make-up practice for the children's choir in the same space at the school.

By lunchtime, he wouldn't have been surprised if someone told him he had steam coming out of his ears like an angry cartoon character.

But his day wasn't over. He had to play at a funeral Mass that afternoon for a beloved teenager who had collapsed and died during a high school basketball game from an undiagnosed heart defect and, God help him, he had adult choir practice at 7:00.

And if someone called him "Andy" one more time, he was going to pack his bags and take the first flight to Nantucket to pursue a career in cod fishing.

In a huff, he started making his way down the hall from his office to the main reception area so he could ~~run away escape~~ go grab some lunch.

Just as he was about to grasp the door handle, Mrs. Gibbons, the receptionist who first took the job back when they still did duck-and-cover drills in the school, intercepted him. Holding her wrinkled hand over the phone receiver, she announced, "Father Steve would like to see you."

She mouthed, "Sorry," while pointing toward the Pastor's door.

Taking a deep breath, he turned and straightened his tie before making his way back down the hall.

"You wanted to see me, Father?"

The middle-aged Filipino priest, who tended to rub the more traditional, conservative members of the congregation the wrong way with his unannounced mid-Mass musical interpretations of the Gospel, waved him in.

"Take a seat, Andrew."

Sinking into the chair, one thought crossed the music director's mind. *If he fires me now, at least I won't have to hold choir practice tonight.*

Father Steve leaned back in his own chair and studied Andrew for a moment before asking, "So, tell me. How do you like it here, Andrew?"

Feeling his face jerk into a forced smile, he replied, "Oh, very much." He followed it with an unconvincing nod.

God forgive me for lying to a priest.

He resisted the urge to twist his face into a wince before asking, "Why do you ask?"

Father Steve drummed his fingers on his desk and narrowed his eyes, "I'll be honest with you..."

That makes one of us.

"...the parish board isn't convinced that we should extend your contract. There have been a number of complaints." He trailed off.

Andrew took a deep breath as the faces of his naysayers, many of whom were in choir, appeared before him. As if their disgruntled faces weren't enough, their whispers and grumbles spoke volumes.

He's too critical.

So rude.

No sense of humor

He works us too hard.

So irreverent.

He doesn't appreciate us.

Now that the grueling Christmas season was behind them, members were bailing on him faster than Protestants on a tour of the Vatican.

"Yes, I know my way of doing things is not what certain parishioners here are used to, but as far as the choir is concerned, with a little more time, I'm sure I can get them to see, well, *hear* the payoff for all of their hard work."

At that, the priest leaned forward. "For the record, I don't agree with the parish board, and I don't think I'm the only one. In case you haven't noticed, 10:00 am Mass—the one your choir sings at—is our most well-attended."

Picking up a little pink piece of paper, he waved it midair and announced, "And Bishop Kramer enjoyed their performance at Lessons and Carols on Christmas Eve so much that he's coming here to celebrate Easter Mass."

The priest's eyes suddenly seemed clouded with visions of overflowing collection baskets.

"Think you can get that choir of yours on board with your way of doing things by then?"

Andrew lifted an eyebrow and nodded. "Sure thing."

Again with the lies.

Father Steve stood. "Of course you will. I'm glad you're here, Andrew, but impressing the Bishop would go a long way toward convincing the parish board to offer you a permanent position. Know what I mean?"

Standing up, Andrew held out his hand. "Yes, I do, Father. Thanks for the heads up. I appreciate it."

So the meeting didn't go quite as he expected.

As they walked into the reception area together, Mrs. Gibbons announced, "Andy, a Mr. Danvers called."

Losing another tenor?

Looking at Father Steve, she explained. "He's in choir. My granddaughter went to school with his sister. As I recall, she was a scrappy little thing. Carried a little box of raisins with her wherever she went in case her blood sugar got too low."

Father Steve looked confused.

Andrew raised both eyebrows. "Message, Mrs. Gibbons? Did he leave a message?"

"Who?"

Forcing a tight smile, he prodded, "Mr. Danvers."

"Right. Yes." She held up her index finger as her cloudy brown eyes scanned the top of the desk for her message pad. "He said he's got a lead on an apartment for you."

Oh.

Locating said pad, she started tearing off the top sheet. "I wrote down the address. He said you should stop by today if you can because it won't be available for long."

She handed it to Andrew. "It's a sublet. Fully furnished. No deposit required."

CHAPTER TWO

———

"Hell is full of musical amateurs."
—George Bernard Shaw

After confirming with the landlord again that the tenant would not be returning to the apartment prior to the lease expiring, Andrew spent an entire day packing up a surprising amount of things that she had left behind. With his brother's help, he loaded up his Jeep and Sam's pickup. The woman's clothes, shoes, and toiletries went to a shelter for battered women. Anything else he didn't need or want went to Goodwill, save for a box of personal effects like photos and letters that he didn't feel quite right about throwing away.

Once everything was gone, he cleaned out the place top to bottom. The next day, he moved his things from Sam's house to his new home.

Home.

A place of his own. Things were definitely starting to look up for the guy who didn't get a very good start in life. He and his brother, just toddlers when their parents died, were bounced around a half-dozen foster families. It wasn't until they were placed in the home of Chuck and Arlene Benet that they felt truly safe. And loved. Unconditionally.

Arlene, a piano teacher, spotted Andrew's talent early on, and Chuck, a police officer, liked nothing more than having Sam ask him all about work and took him to visit the station often. Their already large brood of kids accepted them as if they were blood siblings.

When the boys had been with them for a few years, Chuck and Arlene sat them down and told them two things. First, that they loved them as much as their own children. Second, that they would very much like to adopt them. The memory of it still filled Andrew with a warm glow.

The boys went to court, changed their last name from *McGuigan* to *Benet,* and never looked back.

With the apartment finally arranged just the way he wanted it, Andrew suddenly couldn't wait for his family to come visit.

Maybe for Easter.

On his way out the door to return to the church for the dreaded adult choir practice, he took one last look around. The cranberry, tan, and ivory afghan one of his sisters had made for him as a going away present lay neatly folded across the back of the dark green couch in the living room, and the antique blanket chest he used to keep most of his stuff in served as a passable coffee table. A geometrically patterned area rug and several framed family photos dotting the hallway walls added to the homey feel.

He grabbed his wallet, keys, and shopping list from the kitchen's granite-topped counter, hoping he had the energy after practice to stock his pantry, fridge, and freezer, and locked the door behind him.

* * *

After spending ten very long days squeezed in her car and sharing some rather seedy hotel rooms with Aubrey and Nancy while documenting the sophomoric antics of the fame-hungry Krypto Blight band members on their whirlwind tour of the Midwest in hot spots like Rock Island, Dubuque, Eau Claire, Lafayette, and Florissant—none of which were included in her cell phone provider's network apparently—the last thing Sara wanted to do after dropping her travel companions off was attend the band's final show at the Aragon Ballroom. Yet there she was, concluding once again that their underwhelming stage presence and blatant lack of overall musicality were an affront to indie bands the world over. That she had drawn this conclusion after the first set of their first show on the tour made for one very long assignment.

No, she'd much rather be alone at home, indulging in a pint of ice cream or a bottle of Guinness—or both—followed by a long hot shower and a good couple of hours sleep in her nice comfy bed with the pillow-top mattress pad, butter soft flannel sheets, and perfectly firm but huggable pillows. A chronic insomniac, she relished those first few hours of nocturnal bliss she usually got before troubled dreams stirred her awake. Hence the heavy eye makeup she routinely wore.

Don't leave home without it.

As she drove, Sara's only hope was that Jer was still off at some gig and not too angry with her for not leaving a rent check behind.

It was odd though that she hadn't heard boo from him while she was on the road. The two texts she had sent since arriving back in Cook County went unanswered.

After scribbling a few lines in her notebook, she swiped her black bangs out of her eyes and scanned the crowd around her. A tight pack of fans standing near the stage, apparently tone-deaf, had their arms in the air and were bouncing to the beat while they chanted the lyrics with the band.

Friends and relatives, no doubt.

She couldn't imagine who else would pay to have their senses assaulted like sandpaper on silk. The rest of the crowd stood motionless, their faces reflecting a collective mixture of disappointment and confusion, like they were expecting the Rolling Stones and ended up with this sad excuse for entertainment.

Wanting evidence to bolster what was sure to be a controversial feature on the band, Sara snapped a shot of the disillusioned crowd on her way out.

Worth a thousand words.

* * *

"Come on, people. This isn't the first time you've heard this piece. Let's take it from the top. Everybody up."

Easter was just over six weeks away. With the Bishop presiding over Mass, the pressure was on to get the choir performance ready.

His eyes drifted above the sheet of music in front of him and focused on the stalwart members of the adult choir slowly rising out of their cushioned seats. Some were shaking their heads. Others exchanged exasperated glances with one another. The rest checked their watches or yawned.

Ranging in age from 25 to 87, the adult choir, made up entirely of volunteers, was lacking just one thing. Cohesion.

And enthusiasm.

OK, so two things.

If he had a dime for every time he had to remind them to stop trying to out sing each other, he could fill all of the collection baskets currently sitting empty in the usher's room off of the narthex.

Either they weren't listening or worse, didn't care. After all, why should they? It wasn't their job on the line. It was his.

He swallowed hard, thinking of the lease he had just signed on an apartment he had just sublet.

Far enough from the church so he wouldn't run into any parishioners on his days off, he fell in love with it as soon as he stepped foot in the fully furnished unit—especially the thick plaster walls, original wood moldings, built-ins, and hardwood floors, stained-glass accents in the front bay window, and best of all, the recently tuned upright piano in the living room.

"Ready? Here we go."

He pressed his fingers down on the piano keys and nodded his head, counting the beats. "One and two and—" He gave a sharp nod, signaling the sopranos and altos to start singing.

About half did. The other half started straggling in a beat or three later.

Andrew stopped playing. Several voices kept singing.

"Stop. Stop," he called out, waving his hands in the air.

Forty tired faces glowered back at him.

"Look, I want to get out of here as much as you do, so let's get it right the first time, shall we?"

More grumbling.

"Sopranos. Where should your eyes be?"

"On you," they droned.

"Really? Let's see if you remember that this time. And Altos."

More heads looked up from their music at him.

"Good job starting on time, but there's no need to scoop into the notes. Last I looked, we were in Chicago, not Nashville. Everybody ready?"

Much to Andrew's, and he was sure the entire choir's relief, the second time wasn't half bad.

After the hymn's last chord faded into silence, he looked up with a grateful smile. "That was almost perfect. So close. All right. Let's call it a night. Good job everybody. See you Sunday. Oh, and don't forget to get here by 9:30 so we can warm up before Mass starts."

Clearing the music rest on the grand piano, Andrew retrieved its quilted cover from the choir room and carefully arranged it over the flawless finish of its cabinet.

When he turned, he was startled to find Maureen Higgins, a soft-spoken and, as far as he knew, widowed first soprano, standing behind him.

Surprised anyone would still be speaking to him after that evening's especially contentious practice session, he braced himself. "Maureen. What can I do for you?"

She thrust a small plastic tub at him. "Here. Chicken stew and dumplings."

He fought back the urge to ask if the choir had put her up to it, suspecting it might be poisoned.

It's always the quiet ones.

Still, not having eaten anything since lunch several hours earlier, he eyed it hungrily and said, "How nice. Thank you."

"Oh, it's no bother." With a rare laugh, she added, "I still cook like I have a house full of kids at home. And you look like you could use some home cooking."

At least now I have my own kitchen.

Having spent the bulk of the week settling into his new apartment, he was looking forward to making some of his favorite foods. Just had to stock the pantry and the fridge.

If memory served, there was a grocery store on the way home.

Holding the container up, he smiled at her and said, "Thanks. I really appreciate it."

"Anytime," she said as she pulled on her jacket. "Just don't eat it tonight."

He fought back the urge to ask, "Because the poison won't kick in until tomorrow?"

Instead, he went with, "Why's that?"

Maureen looked aghast. "Because it's Lent, and today's Friday."

Andrew forced a laugh. "That's right. I was just testing you."

Maureen just stood there looking at him like she was about to say something.

He waited, but she didn't. Instead, she turned and picked up her purse and music binder.

"Well, good night, Maureen. See you Sunday."

He had just stepped in the direction of his office so he could lock up when he heard her say, "Ya know, my mother always used to say that you can catch more flies with honey than vinegar. Know what I mean?" she asked as she pushed through the doors with him.

Feeling a dull thud in his chest, Andrew considered sharing with Maureen how he left his honey back at the Stone Arch Bridge last June.

Thinking better of it, he gave her a polite nod. "Be careful going home. Thanks again for the stew."

* * *

Watching where she walked so as to avoid dipping her thigh-high, black boots in puddles of spilled beer, Sara made her way to the closest exit. The pounding bass continued to echo in her ears even as she stepped out onto Lawrence Avenue. Despite the cold, the sidewalk was teaming with pockets of noisy people looking for fun on a Friday night.

Had she noticed the valet leering at her, she likely would not have given him such a generous tip before getting in her car and making her way to Bell's Market for some creamy, frozen deliciousness and a six pack of her favorite dark ale.

Open 'round the clock, the small organic grocery store was popular with the eclectic residents living in the surrounding neighborhoods of Lincoln Square and Ravenswood. Thankfully, on this night, there were only a handful of cars in the lot.

Wedging her on-fumes Honda in between a motorcycle and a dark-blue Jeep, she pulled the key out of the ignition, grabbed her purse, and sauntered into the store. While a frigid wind had picked up outside, the interior felt more like a sauna and smelled of too many overcooked samples of crab puffs and tofu tacos. She slipped off her jacket to reveal a snug bustier as gray as her eyes, flung her leather jacket over her arm, and headed for the frozen food section.

While scanning the many rows of pint-sized cartons, she zeroed in on the flavors trying to find one that had the potential to satisfy her craving. She pulled out one labeled "Red Devil" and read its description. *Red velvet-flavored ice cream spiked with red chili peppers.*

A look of disgust swept over her face, and she shoved it back into place.

Catching the introduction of an old Sheryl Crow hit strumming out of the store's sound system, Sara started idly harmonizing just below the melody. Half the time, she didn't even realize she was doing it. By the time the song finished, she had decided on a pint of Berries and Dream ice cream (black raspberry cheesecake flavor with savory hunks of graham cracker crust).

As she reached for it, her burned-out brain wandered back home to William's Cove where she used to go berry picking in the woods with her mom. But that was before she decided to ditch Sara, her brother, Kerry, and their dad for an airline pilot based in Miami. Didn't even say good-bye.

An all-too-familiar ache weighed heavily in her chest, and a fat tear plopped from the corner of her eye when she blinked.

Hearing the strains of another old acoustic classic fill the air, her memory bank fast-forwarded to the night of her 21st birthday, when her brother, ten years older, entered them in the Bay Shore Club's open-mic contest. While he played guitar and sang lead on James Taylor's "You Can Close Your Eyes," Sara

harmonized on what had always been her favorite bedtime song.
The place was packed with regulars, mostly friends and
neighbors who knew what the family had been through, along
with a fair amount of strangers visiting from towns dotting the
shore of Lake Michigan between Chicago and Milwaukee. As
usual, Sara scanned the crowd for her mother's face and as usual
was disappointed but not surprised.

By the time they finished singing, there wasn't a dry eye
in the house.

All things considered, it was the best night of her life.
And everything went downhill from there.

She stared blindly at the pints of ice cream before her,
amazed that it had been almost three years since she had last
seen or heard from her brother. And how it had been about that
long since she had the opening bars of that song tattooed in a
delicate black strand starting on her upper left shoulder and
ending on her right.

Lost in the haze of a sad memory, the sound of someone
trying to work out the melody directly behind her was more than
disconcerting. Raising her pint of ice cream like she had just
pulled the pin on a live grenade, she turned in the narrow aisle
and found herself looking into the kindest blue eyes she had ever
seen.

"I'm not familiar with that one."

The smooth cadence of his voice gave her pause.

Radio announcer? DJ?

"Is it in cut time?" he asked.

Sara's eyes followed his as they drifted upward to take in
her pint-size weapon.

They were so blue, like robin's eggs (*must be contacts*),
and were fringed with spiky black lashes.

With a sob still lodged in her throat, she warbled, "What
do you think you're doing?"

Before he could reply, she glanced up and down the
empty aisle, disappointed that she came off more like a pussycat
than a piranha.

Even as an odd sense of peace started to envelope her,
she hissed, "You can't just sneak up on a complete stranger
and—"

"I'm very sorry." Lowering his chin, he met her distraught gaze. She watched as a smile curved the corners of his mouth upward, revealing a sparkling row of pearly whites.

He leaned toward her, and for a split second she thought he was going to hug her. As surprising a move as that would've been, what surprised her more was that she would have let him.

Instead, he put his hand on her forearm and gently lowered it.

She just stood there, unable to speak, like he was some sort of sorcerer who cast spells on unsuspecting women shopping for ice cream alone on a Friday night.

"I didn't mean to upset you," he ventured. "I've just never come across anyone with a measure of music tattooed across their..."

As his gaze dropped to the bare skin above her tight, cleavage-baring bustier, his cheeks reddened under a day or two's worth of dark stubble. "Well, shoulders. Across their bare shoulders before."

Dragging his eyes upward to meet hers, he fumbled, "I mean, across *her* bare shoulders. Because you are, of course, a woman."

Sara's eyebrows bunched together under her bangs. The spell was broken.

After an intentionally long minute, she asked, "You don't get out much, do you?"

At that, his cheeks went crimson.

Freakin' adorable...

Eyeing him like a cat does a mouse, she looked the grocery-store stalker up and down. He was barely an inch taller than she was. Granted, the heels of her boots gave her at least a two-inch boost. His thick black hair was on the shorter side, and most of it was combed up off of his forehead. He had a slight overbite, a heart-shaped face, and his eyes tilted down a bit in the corners. As for clothes, topping what she couldn't help but notice were some nicely fitting Levi's, he had on a plain white T-shirt under a thick, tightly woven, navy-blue Henley sweater.

Two words sprang to mind.

Ken. Doll.

He fit the mold perfectly. Ruggedly handsome, Ken dolls were the embodiment of all things competent, self-assured, charming, and wholesome. Sara knew the type well. They'd infiltrate William's Cove on weekends, driving up from their wealthy hamlets dotting Chicago's north shore to sail on gorgeous Lake Compton or golf at one of the nearby resorts. While she never minded the well-mannered breed or the generous tips they usually left when she waited their tables, she always felt so inferior in their presence.

And unworthy.

No matter. With a quick shake of her head, Sara reminded herself that she was already in a relationship with an accomplished musician—albeit an uneducated, rugby-loving, undiagnosed manic-depressive accomplished musician—but still.

Glancing at the Ken doll's cart, she saw that it was full of sensible food like produce, chicken, eggs, pasta, and whole-grain bread along with a bottle of Malbec, a bag of laundry detergent pods, and a box of tissues.

She arched an eyebrow and asked, "Shopping for the missus?"

Barbie, isn't it?

This seemed to confuse him.

Not waiting for a reply, she edged around him, caught a whiff of his cologne, and fought back the urge to make a *yummy* sound.

"Oh, no," he finally replied with a hint of sadness in his voice. "I'm not married."

Two other words sprang to mind. *He's. Gay.* Well, two-and-a-half words.

She noticed him reach into the refrigerated cabinet and pull out a pint without even checking the label.

Make tracks.

When she was several feet away, she heard him venture, "I, uh, heard you singing."

At this she turned to look in his direction, but her eyes dropped to the scuffed black-and-white tile floor. "I wouldn't call that singing."

He approached her, dragging his cart behind him while shaking his head.

"No, I disagree. You have a good quality voice."

Sara scrunched her face like he had just scraped his fingernails on a chalkboard. "That's got to be *the* worst pickup line I've ever heard."

Again, his face twisted with confusion.

"Oh, I'm not—"

Sensing what he was about to say would do more harm to her ego than good, she held her index finger against her pursed lips.

"Shhhh. Stop talking. Let's not spoil the moment."

After all, gay or not, guys like him didn't fall for girls like her. And, as far as she was concerned, the feeling was mutual.

With that, she turned and continued her trek to the liquor aisle. But the Ken doll followed her, cart and all.

"Listen, can we start over? I'm Andrew Benet. And you are...?"

What part of "stop talking" don't you understand?

She turned on him, right there in front of a display of imported marinara sauce. "Listen. Whatever you're selling, I'm not buying, so just do me a favor, and leave me alone, OK?"

She left him standing in her flustered wake and yanked a six-pack of Guinness from the shelf before stomping over to the cashier clear on the other side of the store.

There was only one person in line ahead of her and no one behind her.

Come on, come on, come on.

She wanted to get out of there before Mr. "You have a good quality voice" had another chance to strike up a conversation.

"That'll be twelve dollars and thirty-six cents."

Sara swiped her card in the reader.

Declined.

Frowning, she checked that she was swiping the card on the proper side and did it again.

Declined.

Her frown deepened as she dug in her wallet.

OK, so maybe I forgot to pay my credit card bill again.
"Hang on," she said as she pulled another piece of plastic out of her wallet. "This one will work."
Declined.
She turned her attention to the cashier. "Are you sure this thing is working properly?"
"It worked just fine for the last customer," the multi-pierced woman replied before picking up a handset next to the register and droning, "Assistance needed at checkout."
Out of the corner of her eye, she could see there were at least three other customers in line behind her. She didn't dare make eye contact.
Sara burrowed into her purse and counted the few bills and coins she could find. Kicking herself for tipping the valet at the Aragon as much as she did, all she had left was four dollars and twenty-seven cents. She kept digging.
"I got it."
Oh no.
The yummy-smelling Ken doll with fits-like-a-glove Levis was in line behind her, offering to pay her bill.
Can this night get any worse?
After shoving her wallet back in her purse, she held up her hand in protest. "Absolutely not." With her voice trailing off into thin air, she lied. "I just forgot to activate my new credit card, that's all."
As she watched him take the now ownerless pint of ice cream and six-pack of Guinness from the cashier and place them with his things, he addressed Sara without so much as looking at her. "I wasn't talking to you."
She felt like he'd just punched her in the gut, not that she didn't have it coming.
"Oh. Right. Sorry."
Leaning around him to better see the people standing at the back of the line, she waved and said, "Sorry for the hold up, folks."
A little old lady at the end let out a gasp. "Did she say 'hold up?'"
Not bothering to offer a clarification, Sara slunk out of the store, empty-handed and frustrated beyond words.

She pulled into the Stop-N-Go down the street to fill up, thanked her lucky stars that her gas card was not going to give her any trouble, and headed home.

Well, not her home. Technically, the lease was in Jer's name.

That she hadn't heard a peep from him in over a week—not since receiving his cryptic message, *Ta, darling* was not entirely unusual. Knowing she was already on the road, it was his quick and easy way of letting her know he was off again to New York, London, or LA.

When Bono calls...

She never bothered replying to these announcements. What was the point of calling him up to simply say, "Oh, ok. Thanks for letting me know." Cripes, that sounded so dull, so pedestrian compared to his breezy British vernacular.

It didn't help that he refused to text or bank online.

So old-fashioned.

Still, they always ended up touching base eventually. Especially if she still owed him her half of the rent.

At the next stoplight, she pulled out her nearly dead three-year-old (read: archaic) phone and turned it on. After it buzzed to life, she saw that a little number one appeared over the message icon.

Oh, here we go.

Then it turned into a two. And then a six.

Uh-oh.

She glanced up at the light to make sure it was still red and then punched in her voicemail password. Bracing herself, she put it on speaker and kept driving when the light turned green.

Jer's accent was unmistakable. The first message was brief. "Tell me you remembered to leave a rent check before you left. Give me a ring, love, and let me know where you hid it."

Crap.

She listened to the time stamp.

Nine days ago? How am I just getting this now?

The second message, left a day later, was nowhere near as cheerful.

"Oh, great. Another flippin' recording. Jesus. Look. You know I can barely cover my own bills, love. I'm not coverin' for you this time. I mean it. If you want out, just say the word, but I'm not playing this game with you. You don't want to get married. You don't want kids. I get it. Message received. Not another word. That's what you want, yeah? That's what this is all about, ain't it? Look. Just. Just call me back, aw right?"

Sara didn't notice that her hands had started shaking. What she did notice was that the world around her seemed to suddenly shift into slow motion.

The next three messages were hang-ups.

The anger in his voice was palpable in the last one. "God, what kind of journalist doesn't check her bloody messages? I've been trying to call you all week, for Christ's sake. I'm assuming you're not dead or murdered or... Listen, I'm done. Leaving the States for good this time." After a pause, he softened his tone and added, "Nothing personal, but this just ain't workin' out for us, is it?"

Static cackled over the line, and the rest of the message came in fragments. "Know...afford...my key...bloke...Tuesday." Click.

The message was going on six days old.

Holy hell.

As she turned onto her street, her eyes began to brim, blurring her vision.

Nothing personal? Ouch.

Gripping the steering wheel, she focused on trying to decipher his cryptic message.

Know afford my key bloke Tuesday.

She started talking to her dashboard. "Know afford. Know I can't afford? My key. Bloke. My key bloke."

A knot started forming in her stomach.

"My key bloke Tuesday. My key broke Tuesday?"

Maybe he should've learned how to text and bank online before assuming I walked out on him, huh?

Too tired to think, she steered her sturdy little Honda into the alley behind their, well, soon-to-be her Chestnut Street apartment.

Maybe it's for the best.

As upsetting as Jer's message was, the sight of a dark-blue Jeep sitting in her designated parking spot was ten times more so.

"Aw, not cool," she moaned to her windshield. "Not cool at all."

A wall of dread slammed into her as the ghosts of some of she and Jer's more heated arguments came back to haunt her.

Like when she told him who he could and could not invite over (smokers, no—non-smokers, only if they didn't spill on the hardwood).

Or when she banished him to the couch again after declaring that the thought of being a wife and mother to his children was just a little more than she could take, thank you very much.

That last one was just two weeks before.

As if someone were in the car right there with her, she whimpered, "I can't do a big break-up scene. Not now. Not like this."

Shifting into reverse, she backed out of the slushy alley. After circling the block three times, she finally managed to wedge her car between two minivans stuffed with kids' crap, both of which were taking up way more space than they should have.

She yanked her suitcase from the trunk and dragged it behind her as she marched under the canopy of old oak trees, the roots of which transformed the slippery sidewalk into a dangerous obstacle course lit only by the soft glow of old streetlights.

After she unlocked the heavy glass and brass-trim door to the elegant three-story brownstone, she caught her reflection in the doors as she passed through. Taking in the sight of her bobbed, dull black hair, heavy dark makeup, leather jacket, and aforementioned boots. The first word that came to mind was *scary*.

Great.

Finally in front of the door to her unit, Sara's mind was filled with the dismal prospect of having to secure a waitressing job to supplement her income just so she could keep the apartment.

She shoved her key into the lock.

But it wouldn't go in. Not even a quarter of an inch.

After checking to make sure she had the right key and was holding it right side up, she jammed it back into the keyhole, but it wouldn't go any farther than it did the last time.

Sara stepped back and looked at the door a full minute, her heart pounding.

What. The. Hell?

Why would Jer change the locks before he even moved out? She replayed the voicemail he had left her.

Key bloke Tuesday.

She knocked and waited for a response.

None came.

Leaving the States for good this time.

She didn't think he meant that same day. He was never that brash. Hell, the man could deliberate for five minutes over whether to have strawberry preserves or marmalade on his toast with morning tea.

She threw her hands in the air.

Who the hell am I supposed to call at this hour?

Not ever having been locked out before, she was at a loss. And, since she always made her rent checks out to Jer, she didn't even know the name of their landlord, let alone how to get ahold of him.

She checked her watch. 11:30.

I just want to go to bed.

With her head throbbing and her heart banging in her chest, she pounded on the door.

I am so not sleeping in my car tonight.

A loud thump sounded on the other side of the heavy wooden door.

"Jer?" she ventured, hope coursing through her veins. "Something's wrong with my key. Open up, huh?"

When nothing happened, she pressed her entire body against the door and listened for any sign of life on the other side.

A moment later, she was sorry that she did.

As it swooshed forward, she lost her balance and stumbled into the arms of the man who pulled it open. Not a problem, except that it wasn't Jer.

It was one Andrew Benet.

CHAPTER THREE

———

"I am a marvelous housekeeper. Every time I leave a man,
I keep his house."
—Zsa Zsa Gabor

Tucking his recently acquired staples into their allotted space in his well-organized kitchen, Andrew closed the pantry door and turned to make sure he had emptied all of the bags marked "Bell's Market."

Satisfied, he folded them neatly and pressed them into the confines of a spot he had reserved just for paper grocery bags by the recycling bin.

There. All set.

He cast his gaze around his apartment. For as much as he longed to have his own place away from his horde of siblings, the quiet seemed to press in all around him.

All set for what?

The microwave dinged, signaling that the chicken and dumplings Maureen had given him were ready. He grabbed a fork from the drawer and was just about to dig in to what smelled like really good food when his eyes fell on the six-pack of stout beer sitting on the counter. He wasn't sure what possessed him to buy it. He hadn't had one in years and wasn't especially fond of it then. But when he saw them sitting unclaimed on the grocery-store conveyor belt, the smug satisfaction he anticipated by buying them out from under the snippy woman he'd made a pathetic attempt to recruit in the frozen-food section overcame him.

Uncapping one, he took a swig and closed his eyes. The roasted malt taste filled his mouth, and the face of said snippy woman filled his mind's eye.

The Guinness Girl.

In all of his travels around the globe with youth choirs and choral programs, he had never encountered anyone like her. So abrasive, but somehow, still so fragile and lovely at the same time.

And the way she was picking apart that harmony. Her voice was just above a whisper, but still—it made the hairs on the back of his neck stand on end.

He thought of the occasional prayers he had offered up of late to help him put the past behind him and maybe, just maybe, find someone to share his life with, eventually.

His mind turned to Leanne—the only girl he'd dated since he was 17. Last he heard, she had become a candidate with the Sisters of St. Joseph of Carondelet.

Well good for her. Sucks for me, but, really, good for her.

Then he thought of the Guinness Girl. Hardly an answer to his prayers. More like a punch line to a really bad joke.

Good one, God.

He took another swig and toasted the Almighty's wicked sense of humor.

Still, as the dark ale slid down his throat, he kicked himself for letting her get away.

But after the day I had...

He set the bottle down and ventured into the living room where he found the box of the previous occupant's things waiting for him.

...she's lucky I didn't let the air out of her tires before she left the store.

Setting the box on top of the pseudo coffee table, he started shuffling through its contents, hoping to find clues as to the person's identity. Maybe Sam could help track down whomever this stuff belonged to so he could ship it to her new address.

The landlord said the previous tenant wasn't coming back and that Andrew should pitch everything. But who would leave behind photo albums and hand-written letters?

And a journal?

He looked around the room before slowly lifting the bound notebook with a bright orange cover that was dotted with tiny daisy stickers. The owner's name was written at the bottom in large flowery print. "Sara Annise Cleff." This was followed by one word in large block letters: "Private."

Andrew ran his fingers over the hard-pressed print and was about to turn the page when he heard a knock at the door.

Who could that be at this hour?

Returning the items to the box, he dropped it on the floor with a thud.

A knock sounded again, this time, much louder, and he heard a woman's muffled voice.

As he approached the door in his stocking feet, he realized it didn't have a peephole.

What would Sam do?

He thought for a minute.

Open the door with his gun cocked, that's what he'd do.

He thought about asking who it was.

But what if they didn't answer?

His logic returning, he remembered that residents needed a key to enter the building.

Deciding to go with the element of surprise, he gripped the knob, turned it, and yanked the door open.

The next thing he knew, his arms were full of a woman in a leather coat who backed away from him as soon as he set her upright.

I'll be damned.

The Guinness Girl was standing right there in his doorway.

"What are you doing here?" he asked, incredulous. When she didn't answer right away, he pressed, "Wait—did you follow me?"

She looked just as annoyed and confused as he felt. "Who—? *What?* What do you mean what am *I* doing here. I live here. What the hell are *you* doing here?"

She scowled at him with those big gray eyes.

"I live here."

"No you don't. That's impossible."

"Yet here I am." He stood with his back to the interior of his apartment while keeping his hand on the edge of the open door, ready to shove her back through it and slam the door behind her.

"Yeah, well, I have a key." She held up what was apparently the sole piece of evidence she had to prove her occupancy.

Andrew smirked. "And I have a signed lease."

"But I have a key," she repeated as she shook it at him.

"Yeah, I heard you the first time. How's that working out for you?"

Her face drowning in disbelief, she barged by him.

"Is this some kind of a joke?" she shot out as she edged down the hallway that connected the tiny foyer to the spacious eat-in kitchen, glancing at his family photos with disgust as she passed by.

When he didn't answer, she shot out, "Is that your blue Jeep in my spot?"

"In *my* spot, yes."

"Is Jer here?" she demanded.

He followed as fast as he could, righting any frame she brushed against on her way through. "Who?"

The Guinness Girl spun around to face him.

"Jer Caravelli? My *roommate*?"

Andrew's eyes widened. "Trust me. The only one living here is me."

She stood frowning at him like he had just spoken Mandarin.

"Now look," he started, using the same low, in-control voice that seemed to work so well when corralling members of the children's choir into submission. "I'm sure the landlord would be happy to straighten things out for you in the morning, but as it is, it's been a horrendously long day. I'm exhausted and want nothing more than to go to bed, so if you'll just be on your way...well, that would be great."

Andrew motioned for her to return back though the hallway to the foyer where she had left her suitcase.

Ignoring what he had just said, she turned and slowly looked around. "Where's my bookshelf? And my books?" Stepping into the kitchen, she asked with increasing alarm, "What happened to my coffeepot, and my microwave, and toaster?"

Opening a cabinet, she cried, "And my dishes." She turned and demanded, "What happened to my dishes?" With a hint of a whine, she added, "Some of those were my grandma's."

Before he could answer, she made her way to the bedroom and flipped on the light.

"You know, officially, you're trespassing," he called after her. "The police would be on my side. In fact, my brother is a Chicago cop. I could have him here in no time flat."

At that, the heels of her boots hammered against the hardwood as she stomped out of the bedroom and back into the hallway. "You'd call the police? On me. Seriously? You need backup to handle a woman who's upset because her boyfriend sublet their apartment and left the *country* while she was on the road covering a crappy band from Decatur on their debut tour of the Midwest?" Her voice grew louder with each word.

Then she stared him down, waiting for an answer that he knew better than to give. Of all the hissy fits he saw his sisters pitch over the years, none had ever come close to this.

"Go ahead." Her voice sounded tired and deflated. With a laugh, she quipped, "Maybe they'll put me up for the night."

She was visibly shaken. Dark pools of tears were forming under her eyes and had started to work their way down her rounded cheeks. He watched as she retreated into the bedroom. *His* bedroom.

Not sure what to do next, he stayed in the kitchen waiting for the hysterics to continue once she realized her clothes were gone, but none came.

After a few minutes, he slowly made his way down the hall, passing the dark bathroom to his left, and found her standing in the bedroom with her back to the door. Her head was down, and it looked like she had her face covered with one hand while the other was gripping her waist.

Poor kid.

Ignoring the little voice in his head that had been trying to warn him that she could pull a knife on him, or rob him, or any number of things his suburban-Minneapolis-born-and-raised imagination could conjure since she burst into his apartment, he approached her, careful not to get too close.

"I'm sorry. This must be quite a shock."

Not sure what to expect, his guard couldn't have been any higher when she turned, gripped the front of his sweater with both hands, and pulled him close.

Then she tucked her face into his neck, where he couldn't help but notice how nicely it fit, and started to sob.

At first, he wasn't sure what to do except lightly clasp her shaking shoulders.

"Uh, everything will be all right." he heard himself say without a shred of empathy.

When that didn't seem to help, he tried holding her loosely in an awkward embrace. Feeling the sobs rack her frame, the musky smell of her leather jacket reached his nostrils. It smelled good. Somehow, it suited her.

"Shhhh. Come on. It's gonna be OK."

Much better.

When he heard her sobs turn to hiccups, he pulled her up against him and wrapped her in a full-fledged hug.

"Sometimes the best thing to say is nothing at all," his mom would often advise.

So he just stood there with his arms secured around the complete stranger. Without a clear view of the clock on his nightstand, he had no idea how long they were standing there like that. What he did know was that it felt a whole lot better than buying a six-pack and a pint of ice cream out from under her when she couldn't pay for them herself.

After she had cried enough to fill the Hoover Dam, she rested her forehead against his shoulder, took a deep breath, and sighed. "I'm sorry," *hiccup,* "I was rude to you." *Hiccup.* "It's just," *hiccup,* "this is all a bit much."

You're telling me.

Fishing an unused tissue out of his front pocket, he handed it to her. "Here. I've got a whole 'nother box of these in the bathroom if you need 'em."

"Thanks," she muffled through it while wiping her nose and smearing the spent mascara off of her cheeks with her fingertips. She pointed to his sweater. "Sorry about that too. I'll have it dry cleaned for you."

Feeling a sudden chill as she stepped away from him, he waved her off. "Oh, no worries. It's machine washable."

She gave a little nod and then motioned toward the front door.

"Well, I'm gonna get going. Sorry for the intrusion."

With that, she turned and started down the hallway that led to the foyer.

"Uh, wait," he called after her. "Where are you gonna go? It's after midnight."

The Guinness Girl stopped in her tracks and turned. "My car, I guess. I have a blanket in the trunk."

No longer the mysterious, alluring creature armed with an arsenal of quick quips that he spotted in the grocery store, she looked like someone had just kicked her to the curb, hard.

She grasped the handle of her suitcase, opened the front door, and started pulling it down the hallway behind her.

"Don't let her get away again," the little voice inside of him suddenly shouted.

Standing just outside of his doorway, he blurted, "Uh, wait. Don't go. I'm sure we can work something out."

She stopped. A long moment passed before she turned around. Her eyes were dark, her expression unreadable. Leaving her suitcase in the middle of the hall, she walked right up to him. She studied his face before confronting him, her voice still raw from crying, "What the hell is that supposed to mean? Work what out? This is a one-bedroom apartment."

At this, Andrew straightened up. "Oh. God. No. I'm sorry. That's not what I meant. Honest." He motioned toward the inside of the apartment. "There's a couch. I'm a music director at a church. You can't get any safer than that. Not at this hour anyway."

He could see her mentally debating—couch, car, couch, car...

"Come on," he urged with a tone that usually prompted whoever was on the receiving end to do his bidding, convent-bound girlfriends and adult choir members notwithstanding. "It's below freezing outside. You'll die of exposure."

Her eyes dropped to the now-soggy patch of his sweater and lingered there for several seconds before she nodded. "All right. Just for tonight."

The Guinness Girl retrieved her suitcase, and the two stepped back into his apartment. As they made their way down the tiny hallway, she turned. "Hold on. How do I know you're not a rapist or serial killer?"

He stopped just short of colliding with her. "I was about to ask you the same thing."

This caused her full lips to twitch into a smirk.

I wasn't kidding.

When they reached the open space of the kitchen, she held out her hand. "I'm Sara. Sara Cleff. Music critic, *Chicago Gazette.*"

He took her hand in his, surprised by her strong grip. "And I'm—"

"Andrew." Tugging him a little closer to her, she added with a weak smile, "I heard you the first time."

Pointing to the bathroom, she asked, "Mind if I wash up?"

"No, not at all. There are extra towels in the linen closet."

"I know."

He watched as she casually slipped off her jacket and draped it over the back of a barstool by the counter that served as a divider between the otherwise lofty kitchen and living room space.

Like she must've done a thousand times before.

As she made her way to the bathroom, he titled his head, silently trying to decipher the melody tattooed across her shoulders before she disappeared from view. When he heard the bathroom door click shut, his eyes swept the space around him and fell on the box he had filled with deserted treasures, sitting unclaimed in a corner of the living room.

Owner located.

He put the untouched chicken and dumplings in the fridge and waited for Sara Annise Cleff to emerge.

* * *

Only two things ever really bothered Sara. One was ticket scalpers. The other was being abandoned.

As she looked in the same bathroom mirror she had seen herself in so many times before, she barely recognized the reflection. No longer defiant or too cool for her own good, as Kerry used to say, she looked very much like that little girl who was just told that her mommy was never ever coming home again.

As the tears started to well up, she carefully peeled off her fake eyelashes and dropped each one in a little plastic wastebasket. Sliding her bangles over her wrist, she set them on the edge of the sink. Next, she lathered up a bar of soap that was sitting on a dish next to a toothbrush holder (holding one lonely toothbrush) and scrubbed the makeup off of her face.

The cool water rinse revived her.

And the plush red hand towel she sank her face into smelled just like Andrew, the nice guy who didn't hesitate to hold a complete stranger together while she managed to fall apart over a not-so-nice guy who apparently had no qualms about ending their relationship via voicemail, turning her out of her home, and disposing of her belongings.

And he never ever held me like that either.

She raised her eyes to her reflection and whispered, "Don't go there." The warning hung in the air as she continued to stare at herself.

No Ken dolls.

Taking another deep breath, she combed her fingers through her hair, pulled a fringe of bangs over her forehead, pinched her cheeks to get some color back in them, and made her way to the living room, tissues in hand, uncertain of what awaited her.

The first thing she noticed was a big pillow squeezed into a beige-ish gold pillowcase resting against the far end of the couch. Its owner emerged from the kitchen and pointed to it. "The sheets are clean."

She looked down at the pillow and then back at him. "Sheets?"

"On the mattress."

Again, she looked at him like he was speaking Mandarin.

Gesturing toward the bedroom, she asked, "On my bed?"

"It's my bed now."

She pressed her fingertips to her closed eyes. "Don't remind me."

He pulled his face into a frown. "I meant on the sleeper sofa."

Dropping her hands, she announced with no small degree of certainty, "This couch is not a sleeper sofa."

He looked defiant. "Yes it is."

Incredulous, Sara scoffed, "It's been here longer than I have. Trust me. It's not a sleeper sofa."

After narrowing his eyes at her, he reached over, lifted the middle cushion up, and pointed to what looked like a handle.

"Sleeper sofa."

Her eyebrows shot up. "Well, I'll be damned. I had no idea."

She wondered for a brief moment if Jer knew and then realized it would be better all around if she did her best to stop giving a rat's ass about Jer. As she did when her mother left, she slammed that door in her heart shut and threw away the key.

Andrew returned the cushion to its proper place, explaining, "Yeah, I discovered it when I cleaned the floor." He turned to look at her. "Which was disgusting, by the way."

She cocked an eyebrow in reply.

"It felt heavier than a regular couch," he continued. "So I pulled the cushions off and voila. Sleeper sofa."

She gave him her trademark bored-beyond-belief look.

"So...my stuff? Do you know what Jer did with it all?" It was hard for her to imagine him being so vindictive. Yet his stereo, TV, and cherished collection of CDs and albums were all still there, untouched.

Andrew motioned toward her accommodation for the evening. "Have a seat."

Grabbing an open bottle of Guinness off the kitchen counter, he asked, "Want one?"

Tilting her head as the sting of their checkout line exchange returned, Sara muttered, "I can't believe you bought my goddamn Guinness."

He pulled one out, popped the cap, and held it out to her, then hesitated. With one eyebrow cocked, he asked, "You kiss your mother with that mouth?"

She grabbed the bottle from him with a little more force than intended. "No, I do not."

The Ken doll twitched. "Sorry."

Sara took a swig, gave her head a quick shake, and held up her hand. Making no attempt to keep the emotion from her voice, she replied, "Forget it. Just another sad story and I've had quite enough sad for one evening."

With a nod, he replied, "Got it."

She settled into her favorite spot on the couch, where she'd usually sit when she would tune out the world with a little help from Eric Clapton, Bonnie Raitt, and so many others.

Andrew sat on the couch facing her. "So...your stuff."

"Yeah...?"

"Well, let me back up. Up until a week ago, I was staying at my brother's over in Uptown. Someone from my church, Chris Danvers—do you know him?"

Sara shook her head.

"Oh, I'm surprised. He owns this building."

With a shrug, Sara sighed, "Never heard of him." She took a long pull of her beer, propped her elbow up on the back of the couch, and rested the side of her face in her hand.

"Well, long story short, he called to tell me there was a sudden vacancy in one of his buildings, a furnished sublet, and if I was interested, I'd better grab it fast. So, I cleared my schedule and came to see it."

"Don't tell me," she yawned. Feeling fatigue zap her already-low reserves of patience and civility, she squinted at him. "You fell in love with it."

The Ken doll's freakishly blue eyes opened wide. "Well, yeah—who wouldn't?"

Sara lifted both eyebrows with enormous difficulty given the heaviness bearing down on her eyelids. "My stuff?"

"Yeah, that. Well, according to Chris, the tenant—and he used the singular—had to leave the country suddenly and wasn't coming back."

At that, Sara's body did a weird involuntary twitch, rather like when you're just about to fall asleep and something startles you.

She reached for a tissue.

"That was Jer, was it?"

"Yeah," she whispered.

While she pressed the tissue to her eyes, she heard him continue. "Well, anyway, he told me if I wanted to move in right away, which I did, I'd have to get rid of everything myself. Otherwise he'd need a couple of days to bring it all to the curb."

This is a nightmare.

Now it was Sara's turn to open her eyes wide. "You didn't, did you? Bring everything to the curb?"

The Ken doll shook his head. Not a hair fell out of place. "Oh no. Just some stuff."

In response, she blew her nose and took another swig of her beer. "You know what? I don't think I'm in the right frame of mind for this conversation. Mind if we continue it in the morning? My bad news quota for the day has been exceeded a couple of times over."

The Ken doll looked relieved. "Yeah, sure. But listen. It's not as bad as you think."

At this, she perked up. "What do you mean?"

Pointing to a box in the corner, he added, "Like I said, I didn't get rid of everything."

Sara set her bottle on the trunk and lunged for the box. Kneeling beside it, she pulled the flaps open. As she shuffled the contents around a bit, a feeling of relief washed over her, making her that much more sleepy.

Clothes and dishes she could replace. Pictures and letters she couldn't. She folded the flaps back down again and returned to the couch. When Andrew held her bottle out to her, she glanced in his direction. "Thanks." Feeling a tear drip down her cheek, she pressed the back of her hand against it. "You have no idea."

He handed her another tissue.

"Well, that hardly makes up for the rest of—"

"No, it doesn't," she interrupted. "But it's pretty damn close." Looking down at the box and her suitcase, she exclaimed, "This is all I have left in the whole wide world—a box of memories and a suitcase full of dirty clothes. How sad is that?"

The words had no sooner left her mouth than her host for the evening hopped up and disappeared for a few minutes before returning with a pair of men's blue plaid flannel pajamas. They appeared to be pressed.

Definitely gay.

"These will probably be big on you, but they're clean. You're welcome to 'em. In the meantime, why don't you get a load started before you go to bed? You probably know where everything is. Help yourself to the detergent and stuff. We can figure out the rest in the morning."

Sara looked down at the clothes he had just placed in her lap and smoothed her hand over the soft fabric. "Why are you being so nice to me?" she asked, unable to keep her voice from wobbling.

He shrugged. "Like I said, I work in a church. Occupational hazard." Pointing to the front door, he added, "OK, well, I'm just gonna lock up and head to bed. Do you need help moving the trunk?"

She nudged it with her boot. It moved easily, maybe because he had the four corners of it on casters. "Nah, I got it."

After he passed by her again on his way to her—well, *his* room now—and she heard him call out, "Sleep tight," she hugged the flannel pajamas tightly against her chest.

* * *

Up as usual at the crack of dawn, Andrew trudged to the bathroom, almost forgetting to close the door behind him before he spotted Sara's bangles on the counter next to the sink. Reaching over, he shut the door and locked it.

Fifteen minutes later, he was showered, clean-shaven, and ready to go, except he didn't have to be at the church until four-thirty that afternoon. Unplugging his phone from an outlet in his room, he brought it with him into the kitchen, transferred Sara's clothes that she had washed the night before into the dryer and poured himself some coffee. He sat on a barstool, debated throwing a sweatshirt on over his plain, blue, short-sleeved T-shirt to ward off the chill, but started scrolling through his email instead.

His eyes, however, kept drifting over to Sara, out like a light on the sofa sleeper.

While most of her was wrapped in the blankets like a human burrito, with the sun starting to break through the bare branches of the ancient oak tree blocking the expansive bay window, he could see her face quite plainly.

Without all that the heavy dark makeup, he noted, she looked younger.

And kinda sweet, actually.

But then again, she wasn't talking.

Still, he was glad he invited her to stay the night before.

But what about tonight? And tomorrow night? And the night after that?

While he mulled the possibilities, she rolled over and stretched, arching her back and groaning as she did. Resuming her curled-up burrito pose, she opened her eyes and mumbled, "How long have you been sitting there?"

Looking at his watch, he admitted, "About a minute. Or five. Maybe ten." His cheeks suddenly felt a lot warmer.

With a loud yawn, she sat up. "I slept so good." Patting the thin mattress with her hand, she added, "So comfy."

The words hung in the air between them.

Sarcasm before coffee. Great.

Still, the sight of her in his pajama top seemed to lobotomize him. All he could do by way of a reply was nod.

With a shrug, she added, "Seriously, on a sleeper sofa—who knew?"

Snap out of it.

With no small amount of effort, he turned and glanced at the dryer. "Your clothes should be ready in about twenty minutes."

At that, Sara took a deep breath and yanked the covers back, revealing two impossibly long bare legs as she flung her feet to the floor.

Knowing full well that the sudden blast of heat he felt was not delivered by way of the gilded vents along the floorboards, Andrew got up to check the thermostat on the wall next to the upright piano anyway, mumbling, "Gotta love old buildings."

"Mind if I take a shower?" he heard her ask behind him.

Not about to turn around, he replied, "Not at all. The towels are—"

"In the linen closet. I know."

When he heard the bathroom door close behind him, he turned around and took a deep breath. Walking to the other side of the kitchen counter, he took a sip of hot coffee and debated whether or not to make her bed. Deciding it was best to let his guest clean up after herself, he took the liberty of returning his unused pajama bottoms to their rightful place in his drawer.

On the way back into the kitchen, he could hear the shower running. He was just topping off his coffee when the singing started.

He didn't recognize the song, but it didn't matter. Goosebumps raced up both of his arms.

He set his coffee down but nearly missed the counter completely. Catching his mug just in time, the hot liquid spilled out and scalded his wrist. A few minutes under cold running water, and it was fine. Andrew, on the other hand, felt like he had just tripped over the edge of a cliff and was plummeting like a rock.

He yanked a paper towel off of the holder and was busy wiping up the spill when an idea started swirling in his brain.

She needs a place to stay.

I need her in choir.

By the time he heard the shower shut off, he was fairly certain he knew what he'd propose.

Then the bathroom door opened, and through a steamy cloud she emerged with one towel wrapped around her head and another around her torso, looking like a Vegas showgirl decked out in bright-red terry cloth.

"Have to get my clothes," she sang out as she skirted behind him and pulled a few items out of the dryer.

"Be right back." She waved her clothes, lacey underwear included, in the air as she scampered back to the bathroom, leaving the scent of some indiscernible floral arrangement in her wake.

A bemused smile spread across his face as he tried picturing the reaction the others would have to Sara showing up at choir practice. Her height alone would generate whispers. God forbid they get a peek at her tattoo. And worse, what if she drops an "F" bomb while talking to one of them—in church.

OK, maybe this isn't such a great idea.

Then the image of Marge the Matchmaker and her scary scowl floated before him.

But then again...

Lost in thought, Andrew didn't even realize Sara, wearing a tight, bright-blue, short-sleeved turtleneck sweater and a pair of jeans that left little to the imagination, was already out of the bathroom and had started making the bed. Watching as she attempted to shove it back into the couch with the sheet not tucked in properly around the edges, he practically leapt over the kitchen counter.

"Oh, here. Let me do it. You have to be careful not to force it in there, otherwise you might tear something."

Out of the corner of his eye, he saw her stand straight up.

"I can't believe you just said that."

After he shoved the bed into place, he noted her shocked, but amused, expression. "What?"

Shaking her head, Sara looked right at him for a second, then looked away again muttering, "Never mind."

He stood in front of her and jutted out his chin. "No. What? You're blushing. Tell me."

Pressing her lips together, she just shook her head.

Andrew thought for a minute, replaying what he had said, and then narrowed his eyes. "Get your mind out of the gutter."

He noted her cheeks turn a few shades pinker as she gestured toward the couch and let out a deep guttural laugh, "Hey, I'm not the one who said it."

Walking back toward the kitchen, he asked, "You want some coffee?"

"Yeah. Sure. Thanks."

She replaced the couch cushions and sat on a bar stool opposite him. "So...what happened to my stuff?"

He handed her a mug and pushed a bottle of hazelnut creamer toward her, which she promptly pushed back. "I donated it."

Given the look on her face, he may as well have said, "I piled it high on the parkway, doused it with gasoline, lit it on fire, and roasted some marshmallows."

She pulled her face into a grimace and whined, "That's just as bad as putting it on the curb. I'll never get any of it back now."

"No, probably not," he replied. "But we can stop by the places I dropped stuff off at and see if any of it hasn't been claimed yet."

"Claimed? By whom?"

"Needy people. I gave your clothes to a women's shelter over on Damen and the rest to the Goodwill up on Sheridan."

She got up and pointed in the direction of the front door. "Well, let's go."

When he didn't move, she asked, "What are we waiting for?"

He set his cup down and leaned across the bar counter toward her. "Before we do, I have a proposition for you."

Drawing in a deep breath, her expression grew serious. She sat back on the barstool and with her voice almost lower than his asked, "What?"

"You need a place to stay..."

Dropping her chin, Sara's eyes met his. "Yeah...."

"And I need—"

She narrowed her eyes into thin slits. "Be very careful. Your next word may just be your last."

He lifted both eyebrows. "An alto. I really need an alto."

There. I said it.

Clearly this was not what she was expecting to hear. She turned her head and looked at him sideways with a sneer pulling at her lips. "For what?"

"The adult choir at St. Matthias."

At this, she let out a loud laugh. "You're joking. Me, in a church? Not gonna happen."

Coulda swore I put a rosary in that box.

"Why not?"

"Well, for starters, lightning will strike the moment I step foot across the threshold, killing dozens of innocent bystanders instantly."

Andrew raised his coffee cup to his lips and then lowered it. "Which is exactly why I keep a fire extinguisher right next to the entrance. And if that doesn't work, I can always hose you down with holy water."

Suddenly his mind was filled with an image of her standing there soaking wet.

He took a fortifying swig of steaming, hot liquid and set his mug down with a loud clank. "Seriously. It would only be until Easter," he croaked through scalded vocal chords. "After that, you'd be off the hook."

He watched as she pursed her lips and studied him through narrowed eyes that made him feel like she was scanning him with x-ray vision.

Her voice oozing with caution, she asked, "Why? What happens at Easter?"

"The Bishop is coming to our parish to say Mass. It's a huge deal. I wouldn't be surprised if he showed up for parts of the Triduum as well. If he's impressed by the choir, I have a much better chance of landing a full-time job there."

A grimace tugged at Sara's mouth.

Taking in her pained expression, he started to explain, "The Triduum is the three days before Easter—Holy Thursday, Good Friday, and the Easter Vigil on Saturday night."

She pressed her lips into a thin line and rolled her eyes. "Yeah. I know what it is. I sang in choir at St. Xavier's up in Williams—well, where I grew up."

"Ha." Andrew pointed at her like he just won a bet. "I knew it."

Sara clasped her coffee mug with both hands and hunched her shoulders, scowling at him.

"And if I refuse?"

Her response took him by surprise.

To bolster his position, he could state the obvious. *You'll be homeless.*

Instead, he countered. "You clearly enjoy singing, and my guess is you want to keep living here as much as I do."

Her face twitched into a sneer again. "I wouldn't go that far."

He couldn't help but notice that her eyes darted to her left as she said it.

During the course of his brother's police academy training, Sam taught him how to tell when someone is lying. "If they look to their left when they answer your question, they're lying. If they look to their right, they might still be lying, but probably not."

Not an exact science, but still—*Busted.*

He continued to study her over the rim of his mug, wondering why else she would have willingly stayed with a guy who ended up walking out on her while she was out of town and clearly didn't give a crap what happened to her things.

He set his mug down. "Come on. You help me; I'll help you. You come to practice every week—"

"Wait, what?" she shot out.

He held up his hand. "Let me finish. You come to practice every week and sing at 10:00 am Mass each weekend, and you can stay here for as long as you like. All you have to do is pay your half of the rent. The rest we can figure out as we go along."

I probably should've thought this through a little better.

Andrew paused for effect before concluding, "Take it or leave it."

He did his best to look like he didn't care either way.

With her arms folded in front of her, Sara propped her elbows on the counter. "Let me get this straight. I pay half the rent to keep living here, with you—" She stopped and gave him a slow once-over before continuing. "*Plus,* I have to go to choir practice and Mass every week from now until Easter?"

He shifted on his feet before nodding. "That's right."

She arched her eyebrow and leaned across the counter with a smoky stare.

Unable to hold it, Andrew coughed and looked at his feet.

"OK, I'll do it, but only if I get the bedroom."

His head shot up. "What? Uh-uh. I've been sleeping on my brother's couch since I moved to Chicago. I am not giving up the bed."

Sara glowered at him. "Oh, *and* I have to sleep on a crappy sofa sleeper for what, a month?"

Under his breath, Andrew hedged, "Well, a month and a half. Six weeks from tomorrow, actually."

He watched as Sara clenched her jaw and glared at him. Then, doing that getting louder as she talked thing again, she spouted, "Six weeks? You expect me to sleep on a crappy sofa sleeper for six weeks? After just having gotten back from ten days of having to share a room with two other women in some of the Midwest's finest one-star hotels?"

She can definitely crescendo.

Pointing her finger at him, she warned, "You're pushin' it, pal."

Andrew watched as she slipped off her barstool and swooped behind him to retrieve the rest of her things from the dryer. "Maybe I do love this apartment," he heard her grumble before she slammed the dryer door closed. "But not that much."

A vague sense of panic welled up inside of him. He wasn't used to having his ideas shot down—not like this. Compromise was not his strong suit, and he knew it. Still, not wanting to lose her, his mind started to fire on all cylinders, trying to think of ways to get her to stay.

Just as she dumped her things back in her suitcase (*without even folding them? really?*), he asked, "Can you sight read?"

"What?" She was busy trying to tug the zipper closed. Sitting on the stool she had just abandoned, Andrew asked again, "Can you sight read?"

Giving up on the zipper, Sara stood up and put her hands on her hips, looking just as defiant and abrasive as she did when she rebuffed him the night before in the ice cream aisle at Bell's Market. "Yeah. So what?"

"OK, hear me out. Don't make up your mind just yet. Let's go grab some breakfast, my treat, and we'll go look for your things. Then when we get back, let me run you through the pieces we'll be doing at Mass tomorrow morning so you can sing with the choir."

When she pulled a face, he held up his hand, "Just this once. And then afterward, if you don't want anything to do with it, or me, no hard feelings."

She relaxed her posture and started examining her fingernails.

"But," he continued before she could reply, "If you want to give it a go, we can take turns in the bedroom."

This time, he corrected himself before she had a chance to react. "Take turns *with* the bedroom, I mean. A week on, week off—whatever."

With the exception of pursing her full lips again, which Andrew was beginning to realize triggered certain reactions in him that, should he ever divulge them in confession, would prompt even the pious Father Steve to rethink his vocation, her expression was indecipherable. Without a word, she just reached over, slipped on her leather jacket, and started buttoning it up.

Feeling more deflated than an off-season beach ball, he got up and set his coffee cup in the sink.

Can't say I didn't try.

When he turned to face her again, the last thing he expected to see was her dangling her car keys midair. "Well, come on. I know a great breakfast dive about ten minutes from here."

CHAPTER FOUR

---

*"I have six locks on my door all in a row. When I go out, I lock
every other one.
I figure no matter how long somebody stands there picking the
locks, they are always locking three."*
—Elayne Boosler

Ferndell's was one of those storefront dives that people
pass by every day without appreciating or even realizing the
culinary treasures that could be had for a song within. That was
how Sara put it to Andrew anyway when she pulled him through
the door.

"Trust me," she said as she handed him a large, plastic-
coated menu. "This is the place to come if you're hungry."
Scanning the breakfast entrees, she mumbled, "And I'm
starving."

After placing their orders with a gum-popping waitress
and watching as she filled their coffee cups, Sara looked across
the booth at Andrew, who was just staring at her with those
beautiful blue eyes, clearly amused.

Her guard shot up, and she suddenly realized she was
sans makeup. In public. Despite feeling completely undressed
save for the color rising in her cheeks, she met his gaze. "What?"

Eyebrow arched, "I can't figure you out," was all he said,
with a hint of a smirk, making her feel like she was a problem
that required solving—like a human Rubik's Cube.

Is it that obvious?

Not sure how to respond, she reached for her cup. "I'll
take that as a compliment."

"Go for it."

In the awkward silence that followed, Sara tapped her fingers against either side of her cup. "So...do you go by anything other than Andrew? Sounds kind of stuffy."

He answered with his eyes and a slow shake of his head. "Really? Not Drew? Or Andy?"

At this, he pulled a face, "No. Please. Do not call me 'Andy.'"

"No worries," she murmured as she brought her cup to her lips, noticing for the first time that she found his slight overbite and the way his eyes angled down a bit in the corners when he wasn't smiling really rather endearing.

Taking a sip, she held the warm cup in her cold hands. "You don't look like an Andy. You could definitely pull off 'Drew' though."

With his cheeks taking on a decidedly pink hue, he said through a shy smile, "Nope. Just Andrew."

After a minute, he cocked his eyebrow. "What about you? Any nicknames?"

Suddenly the memory of her dad's trademark wolf whistle slicing through the woods behind their house up in William's Cove rang in her head. Sounding more like someone calling their dog in—not their child—he'd holler, "Trouble! Come on home now. It's gettin' dark."

She set her cup down on its saucer with a wobbly clank.

Looking around for their waitress, she asked, "Where's our food? It normally doesn't take this long."

Andrew, seemingly concerned that he had tripped a nerve, lowered his voice and asked, "Is that a yes?"

Flustered, she picked up her fork and examined it. "Yes, I have a nickname but no—" She put her fork down and looked at him with the most serious expression she could manage. "You'll never get it out of me."

He lifted his chin. While the glint in his eye said, "Challenge accepted," out loud he just said, "Fair enough."

Sara nearly leaped up and hugged their waitress, who had just arrived with their food.

Digging in to her omelet, she looked around the restaurant at the other patrons, the busboys milling about, the light fixtures—anything but him.

Not until he asked, "So what made you want to become a music critic?"

After she finished chewing her food, she finally met his gaze. "I don't know. I always liked analyzing performances and then writing about them."

Eyebrow arched, she continued, "Over time, I've gained some credibility. Now people check what I have to say about a performer or group before they buy a CD or plunk down big bucks for a show. It's pretty cool actually."

He didn't seem nearly as impressed by her as she was.

"You have that kind of power over the masses?"

There was something in the way he said it that made her feel like the most pompous person on the planet. She felt the color rise again in her cheeks.

With a shrug she replied, "Occupational hazard. How about you? What made you choose your profession?"

He thought for a minute. "I don't know. In some ways it chose me."

Her interest piqued, she asked, "What do you mean?"

"When my brother and I were kids, Dad would take us to church where Mom played the organ, still does, and a couple of our older siblings sang in the choir. I couldn't wait to take lessons and join in. Sacred music has always intrigued me. And the pipe organ, how it works? I find that fascinating."

Sara felt herself slip into interview mode. "How so?"

"Well, like an orchestra, the organ can have nearly endless possibilities for sound. Same thing with choral music. There are so many possibilities."

He held a hand out to her. "Well, what am I telling you for? You've sung in a church choir before, so you know what I'm talking about. Sacred music can always touch the soul." With a shrug, he added, "Once it does, there's no turning back."

Watch me.

After polishing off his French toast, he pointed to her shoulder and started, "So what's the song tattooed on your—"

Sara nearly choked on her food. After swallowing it down, she held her fork midair and croaked, "Next question."

He narrowed his eyes and looked down at his plate. "I'm only asking because it looks like it's—"

"Not up for discussion, OK?" A sudden longing to see Kerry again welled up inside of her. She tried blinking away the moisture pooling in her eyes before actual drops formed.

Too late.

With a quick brush of her fingertips, she swiped at them, clenched her jaw, looked across the room and whispered, "Next question, please."

"I'm sorry," she heard him say with his voice soft and low.

She had to blink a few more times, dab at the corners of her eyes with her napkin, and take a swig of her ice water before she was ready to look him in the eye again.

When she did, he asked with a teasing smile, "Does this mean you don't want to see mine?"

With that, the water she had just gulped threatened to resurface. She held a napkin to her mouth while she forced it back down before rasping, "You don't have a tattoo."

Leaning back in his seat, he raised an eyebrow. "Oh, but I do. Wanna see it?"

He slowly pulled his sweater up over his right hip and started tugging the hem of his T-shirt out of his jeans. Right there in the middle of a restaurant. She was mesmerized, wanting to see what kind of tattoo a Ken doll would get.

A heart with "Barbie" written across it?

Just as she was about to lunge across the table to get a glimpse, the gum-cracking waitress returned with their check.

Dammit.

"Can I get you anything else?"

Andrew, with his eyes still on Sara, plucked his T-shirt and sweater back down. "Had enough?"

Not nearly.

Four hours later, Sara and Andrew returned to his apartment with a few of her prized possessions that he bought back for her, including, but not limited to, her grandma's kitschy green glass relish dish, her fruit-themed shrimp forks, and four royal-blue, ceramic coffee mugs each bearing the shiny gold Cleff Marina logo. The plates went fast, the staffers at Goodwill told them, as did her perfectly good coffee pot, toaster, and microwave.

From there, Andrew had taken her to the women's shelter. As soon as they stepped inside to inquire if anyone had dipped into her belongings yet, Sara spotted several of the residents already wearing some of her favorite pieces of clothing, like the khaki-green, fisherman-knit sweater she stole from her brother years ago, the pretty pink and gold scarf she picked up at an Old Town art fair that summer, and a long, crinkled, floral-patterned skirt that never ever needed ironing.

"Can I help you?" a volunteer asked Andrew.

"Yes, I was here the other day to drop off—"

Sara interrupted. "Never mind." To Andrew, she just said, "Let's go."

She didn't say a word to him the entire way back. Instead, she thought of how her pal Mattie Ross always said the whole world could be divided into two groups: givers and takers.

Sara had always considered herself a taker. There were times even when she prided herself on it or, worse, used it to justify her actions.

What else could people expect of someone whose own mother abandoned her for some schlep named Wally who somehow managed to convince her mother that she'd be so much happier flying around the world with him than raising her and her brother while running the Bay Shore Bar and Grill next to her husband's smelly marina?

But when she saw those women at the shelter—some with visible bruises, some not so visible—wearing her clothes, painful memories of her parents arguing *all the time* surfaced. How many of those women, she wondered, felt obligated to stay in abusive relationships?

She continued to stare, recognizing more than just her mother in those women. She saw herself.

As she drove Andrew back to the near-northside apartment building, she tried labeling the emotion she was feeling. Unable to find the right word, she said nothing at all.

When they approached the door to the unit, Andrew, his arms filled with a box of her things, simply tilted his head to the right and said, "This side."

Sara plunged her hand into his warm, fleece-lined coat pocket to retrieve the key and slid it into the lock. Once inside, as soon as he set the box down, she leaned in and kissed him on the cheek.

Turning five shades of red, he asked, "What was that for?"

She shrugged. "No idea." All she knew was that it made the pain of her past subside. Just a little.

His eyes bright, he asked, "Ready to run through some music?"

She slipped off her jacket and exhaled a dramatic sigh. "Sure. Why the hell not."

Sara was eight years old the first time her father had shoved a microphone in her hand. They were at the helm of the big old paddleboat on which the marina used to give tours of Lake Compton, at the east end of which Williams Cove was tucked. Looking out at the crowd of smiling, expectant grown-ups, she froze, unable to think of a single song, despite belting out Top-40 hits at the top of her lungs whenever she thought no one was listening.

"Come on, Trouble. You can do it. Make me proud now," her dad had urged as he steered the boat away from the dock.

The microphone had felt as heavy as a brick in her little hand. The urge to drop it and run away had started to overtake her. She was about to do just that when the sound of a guitar strumming a familiar melody behind her signaled that Kerry had come to her rescue. Again. Turning, she'd seen her older brother, just about 18, sitting there on a chair bobbing his head, counting her in.

"One and two and..."

Sara blinked.

The music stopped.

"You OK?" Andrew was sitting right there next to her on the piano bench.

"Oh. Yeah. Sorry. Go ahead. I've got it."

His hands poised over the keys, he asked, "You sure?"

She nodded. "Yep."

He started again, and she followed along, leaning in to read the tiny print, but trying at all costs to avoid any additional physical contact.

After making it all the way through once, she was feeling pretty good about herself until he said, "OK, now this time, watch the dynamic markings. Don't be afraid to crescendo when it tells you to, otherwise, you're just flatlining."

She gave him a look. "I thought I did pretty fan-frickin'-tastic, thank you very much."

Flipping the music back to the first page, he said without looking at her, "You sounded better in the shower this morning. Come on. Again."

So she did. When they finished, he looked at her with his eyebrow raised. "That's more like it."

For reasons unbeknownst to her, acing the alto part of that simple little hymn made her feel a thousand times prouder than when she snatched the karaoke trophy away from the guys in Sports a few weeks back.

"OK, we'll be singing that during offertory tomorrow," he explained as he put it back in his folder and pulled out a larger binder. "Now, let me run you through the rest of the Mass."

When they had finished, he slid off the bench and checked his watch. "Oh, I'd better get going. I've got five o'clock Mass tonight."

He had no sooner left then returned again.

"Forget something?" Sara asked as she plugged in her laptop, debating whether she should get some work in or take a nap.

"Yeah. Here." He held out a key.

He may as well have whipped out an engagement ring. She felt herself shrink away from him. "But I haven't made up my mind yet."

A barely perceptible flicker of disappointment crossed his face. "I know. But if you want to go anywhere while I'm gone, you'll need a key to get back in, right?"

"Oh, yeah, right." She snatched it from him and set it as far away from her as possible on the kitchen counter, like it was some ominous token of doom.

"Catch you later."

"Later," he called from the foyer before closing the door behind him.

While she knew she should put the finishing touches on her Krypto Blight piece that was due first thing Monday morning, with the place finally to herself, all she wanted to do was process the titanic shift in her universe.

She stood and took a good look around the apartment. The addition of Andrew's personal touches —a couple of plants, some throw rugs, and pictures on the walls, made the place seem so much more warm and inviting. While she had only been away for a week or so, it was a far cry from what it was when she left—basically a high-end flophouse for wayward musicians.

And music critics.

Why, not twenty-four hours before she had been dropping Nancy and Aubrey off before she headed to the Aragon Ballroom. As far as she'd known, she was still living with Jer, stringing him along so she could keep living in an apartment she loved but couldn't afford. Now, most of her belongings had been cast to the wind, and her only hope of retaining her prestigious address was to step foot in church twice a week for the next six weeks.

Claire was right.

Her pal, an advice columnist extraordinaire, knew Sara's scheme would come back to bite her in the butt, and boy did it. With fangs.

Flipping on the stereo, she gently pulled *Dark Side of the Moon*, the only album with the power to anesthetize her, out of the bin she noticed was now alphabetized. Removing the vinyl disk from its plastic sheath, she lowered it onto the turntable with side two up, and carefully set the needle to the smooth band between the first and second tracks.

Then she lay down on the couch and closed her eyes.

Two hours later, she was roused by a growling stomach and the enticing aroma of kung pao chicken. Sitting up, she found that the crocheted afghan from the back of the couch was draped on top of her.

Must've fallen on me.

The apartment was dark, save for the soft light coming from the kitchen where Andrew had set two plates on the kitchen counter.

"Hey. You like Chinese food?" he asked as he pulled little white boxes of steaming hot food from a brown paper bag. *Jer never brought home take-out for the two of us.*

"Love it." She eased onto a barstool. "How was, uh, Mass?"

Seeing as it had been several years since she'd been, she couldn't find the words to express how much she was dreading what she was sure would be a fiery reentrance into the building.

"Father Steve's sermon was riveting as always," Andrew replied as he pried open the boxes and plunged serving spoons into each. With a wink, he added, "But I don't want to spoil it for you."

She pursed her lips together. "I don't suppose you kept my chopsticks...?"

Reaching into a different drawer, he held up two sets. "Is that what these are? I thought they were really big toothpicks."

At that, she laughed out loud. "Dork."

With the kitchen lights behind him, his eyes were dark as he flashed her a grin that might've otherwise made her knees buckle if he wasn't—well, wearing a stuffy shirt and a tie.

"You're wearing a shirt and a tie," she observed out loud. "You left here in jeans and a T-shirt."

He pushed two of the large boxes toward her plate. "Help yourself." Settling onto a stool across the counter from her, he heaped some fried rice onto his plate and explained that he kept extra work clothes in his office just in case he was ever running late or something came up.

Sara's eyes lit up. "Oh, I do that too," she remembered with her voice full of hope. "Which means I have at least two pairs of shoes and some clothes in my cube." Spooning food onto her plate, she added, "This day just keeps getting better and better."

When she looked up again, with her mouth full of food, she was surprised to see he wasn't eating. He was just looking at her, his elbow on the counter with his fingers wrapped loosely around his chin. She could see the questions swirling behind those narrowed baby blues. Questions she was pretty sure she did not want to answer.

"So," she started, "you want to give me the lowdown on this choir of yours? Will I be the only one under the age of 50? Anybody you want to warn me about? And, before you answer, are you sure you're not setting me up for a major choir fail?"

He looked amused. "No, yes, and no. We've got a couple of high school seniors this year. A soprano and a bass. You'll want to be ready for Marge. She's the librarian. She'll get you your music and binder and record your contact information. Probably ask for finger prints and a retinal scan."

Then he set his chopsticks down and leveled her with another look that had her starting to think some very unholy thoughts. "And I will never put you in a situation that you're not ready for, so no—no choir fail. Not tomorrow, anyway."

Surprised by a wave of warmth that started from her scalp and swooshed down to the tips of her toes, she struggled to find her voice. "Good to know."

"Oh, and that reminds me. I think it's best if we don't tell anyone we're, ya know, um—"

Cocking an eyebrow, she offered, "Living in sin?"

"Roommates." Despite his smirk, his cheeks were a lovely shade of embarrassed.

Pointing her chopsticks at him, she said, "You sure blush easy for a guy."

Flicking open the top button of his shirt, he loosened his tie and replied, "No, I don't."

"Like hell," she argued. "You're bright red. Go look in the mirror."

While he didn't follow her directive, he did stand up. "That reminds me. I got you something at Goodwill today."

Sara watched as he opened a lower cabinet, produced a large brandy snifter, and set it on the counter next to her plate.

"Sweet. A tip jar." Forget waitressing. She could beg tips at karaoke bars.

Andrew shook his head. "Nope. This will serve as a swear jar."

The smile left Sara's face. "What for?"

Locking his eyes on hers, he replied, "Every time you swear, you have to put a quarter in."

Heh, you better get a bigger frickin' jar.

"I don't swear."

"You cuss like a sailor."

She stabbed at her food with her chopsticks. "Like hell I do."

D'oh.

Andrew just pointed to the snifter.

Growling, she dug in her pocket and dropped a coin in, listening to the clink echo after it landed at the bottom. "Do hand gestures count?" Shifting in her seat, she mumbled to herself, "Who gives a rat's ass if I swear?"

Jer never complained about it.

"That's two." Pointing once again to the snifter, he suggested, "Why don't you just put a dollar in, and take the quarter back."

"That's not a swear," she protested. "It's a rodent and a body part. I hardly think that counts."

Andrew thought about it for a minute. "OK, I'll give you that one."

Sara chortled, "Damn straight."

Out of quarters, she shoved a dollar bill in the snifter. Tired of this little game, she held her chop sticks midair and said with a voice that one might use if one were pretending to be sweet and cheerful when all they really wanted was to throttle you, "Here's a tip. Next time you ask a girl to be your roommate, you might want to wait until after she agrees before pulling this little puppy out."

With his eyes on her, he slowly pulled his chopsticks out of his mouth. "Duly noted," he mumbled. Then, in one deft move, he lifted the snifter by its base and dumped her cash on the counter.

As she grabbed the money back, he cautioned, "You might want to hang onto that. I have a feeling you're gonna need it. And a whole lot more." After a somber wink, he added, "In fact, you might want to think about taking out a loan."

* * *

Across town, Claire and her husband Paul were hosting some relatively new but very special friends of theirs, Mattie

Ross and her fiancé, Nick DeRosa. Mattie, Claire's *Plate Spinner* predecessor, played a big hand in rescuing her from a severe case of career burnout. Nick, in the meantime, helped Paul jump back on the corporate treadmill after doing time as a stay-at-home dad to his and Claire's four boys.

Having fed said boys earlier, Claire served up hearty braised pot roast with pappardelle noodles, salad, and warm rolls. As the two couples sat around the table in the spacious mission-style dining room, Mattie moaned and wiped her mouth with a rust-colored cloth napkin.

"Claire, you have got to put the recipe for this in your column. It's so good."

Having just polished off his second serving, Nick nodded emphatically.

Claire beamed. "Yeah, I was thinking about it. Maybe something like: *Here's the perfect recipe for a hearty meal on a cold winter night. Not only does it warm the house up, it makes it smell scrumptious in the process.*"

"Perfect," Mattie laughed.

"There's plenty left if you guys want more," Claire announced.

Paul put his fork down and eased back in his chair with a satisfied sigh. "I'm good."

"So, Nick," Claire started. "Mattie mentioned you're up for a teaching job at Knollwood?"

Wiping his mouth, Nick nodded. "Yeah, that's right. One of the PE teachers is retiring, but if I can do that plus keep coaching cross-country and track," he glanced at Mattie before continuing, "we'd be able to get a house of our own sooner rather than later."

Smiling back at him, Claire replied, "Well, best of luck. When will you know?"

Nick pressed his lips together. "No idea. I would think soon though. I know a couple of teachers have already gotten their contracts for next year."

Claire smiled at Mattie who was beaming at Nick. "How exciting. Be sure to let us know, so we can celebrate."

When the others had finished eating, Nick picked up his and Mattie's empty plates and addressed Paul. "Why don't we clean up tonight?"

Paul cocked an eyebrow at his young friend who was nodding toward the kitchen. "Uh, yeah, sure."

Taking Claire's plate that she had just wiped clean with half of a roll, he leaned down to kiss her on the cheek. "That was so good," he whispered before whisking it away.

After he closed the pocket door to the kitchen behind him, Mattie sighed, "I hope Nick and I are as in love as you guys are after being married for fifteen years."

"Heh, let's not forget what we had to go through to get here." Why just six months earlier, Claire was a burned-out breadwinner, ready to divorce Paul because he refused to go back to work. After writing to the Plate Spinner—Mattie at the time—for advice, she had responded with an offer that not only redirected the trajectory of Claire's career, it saved her marriage in the process. Well, that and Nick, cross-country coach to Paul and Claire's oldest son and Mattie's marathon trainer, landing Paul a position at Griffin Media, the *Chicago Gazette's* parent company.

Claire reached over and patted her hand. "Marriage isn't easy. You really have to work at it. But if the stars align just right, love will prevail."

Mattie narrowed her eyes. "I can't believe you just quoted your own column."

"Too Hallmark-y?"

"Yeah, a little."

Claire leaned back in her chair and rubbed her expanding belly. "So how are you doing? How are the wedding plans coming along?"

"Oh. Major developments on the wedding front." With her eyes wide, Mattie briefed Claire on how, when she went up to ask Lester Crenshaw, the *Gazette's* publisher and a dear friend of the fatherless Mattie and her fiancé, to give her away at her wedding, he not only said yes but insisted that he host the reception at his posh north-shore country club.

With her eyes as big as Mattie's, Claire couldn't help but ask, "How awesome is that? Is Nick on board?"

She nodded, causing her long red curls to bounce on her shoulders. "His cousin Vito's banquet hall just can't compete."

Lowering her voice, Claire asked, "And his mother?"

Mattie waved her off. "Oh, yeah—Nick talked to her. She agreed, as long as she can still do the rehearsal dinner in their backyard the night before."

"The only downside is, Nancy has to pull out of the wedding party. Thank God Nick didn't ask all of the guys yet."

Even the baby did a little happy flip at that bit of news. Still, Claire felt compelled to reply, "Oh, how come?"

"Her mother called. She's getting married the same day. To husband number six, and she wants Nancy to be her maid of honor."

Well, there you have it.

Then Mattie leaned across the table, her eyes a little more sparkly than usual. "Claire, I have a big favor to ask."

Forever indebted to Mattie for picking her to succeed her as the Plate Spinner, she would do anything for her. Defend her against an overbearing future mother-in-law. Go wedding dress shopping with her. Donate a kidney.

"Absolutely. Anything."

"Be my bridesmaid?"

Except be a bridesmaid.

"Oh, honey. I don't know what to say."

Which was a lie. There were lots of reasons why Claire didn't want to stand up in Mattie and Nick's June wedding. For starters, she'd be going on eight months pregnant.

Well, OK, that's the only reason.

As if reading her mind, Mattie seemed to know exactly the right thing to say. "Claire, I know we've only known each other for a short time, but I really feel like we've become close friends. Without you, I wouldn't have been able to go back to investigative journalism—which I *love*—and since then, I don't know—I just think we've grown really close, and it would mean *so* much to me to have you be a part of the most important day of my life."

Truly touched, Claire blurted, "Well when you put it like that...of course. I'd love to."

They were locked in a hug when the guys passed through the dining room on the way to the family room to catch the Bulls game, beers in hand. Their in-transit conversation went as follows:

Nick: "Oh, hey. I've been meaning to ask, would you mind being an usher in our wedding?"

Paul (with a quick shrug): "Yeah, sure. Why not?"

Before sitting back down, Claire darted into the kitchen and returned with a wall calendar and a small notebook. "OK, so what's the date?"

"June 6th. It's the first Saturday after the Illinois High School Association track and field finals are over. When's your due date?"

"August 12th."

Visibly relieved, Mattie put both hands palm down on the table. "So we're good, right?"

"Well, considering I'll be around 31 weeks, yeah, we're good. Have you started looking at bridesmaids' dresses yet, because by then I'll be ready for a tent."

With a nervous laugh, Mattie replied, "As long as it comes in daffodil."

Claire looked up from her notebook. "I'm kidding, Matt. It's all good. Hey, didn't you say Nick's mom is a seamstress? Have you asked her about doing alterations?" Which led her to ask, "And how many bridesmaids are there? Who else have you asked?"

Mattie picked a little chocolate cupcake up from a tray Claire had placed in the middle of the table and popped it in her mouth. "Oh my gosh, I have so much to tell you."

By the time she was done catching Claire up on all things wedding related, the Bulls had beaten the Cavaliers in Cleveland which would explain all of the cheering coming from the family room, especially after Paul and Claire's two oldest boys had joined them.

And Claire was exhausted.

"Well, we should get going," Mattie suggested as she pulled Nick away from watching the post-game coverage. After they said their good-byes, Claire melded into Paul's open embrace. "I'm wiped."

"Hey, well at least we get to sleep in tomorrow."
Claire looked up him. "Ten o'clock Mass?"
"Sounds like a plan." After planting a kiss on her head,
they shut off the lights and headed up to bed.

* * *

After stuffing themselves with Chinese food, putting
away the leftovers, and hand-washing Sara's hand-painted
chopsticks, she and Andrew spent several long minutes
suspended in the "we're living together, but not *living* together"
awkwardness as they stared down the Saturday night that seemed
to sprawl out in front of them like eternity.
"So," Sara started. "What's a music director do for fun on
a Saturday night? Movies? Plays? Concerts?"
When he responded with another one of his penetrating
stares, she continued, "Uno? Yahtzee? Poker?"
"Actually," he said, his voice low and his eyes kind,
"I've got to be at church pretty early tomorrow."
Sara studied him for a moment before responding.
Just roommates. Nothing more. Message received.
"Oh, yeah, sure. I'm still kinda beat from being on the
road."
Andrew raised both eyebrows. "Right. Well, OK then.
Good night." He flashed her a quick smile, cupped a hand
platonically on her upper arm, and gave it a gentle squeeze.
In return, Sara gave him a little wave as he turned and
started down the hall. "Toodles."
An hour later, she was still wide awake, dressed in his
pajama top, sprawled out on the hide-a-bed, dreading going to
church in the morning, and wondering where in the hell she
could sleep tomorrow night after she informed Andrew that she'd
take a pass on his proposition, thank you very much.
On hearing her phone that was recharging on the kitchen
counter chirp, she hopped out of bed and read the text. It was
from Nancy. *Where r u? Sports staging a comeback. Hurry!*
Sara glanced at the oven clock. It was only 10:00. If she
took the train, she could make it to Kildare's, a popular Lincoln
Park bar, by 10:30.

After texting *on my way*, she slapped on some makeup and changed into a billowy white blouse, black tights, her boots, and jacket. She grabbed her purse and carefully closed the front door behind her so as not to make a sound.

It wasn't until hours later, when Sara returned to the apartment feeling a little dizzy and very fuzzy from downing a couple of celebratory shots, that she realized she had left the extra key Andrew had given her on the kitchen counter. On the other side of the locked door.

Well, shit.

She rested her head against it and knocked softly for she didn't know how long. Not expecting him to answer, she turned her back to the wall next to the door, slid to the floor, and folded her arms over her bent knees. Letting her head fall forward, she was almost fast asleep when she felt two strong hands gripping her elbows.

A groggy voice asked, "Sara, you all right?"

She lifted her head, opened one eye, and then the other. Squinting in the dimly lit hallway, she whispered, "Forgot my key."

Seeing the concern in his eyes, something twisted deep inside of her.

"And to leave a note," he muttered.

She took a deep breath and exhaled, "Sorry."

Watching him grimace, he chuckled, "It's all good."

She reached over and patted his cheek. "You look tired."

His smile broadened. "Because it's two in the morning. Come on. Let's get you up."

Once she was standing, she took in his rumpled hair and bare chest.

As he ushered her back inside, she thought to herself, "Kinda hot for a church guy."

That she actually vocalized this sentiment out loud was indeed unfortunate.

Making her way down the dark hallway to the kitchen, she heard him mumble behind her, "Yeah, I get that a lot."

There was something in his tone that caught her ear. Self-deprecation? Loneliness?

Whatever it was, it prompted her to turn, take his face in her hands, and plant her lips against his. Knocking him back against the wall, she leaned into him, taking much longer than it would have if she were sober to realize he wasn't kissing her back. Not really.

Oh.

She pulled back and looked in his surprised eyes. "Sorry about that."

When he didn't respond, didn't say anything at all, she turned toward the open sleeper sofa, and sighed, "Sara strikes out. Again."

Then she flopped down on it face first.

What seemed like a second later, she thought she heard someone whisper her name, but managed to ignore it. Then she felt someone sit on the mattress beside her and something warm press against her exposed neck.

Holy shit.

Nearly jumping out of her skin, she banged it away with her bauble-laden hand and sat up, eyes wide and panting.

"Easy," the Ken doll winced, examining his fingers. "I was just checking to see if you still had a pulse."

Through her smudged, makeup-caked eyes, she noted that her jacket was folded over the arm of the couch, and her boots were sitting together neatly against the wall.

When Andrew shifted his focus from his hand to Sara, he gave her a warm smile.

Again with the blushing.

"I, uh, also wanted to remind you to be at church by 9:30 this morning. I left the address on the counter. Just come right in and find me up near the front, okay?"

Barely registering what he was talking about, she reached over and grasped his hand. "Did I hurt you?"

"I've had worse."

She glanced at him. He was back in a shirt and tie, but this time coupled them with cords and a V-neck sweater.

Such a Ken doll.

A Ken doll that was still sitting on her bed. And still with that smile on his face.

Releasing his hand, she tried to edge a comfortable distance away from him, but he was on top of the blankets, effectively trapping her. Instead, she slid back under them.

"You're being awfully chummy this morning." She yawned. "If you wanted to check my pulse, you could've just grabbed one of my wrists."

Turning his head so he could maintain eye contact, he asked, "So you would've preferred that I grope around under the blankets looking for your wrist? I'll remember that for the next time."

Wondering what had happened from the time they went to bed the night before to now for him to be acting like this, she propped herself up on her elbow and asked, "What's with you?"

After another penetrating, but so-not-smoldering stare, his smile faded, and the gleam left his eye. Then he stood up.

Finally.

"Nothing. I'll, uh, see you at church."

"I'll be there," she replied with a mock salute, well aware that she didn't sound very convincing.

With a quick nod, he was gone.

Taking a long look around the empty apartment, she laid back in bed and moaned, "Do I have to?"

It wasn't until she had gotten up and was making the bed that she realized she wasn't wearing his pajama top. She was wearing what she'd wear to work. Or a club.

Fragments of memories started flashing through her groggy brain.

Being at the bar.

Was that last night?

Singing some old Heart song. "Crazy on You?" "Magic Man?"

Winning the trophy.

Damn straight.

Drinking shots.

Way too many shots.

Nancy putting her in a cab, so she didn't have to take the train.

Hope she paid the guy 'cause I sure as hell didn't.

But she was certain Andrew was asleep the whole time.

Wasn't he?

After she had taken a long steamy shower, Sara used her fingertips to wipe the steam off of the medicine cabinet mirror.

Starting at her bare face, she wondered how much makeup was too much for church.

Brushing on some blush and flicking a bit of mascara on her lashes, she had just leaned in to apply her lipstick when it hit her.

Oh, good lord. I kissed him.

And he didn't kiss back.

CHAPTER FIVE

———

"I used to be Snow White, but I drifted."
—*Mae West*

On autopilot for the first two Masses of the morning, Andrew immersed himself in the music, doing all he could to not think of Sara's middle of the night ~~greeting assault~~ kiss. He tried reminding himself that she had been drunk at the time. Why else wouldn't he have kissed her back?

But then again, why else would she have kissed him in the first place?

Girls like her don't fall for guys like me.

On the outside, she was all wild child what with her Goth-like appearance, foul mouth, and heavy drinking. He couldn't imagine bringing her home to meet mom and dad—especially when dad is a cop and mom is a church organist who is still in touch with his former fiancée.

Try as he might, he couldn't keep his thoughts from wandering to the feel of Sara's hands holding his face.

And the way her breath tasted of whiskey as she moved her mouth over his.

Leanne never kissed me like that.

In hindsight, not a big surprise. While pretty, kind, and able to silence a room full of misbehaving four-year olds with just one look, she was above all chaste.

When he thought of Sara, right or wrong, the word chaste just didn't come to mind. Unable to come up with a word that did, he knew in his heart of hearts that she wouldn't be trading her leather coat and boots for a nun's habit anytime in the near future.

So, advantage, Sara.

As the crowd from the 8:30 am Mass cleared out, he kept his eyes trained on the back of the church as members of the adult choir began trickling in for warm-up. He greeted each as they passed him on the way to their seats. When he spotted Marge, he called her aside.

"You OK this morning?" she asked as she peered at him over the rim of her reading glasses.

"Yes. Why?" Again, his eyes darted to the back of the church.

"You seem jumpy, and your face is flushed. You feeling OK?" the retired nurse asked again as she pressed the back of her hand to his forehead. Before he hand a chance to dodge away, she reported, "No fever. Maybe you should have your blood pressure checked."

He started leading her back to the choir room. "I'm fine." Then, in a hushed voice, he instructed her to fill an empty binder with music they'd be singing for that morning's Mass.

"Find yourself a new hostage?" she asked before ducking through the door.

As he turned back toward the rest of the choir, he noticed, while some were getting their music ready, most had their eyes on the back of the church.

Taking a deep breath, he followed their collective line of vision.

Oh, thank God.

Until he laid eyes on Sara, he wasn't aware of how anxious he had been about whether or not she'd show, what she'd be wearing, and if she'd be on time.

She seemed rather stupefied, if that was even possible. He watched as she gingerly dipped her hand in the Baptismal font and made the sign of the cross, then slowly started making her way up the side aisle with her eyes fixed on him.

A long black skirt that she had topped with a belted greenish-blue, long-sleeved blouse swooshed against her legs as she moved. No heavy makeup. No visible tattoo to render the bass and tenor sections mute. His relief was without bounds.

As she approached, he noticed the soprano section was already whispering like they'd just seen a streaker run through the narthex. The tenor and bass sections, on the other hand, were silent if not slack-jawed.

OK, so this probably wasn't one of my better ideas.

Coming straight up to him, she said a little too loudly, "New alto, reporting for duty."

Not wanting to throw fuel on the rumor mill inferno, he avoided making eye contact with her, instead pointing to Marge who was coming out of the choir room. "OK, great. Marge there can set you up."

With binder in hand, Sara returned Marge's stare up until the moment the librarian nearly tripped on the step leading up to her chair.

Sara, in the meantime, turned toward the other altos and said, "Hello."

The collective question on their faces asked, "Where in the world did you come from?"

Andrew rushed over and said loud enough for all sections to hear, "Everyone. This is Sara. She'll be sitting in with the altos this morning." Gesturing to the rest of the choir, he clipped, "Sara, everybody." Then, turning to her, he instructed, "Go ahead and sit on the end here, next to Glynnis."

Once everyone was in place, he started running them through a warm-up exercise. He could hear Sara loud and clear. A quick glance at the group, he saw that they heard her too and seemed to approve.

"OK, let's run through 'The Lord is My Shepherd.' Everybody up." The choir knew this one well and seemed to like it. Sara had already sung it twice the day before and nailed it. Fingers crossed, all would go smoothly.

He sat behind the piano and started playing. At the start of the measure in which sopranos and altos were supposed to start, together, he gave a hard nod and held his breath.

Perfect.

While he could tell Sara was holding back, he heard her gain confidence as the hymn progressed. With the last chord reverberating through the church, he gave one last nod, signaling them to stop. And they did. All together.

Perfect.

When he looked up, he didn't bother masking his surprise. "That was fantastic. The congregation will be throwing their credit cards at the collection basket if you sing it like that during Mass."

In reply, he actually heard chuckling and saw several happy faces looking back at him.

Well, that's a first.

Then his eyes fell on Sara. She was staring at him, looking a little glassy-eyed.

As he slid off of the piano bench, he saw Glynnis hand her a tissue from her purse when they both sat back down. "It's a very pretty piece, isn't it? I cried the first time I heard it too."

Andrew leaned down and whispered, "You all right?"

She gave him a quick nod, but he had a feeling that was far from the truth, especially when he caught her eyes sliding to her left.

* * *

When she had pulled into the St. Matthias Church parking lot that morning, Sara backed into a spot as far away from the doors as she could find, hoping to not get caught in the congestion of cars leaving after Mass. Before getting out, she sat and stared at the tidy red brick building, watching the shiny, happy parishioners come and go, all the while asking her dashboard a series of questions.

Why am I here?

What if I mess up?

What if I don't remember the prayers?

What if they expect me to go to communion, or worse, confession?

As she sat hunkered down in the front seat, her hands gripping the top of her steering wheel and a hornet's nest of emotions churning in her empty belly, she was still staring at the doors leading to the church when a familiar face caught her eye.

Claire?

What the hell is she doing here?

Sure enough, she was followed by four boys, one of whom darted ahead of her and pulled open the door. Her husband, an accountant with Griffin Media, came up behind her and grasped her hand as they went in.

A not very Christian-like pang of envy tore through her. *I'll never have that.*

Tempted to drive her car—already packed with her clothes, the box of her personal effects Andrew had retained, and the things he had bought back for her from Goodwill—over to Nancy's and see if she'd be willing to put her up for the night, her eyes fell on the stained glass window near what she presumed to be the front of the church. On the other side of which, she presumed, Andrew was waiting for her.

Picturing the intoxicatingly lovely floral motif stained glass over the bay window in her, ugh, make that *his* apartment, she grimaced, took a deep breath, and got out of the car. Not seriously expecting lightning to come out of the beautiful blue morning sky and strike her down on her way into the church, she made a beeline to the door just in case.

In the lobby, or narthex, several people were milling about, mostly older and clearly all acquainted. After she hung up her leather jacket in the coatroom, she could feel their eyes on her as she passed by and was grateful she hadn't worn anything too eye-catching. All was going well until she passed through the doors to the church itself.

Her senses were accosted by the quiet stillness. Picking up the slightest scent of incense, she was flooded with memories of attending Mass as a kid, every Sunday and holy day up until she graduated from high school, and then it just didn't seem to matter any more. Dad had stopped going after Mom left, and Kerry only went on occasion.

She dipped her fingertips in the cold holy water of the baptismal font and made the sign of the cross, feeling like the biggest hypocrite on the planet. The nearly empty pews were dotted with people already there. Some were on their knees. Some were clutching rosaries. To her right, a short line of people waited for their turn in the confessional. Her eyes zeroing in on that door, she felt the blood start to drain from her head.

Turning, the first thing she saw was Andrew, right where he said he'd be, and she felt a giant whoosh of a welcoming sensation wash over her.

It took her by surprise.

And it felt good. Weird but good.

So, despite the drunken line she had crossed with him during the night, she ventured forward, oblivious to the stares of others.

Once she was in place, he ran them through the same hymn he practiced with her the day before. The sound of the beautiful harmonies the choir produced gave her goose bumps and made her eyes water.

Fumbling through the rest of the Mass, by the time choir had finished the recessional hymn at the end, the words Andrew had used at breakfast the day before came back to haunt her.

There's no turning back.

And it scared the shit out of her.

"It was so nice to meet you, dear," she heard the older woman next to her—*Glynnis, was it?*—say before stepping away to gather her things. But Sara was already scanning the crowd leaving the church, hoping to catch Claire before she left. While the other choir members were busy putting their music-filled binders away and getting their coats, and Andrew was still playing some lovely instrumental piece, she left without so much as saying good-bye to anyone.

"Claire, wait up."

Her friend had just made it into the narthex when she heard Sara's voice. With eyes wide, Claire exclaimed, "Hey. What are you doing here?"

In a hushed voice, Sara started, "Oh my God, Claire—you have no idea. Can we talk?"

Claire looked up at her husband, who had his eyes on Sara.

"Honey." He didn't seem to hear her.

"*Honey*," Claire tried again while giving his arm a hard squeeze.

That did the trick.

"What?"

Nodding at her friend, she asked, "You remember Sara? From the *Gazette*?"

With a smile, he nodded. "Yeah, sure. How are ya?"

Sara breathed out. "Hey, Paul. I've been better." She then looked imploringly at her friend.

Claire turned to Paul. "Why don't you take the guys down for donuts without me? I'll meet you there in a bit."

With a quick nod, he herded their sons and directed them to the stairwell leading to the lower level where the Holy Name Society was serving coffee and donuts after each of the services that day.

Leading her to a quiet corner, Sara sputtered, "Claire. You would not believe the weekend I have had." She tried to keep the emotion out of her voice but clearly did a poor job of it.

"Are you OK? What happened?"

Sara spent the next several minutes recapping the highlights starting with her encounter with Andrew at Bell's Market and ending with the reason she was at St. Matthias, of all places, on a Sunday morning.

When she had finished, with eyes wide, Claire gasped, "You're *living* with Andrew Benet?"

With a quick look over her shoulder, Sara shushed her. "No! I don't—*no*. Oh, I don't know. My whole world has been completely turned upside down, and I can't think straight. All I know is you called this, Claire. Now that it's happened, you've got to tell me what to do."

"OK, calm down. Let's see. So, to recap, if you want to stay in your beloved apartment, you just have to join choir—"

"Just until Easter."

Claire nodded. "Right. Just until Easter. Which is over a month away."

"Six weeks. It's six weeks away," Sara countered, breathless.

"Okay. Six weeks. What happens after that?"

Sara stopped fretting long enough to realize that she should've asked Andrew that very same question. "I suppose we'll cross that bridge when we come to it. What I need to know is what to do *now*."

"Well, listen, that's entirely up to you, hon, but I will tell you this. What I know of Andrew, and mind you, it's not a lot—"

"Yeah...?" Whatever Claire was about to tell her, Sara hoped it would either make or break the entire deal. She braced herself. "Go ahead. Tell me."

With a smile, Claire finished. "What I have heard from other parents here and have seen with my own eyes, is that he's a really great guy. Very decent. Wildly talented. He came from...oh, I can't remember. Somewhere in the Midwest. Oh, Minnesota. He's got a brother who's a cop. Had him come in and talk to the 7th and 8th graders in the fall about safety, the internet, bullying, that sort of stuff.

"And," the advice columnist continued with a protective edge in her voice, "I'm pretty positive he would never sublet the apartment while you were on assignment, leave the country, and tell someone to pitch all of your things." She looked into the distance and added, "What a schmuck."

She squeezed her friend's shoulder. "You should've called me. I'm so sorry you had to go through that alone."

With that, Sara felt a smile pull at the corner of her mouth. "Well, technically, I wasn't."

Looking out at the still-crowded narthex, she shook her head before whispering, "It's just, he's so not my type."

Claire smirked. "Andrew? What's wrong with him?"

Sara, rolling her eyes, sputtered, "Nothing. Everything. He's so stoic. So proper and self-righteous."

With a frown, her friend interjected, "Really? He doesn't seem the preachy type."

"No, that's not what I meant." Looking Claire in the eye, Sara tried to clarify her thoughts. And stop blithering. "But he works *here*."

"Yes, I totally get that, believe me. But," Claire tried reasoning, "just because you're living together doesn't mean it has to be anything beyond that."

With a pained expression, Sara whispered, "Too late."

Gripping her arm like a vice, Claire nearly shrieked, "What?"

Unable to tell if her reaction was the result of admiration or just plain shock, Sara did her best to tuck even deeper into the corner. "It's not what you think. I was out with Nancy last night—"

With a disapproving look, Claire interrupted, "Ach, say no more. I don't care if she's an award-winning journalist, that woman is a tramp."

Well aware Claire didn't think well of the assistant food editor, Sara looked at her friend like a rebellious teenager would a disapproving parent.

Claire relented. "Sorry. Probably should've kept that to myself. Go ahead. You were with Nancy..."

"Well, I had a few drinks. When I got back to the apartment, I realized I didn't have the key he gave me, so I had to wake him up to let me in. That's when I kissed him."

Claire's eyebrows shot up. "Oh really?" Leaning in conspiratorially, she asked, "How was it?"

Forgetting where she was, Sara said perhaps a little too loudly, "I thought it was pretty great." Then she whispered, "Until I realized he wasn't kissing me back."

Her friend looked at her sympathetically. "Oh, sweetie."

Emerging from the dark corner, Claire started walking her friend to the stairwell her boys had used on their hunt for sugary goodness. "Can I ask you something?"

Sara nodded.

"If you don't think he's your type, why did you kiss him?"

Sara looked down at the tips of her boots peeking out from under her skirt for a long while before she raised her head. "I know I've only just met him, but he makes me feel—" She squinted into the distance, unable to finish. After a few seconds, she laughed at herself, then returned Claire's concerned expression with glistening eyes.

Her friend prodded, "He makes you feel..."

When Sara finally replied, the words caught in her throat, but Claire heard them loud and clear all the same. "Like he gives a shit, ya know?"

Claire gave her a sweet smile that somehow made Sara feel that much more conflicted. "Oh my."

"I know, right?" With another wave of panic rising within her, Sara pleaded. "So what should I do?"

Tilting her head, the advice columnist replied, "Sounds to me like you've already decided."

* * *

Begging out of coffee and donuts with Claire and her family—her adorable, perfect family—Sara got in her car and drove. And drove and drove and drove. She edged through Ravenswood and Uptown before making her way to Lake Shore Drive. Given that it was a dismal, gray March day filled with low dark clouds that threatened snow, traffic was light as she pulled on at Foster Avenue.

For the entire way down to the 57th Street exit where she got off and parked in the Museum of Science and Industry parking lot, she tried convincing herself that agreeing to Andrew's terms for cohabitation would be yet another in a long line of mistakes she'd already made during the course of her screwed-up life.

Before this weekend, there were only two other people who Sara could say with any confidence had ever made her feel cared for: her mom and her brother. While her mother had actually walked out on her, her brother may as well have. When he had found out what she had done...

Sara sat there for a very long time, staring out her windshield, seeing nothing but the expression on Kerry's face when he confronted her with a rumor he'd heard down at the garage, contorted with anger because she hadn't come to him for help first, and hurt that he had to find out from someone else. Jimmy Mabry of all people.

While he said very little, his words hurt more than she could've ever imagined. "I'm done."

She accepted Mike Teegan's internship offer the very next day, and she hadn't seen nor heard from Kerry since.

Because I'm pond scum.

She took a deep breath and gripped the steering wheel with both hands.

"And I'm really tired of this pity party," she said to absolutely no one as she shifted her car into drive and pulled back onto Lake Shore Drive, heading north into the oncoming wind-whipped flurries and thinking of little more than that weird welcoming whoosh she felt when she stepped foot into the nave of the church that morning.

* * *

In the post recessional-hymn commotion brought on by thirty-some adults trying to funnel through the narrow choir room door to return their music binders and retrieve their coats, Andrew stayed out of the fray by playing one more solo piece, usually a nice long one. He'd even play it twice if he had to.

But not today.

After catching Sara make a quick exit after Mass, he was eager to see if her teary eyes after the warm up and strong vocals through the rest of the Mass were indicative of her willingness to accept his offer of joining the choir.

And living with me.

When it seemed the last of the choir members had passed by on either side of him, making their way toward the exit as he played, he slid off the bench as soon as he finished.

"So who is she?"

It was Marge, standing there with her plaid wool coat, trying to work her leather gloves onto her arthritic hands. While she sounded friendly, her ever-present scowl gave away her true mood.

Feigning ignorance, he asked, "Who?"

Marge's scowl deepened. "I asked around. No one's seen her here before."

Andrew stood in front of her. "When I started here, you mentioned you had just retired."

Nodding, she said, "Yes, that's right."

"Was it, by any chance, from the CIA?"

"Oh." She swatted him with her gloves that she had yet to put on.

Gathering his sheet music, Andrew edged around the trifocaled obstacle and said, "She's a friend, Marge. Just a friend."

He ducked into the choir room to store his music and retrieve the cover for the Steinway. On his way out, armed with a change of subject, he announced, "I heard we're supposed to get some heavy snow today," but Marge had already gone.

After he covered the piano, he switched off the organ console and pulled on his coat, hoping to duck through what he could see was a still-crowded narthex without encountering any disgruntled parishioners who still asked him inane questions like, "When is Mr. Greely coming back?" and "Can't you play any faster so Mass won't take so long?"

I hate donut Sundays.

He was almost at the doors to the parking lot when he thought he heard Sara's voice.

"It was pretty great."

Stopping in his tracks, he turned his head in the direction he thought it came from but didn't see her—just a bunch of adults trying to visit while keeping an eye on their sugared-up kids.

Huh.

He left, hopped in his Jeep, and hoped for the best. As he made his way home, he tried anticipating what he'd find. Would she be excited? Grateful? Maybe she'd be making lunch or napping. One thing he did know, she sure as hell wouldn't be cleaning.

Maybe he'd create a chore chart like the one his mom had used.

That would probably go over as well as the swear jar did.

Light snow started dotting his windshield. Flicking on the wipers, his thoughts drifted to what he'd make for dinner later, which prompted him to consider swinging by the grocery store while he was out. Then he started wondering what kind of food Sara liked, if she cooked, what kind of schedule a music critic kept during the week, and whether coming up with a dinner schedule would be too much.

I ought to write all this down.

After pulling into his spot behind the building, he leaned over and popped open the glove compartment to look for a little pad of paper and pen he usually stored there for logging mileage and maintaining the Jeep's service schedule.

With a list of questions in hand, he took the stairs two at a time.

I have a very good feeling about this.

Not two minutes later though, that very good feeling was gone. Not only was Sara not there, none of her things were either. Not her clothes, her toiletries, her box of personal effects he had saved. Not even the items of hers that he had bought back for her from Goodwill.

It was like she was never there, and the emptiness crushed in around him.

* * *

"Hey, Charlie. What are you doing here?" Sara asked the *Gazette* staff photographer as she passed by his cube on the way to hers.

The clip-clop of her boot heels echoed through the office that was sparsely populated even for a snowy Sunday afternoon.

Leaning back on his chair to watch her go by, he called out, "I don't have a life. What's your excuse?"

I'm hiding.

"Deadlines, Charlie. Always a deadline."

As soon as her laptop booted up, she uploaded the photos she'd taken of the Krypto Blight tour and finished refining her lengthy piece before sending it to Mike Teegan. Taking a closer look at her email inbox, she spotted a reply from him on her assessment of Ellie Klein's disastrous foray from the top of the country charts to the bottom of the pop charts.

She clicked Open and held her breath.

All it said was, "Thanks for this. Stop by tomorrow, and we'll talk."

She frowned at her screen. Considering Mike's typical responses were more like short opinionated essays than emails, the brevity of this one didn't sit well with her.

Hitting the reply button, she typed, "Looking forward to it," and hit send.

"You'd better get home, Sara," Charlie said as he passed her cube. "The snow's getting heavier, and it's already dark."

She looked up at him. "No worries. I'll be right behind you."

As she made her way down the street toward the parking garage, she braced herself for life with the type of man who pressed his pj's and used flavored creamer in his coffee.

Six weeks is a very long time.

Glad she had worn her boots, she quickly realized they were more suited for fashion, not function. And she wished she still had her nice long wool overcoat. While the leather of her jacket kept out the wind that was racing down Michigan Avenue, it offered little protection against the bitter cold. Even after she ducked into the parking garage around the corner, without a hat, scarf, or gloves, the chill sank into her bones. She slammed her car door, turned the key in the ignition, and put her defroster on high before heading down the ramp and onto the unplowed street.

Having grown up in Wisconsin, she was a pro at driving in the snow. It was the ice underneath it that scared her. She took a wide berth of buses as she edged down the nearly empty avenue before turning onto Chestnut and heading west. She slipped her snow-caked Honda into Jer's old spot behind the apartment building as far as she possibly could, hoping it wouldn't get nicked by any snowplows or overzealous shovelers.

Before getting out of her car, she looked in the backseat at her boxes of belongings and debated about lugging them back upstairs.

Later.

She grabbed a stadium blanket that lay folded on the floor behind the passenger seat and draped it over both boxes, grabbed her overnight bag and purse, and got out of the car.

It was dark, and the light that was supposed to illuminate the parking lot was only giving off a dim glow through the heavy flurries.

Her high-heeled boots, still damp from her walk through the unshoveled sidewalk to the parking garage did little to keep her steady and her feet warm as she slogged through the heavy, wet snow. By the time she made it around to the front door, her hair was soaked, and a thick wedge of white stuff had packed itself between the collar of her jacket and her bare neck. She was shivering so hard, she could barely fit her key in the front door lock.

Once in front of the apartment door, she found that trying to slide the key in the lock proved to be more difficult than she could manage. All she seemed able to do was poke at the door with the tip of the key. On her third attempt it opened while she was still hunched over, squinting at the lock.

Straightening up, she saw Andrew standing before her, a sight for cold eyes, still in his dress shirt and sweater, but he had ditched the tie and swapped the cords with jeans.

Other than that, he looked like hell. And she told him as much through her chattering teeth.

With his face breaking into a relieved smile, all he said was, "Hey."

Still shivering, she asked, "Can I come in?"

As if finally noticing that she was covered in snow and turning blue, he took her purse and suitcase from her and set them on the floor in the foyer. "Of course. Come on."

Locking the door behind them, he ushered her through the hallway and motioned for her to sit on one of the kitchen barstools so he could help her off with her boots.

She pressed her bare, raw, red hands against his nice warm shoulders as he unzipped them and pulled.

"Your socks are soaked. Your feet must be freezing."

Sara hunched her shoulders up and nodded.

Next, he peeled off her coat and draped it over the back of a chair on the kitchen's tile floor so it could drip as it thawed.

Letting out a gasp as the snow wedge escaped down her back, she heard him say, "Stay right there." He disappeared for a minute before returning with a nice fluffy towel that he handed to her. "Here."

Setting it in her lap, she arched her back and pleaded, "Get it out?"

"Oh, uh, let me see." First he gingerly peered down the back of her blouse but saw that it was stuck against her skirt's belted waistline. "I'm just gonna..."

"It's OK." She shuddered. "Just get it out."

In a flash, he reached down her back, pulled out the offending snow pack, and tossed it into the sink. The feel of his warm hand brushing against her cold skin prompted her to gasp.

Covering her hands with his nice toasty ones, he whispered, "You're frozen. What were you thinking?"

She gave her head a quick shake. "Didn't know it was gonna snow."

He stood in front of her and stated the obvious. "You're completely soaked. You better get out of those wet clothes before you catch a chill."

At that, her breath hitched. "Too late."

"Right. OK, then a hot shower. Give me a second, and I'll get it ready for you."

"Not too hot," she chattered. Every Wisconsinite knew you should only use lukewarm water on frostbitten skin, and she felt frostbitten from head to toe.

Thirty minutes later, she was on the couch dressed in his blue plaid flannel pajamas, tops and bottoms this time, her feet were tucked into his wool socks, and her entire body was wrapped in the afghan. The shaking had subsided, but the chill wouldn't release its grip on her.

Handing her a mug, Andrew instructed, "Drink this."

She looked up at him. "Will it make me larger or smaller?"

Placing it in her outstretched hands, he answered, "Warmer. It will make you warmer."

Before she took a sip of the hot liquid, she asked, "Not a fan of Lewis Carroll?"

"No. I tried watching the movie, but I just couldn't get into it."

She gave him a disapproving look as he sat down beside her and said, "Come on. Drink up."

"So bossy," she whispered as she raised the mug to her lips and took a swig.

The hot, sweet and sour mix of honey and lemon, coupled with the warm familiar buzz of whiskey, filled her mouth.

Swallowing hard, she tried handing the mug back to him. "This isn't tea."

He held up his hand. "I never said it was. It's a hot toddy. Finish it."

She took a big gulp. "There's whiskey in this. Are you trying to get me drunk?" While protesting over such a thing seemed out of character, her tired brain told her it was good form.

His eyes dark, he let out a low chuckle. "Heh, no. People drink this to warm up, relieve cold symptoms, that sort of thing. It's an old Minnesota recipe."

Sara just clutched the mug and nodded before opening her mouth to accommodate an enormous, jaw-popping yawn. After taking another swig, her stomach grumbled, reminding her that she hadn't eaten anything since downing a vending-machine bag of peanuts at work earlier. But she was too tired to think about food. Come to think of it, she was too tired to think about anything...anything at all.

CHAPTER SIX

———

"You can't have everything... Where would you put it?"
—*Steven Wright*

On Monday morning, Sara woke up with a start.

"What time is it?" she whispered, looking around her bedroom. Her face slowly creased into a frown.

The closet doors weren't hanging open, and her clothes weren't strewn about as usual.

I don't remember cleaning up in here.

Sinking back into her nice comfy bed with the pillow-top mattress pad, butter-soft flannel sheets, and perfectly firm-but-huggable pillows, she closed her eyes, hoping to catch the tale end of a dream. Already she was having a hard time remembering the details, but it was the type of dream in which you wanted to stay forever.

It took place there in the apartment.

What she wanted more than anything was to dive back into the feeling of being light and happy. And loved.

Her eyes popped open again.

Somebody else was in the dream with her. She squinted, trying to remember before the details disappeared for good.

It wasn't Jer, that's for sure. She never felt light and happy around him. Dark and moody was more like it.

Resting her head back on the pillow, she stared at the ceiling.

Nope. It was gone.

With a wave of despair about to crest over her, she peeled back the blankets, remembering a promise she made to meet Mattie, Aubrey, and Nancy for breakfast before heading into the office.

Glancing at the other side of the queen-size bed, she was glad to see it was unoccupied.

Claire's right. I've gotta ditch Jer.

The thought had no sooner crossed her mind, then it all came flooding back.

Wait. He ditched me.

She held her hands to her face as the entire weekend flashed before her eyes in a rapid-fire sixty-second replay.

Oh my God.

She looked down at her blue-plaid, flannel-wrapped legs and whispered, "Oh my God."

Stepping over to the closet door, she carefully pulled it open, knowing full well it would squeak if she forced it. As she took in the row of neatly hung men's shirts and suits, she grimaced.

I can't believe I'm living with a Ken doll.

Eager to get in the shower and out of the apartment, she slowly turned the doorknob and stepped into the shadow-filled hallway. Not yet six, the morning light was just starting to filter in through the front bay window. Tiptoeing into the living room on her way to the foyer to retrieve her carry-on bag and purse, she saw the sleeper sofa was open. And occupied. She sucked in a breath.

Andrew was on his side, wrapped snuggly in the blanket, save for a bare arm that was tucked in front of him. His hair was a complete mess, a shadow of scruff darkened his face, and his mouth was open, just a little.

Adorbs.

But, then again, he wasn't pointing at a brandy snifter because she had just uttered an expletive.

As quietly as possible, she got her things and ducked into the bathroom to get ready. Finishing with time to spare, she crept back into the kitchen, poured a cup of the coffee her rather hunky roommate had readied the night before, and checked her phone.

But her eyes kept drifting over to him, still in the same position, thinking of how he took care of her the night before and, she assumed, the night before that. No judgment. No scolding.

"No expectation of payback," she thought grimly. And no cold shoulder afterwards.

What's with that?

Perched on a barstool, she was still studying him, coffee mug in hand, when his eyes fluttered open.

"How long have you been sitting there?" he mumbled.

She picked up her phone to check the time. "I don't know. Five, ten minutes?"

He sat up, and her eyes honed in on his arms, the muscles of which flexed as he clutched a pillow in front of his chest.

Oh my.

"Do ya mind?"

She caught herself. "What?"

He motioned for her to turn around.

"Oh. Sure."

He's shy? How cute is that?

Pressing her lips together, she turned and averted her eyes to the kitchen—which had all sorts of shiny, reflective surfaces.

"Be right back," she heard him say.

Uh-huh...

The feel of hot liquid spread over the top of her thighs.

"Shit."

Freshly brewed coffee soaked into her one good black skirt. With no time to wash it, she hopped up and blotted it with a kitchen towel.

Hearing the bathroom door open, she set it on the counter and watched as Andrew approached wearing the T-shirt and pajama bottoms that he had apparently forgotten to wear to bed the night before.

"How'd you sleep?" he asked, combing his hand through his hair.

"Really good, thanks."

Feeling the color in her cheeks rise, she continued, "That hot—what did you call it?"

"Hot toddy."

"Good stuff."

One side of his mouth curved into a smile, and a little zing sped through her. "Glad to hear it."

"There's just one thing," she said as he started making up the sofa sleeper.

"What?"

"How did I get into bed?"

While he tucked the sheets and blankets between the mattress and bed frame with the speed and precision of an Army nurse, Andrew replied, "I carried you. You were out like a light."

She looked at him sideways. He looked strong but not that strong. "You did not."

He stopped what he was doing and turned to face her. Putting his hands on his hips, he asked, "Want a demonstration?"

Yes.

"Oh, no," she laughed nervously as she shifted on the stool, sweeping him up one side and down the other with her skeptical eyes.

He certainly didn't seem to be suffering from any pulled muscles or a hernia. Maybe he was telling her the truth. Unable to stop blushing like a moron, she checked the time on her phone. "Oh cripes. I'd better get going."

Cripes?

Slipping off her barstool, she watched as he took a coffee mug down from the shelf and started filling it. Then she edged into the kitchen behind him to pull her now-dry jacket off of the chair. "Catch you later?"

He stopped mid-pour. Setting the pot down, he turned toward her but didn't go out of his way to make eye contact. "Does this mean we have a deal?"

Before he was able to get the last word out, she clipped, "Yes." Then she just stood there looking at him like an idiot, waiting for him to say something, anything.

After an interminably long minute, he unleashed another sleepy smile and nodded. "Great." Then he locked his baby blues on her. "Catch you later."

Sara pointed at him. "Right."

Coat on, she was almost at the door when she heard him call her name. She stepped back into the kitchen, trying not to look too annoyed at the delay. "Yeah?"

He was examining the kitchen towel she had used to blot her skirt. "What happened here?"

Uh...

"Oh, I spilled some coffee on my skirt, so I used that to blot it up."

He tilted his head at the stained towel. "So why didn't you throw it in the hamper?"

All she could manage by way of a reply was one very arched eyebrow.

Tossing it to her, Andrew added, "You should probably spray some pre-wash stuff on it too to get the coffee stain out."

With both eyebrows raised, Sara pressed her lips together and nodded. "Right."

Definitely gay.

Depositing her bag on the kitchen table, she grabbed a squirt bottle from the top of the washing machine and doused the towel with it on her way to the hamper. After silently washing her hands in the kitchen sink, she accepted the clean towel Andrew handed to her, then turned her back on him and left.

What in God's name have I gotten myself into?

* * *

By the time Sara made it to Chez Doug's, a hopping coffee shop next to the Gazette Building that had red walls, lots of dark wood, and deep, high-backed booths, she found her friends comfortably ensconced in a corner, deep in conversation. Slipping in next to Mattie, she watched as the newest investigative reporter on the *Gazette* staff leaned across the table toward Nancy and Aubrey sitting together on the other side.

"She's making me crazy."

"Who?" Sara asked. "Your future mother-in-law?"

She watched as Nancy shook her head. "Wedding planner."

"Aren't they supposed to do your bidding?"

Turning to her, Mattie exclaimed, "That's the thing. She isn't. In fact, she isn't doing anything. And the wedding's in June! She came so highly recommended. Maybe she's overextended."

"So fire her."

"I can't," the bride-to-be replied glumly. "I signed a contract."

Feeling protective of the former advice columnist who had always empathized entirely with Sara's inability to feel that she deserved any of the good things life had to offer, Sara nudged against her and, like a genuine Mafioso, asked, "You want I should go, uh, talk ta her...?"

With a quick laugh, Mattie replied, "Thanks, but I think I'm gonna unleash my Sicilian future mother-in-law on her." Pointing to Sara and Aubrey, she continued, "Oh, and don't forget—I hope you two can still make it to her house this Saturday."

Aubrey shrugged. "Yeah, sure."

Mattie turned to Sara. "Think you can make it?"

"Why do we have to go to Mrs. DeRosa's?"

"Oh, sorry. You weren't here yet. After my sister and I checked out every bridal shop in the entire Chicago Metropolitan area, we still couldn't find any bridesmaid dresses we like, so Lucy, uh, Mrs. DeRosa, offered to design whatever we want and make them. We just have to get the fabric and stuff. *Whatever we want.* Isn't that fantastic?"

"Wow. She can make—what—five dresses by then?"

Mattie nodded. "Well, just four. Nancy has a conflict."

Nancy put her phone down. "Yeah. My mom's getting married again. Same day. What are the chances?"

After a moment, Mattie continued, "You know, I know mothers-in-law are supposed to be awful, but I'm really kinda crazy about mine."

Sara was about to ask what time they were meeting at Lucy's when Chez Doug himself appeared at their table, holding a small pad of paper. "Ladies. What can I get you this morning?"

"Hi, Doug," they said in unison to the middle-aged former parochial school teacher who owned and operated his namesake establishment.

Sara noticed Nancy suck in her cheeks as her eyes raked over the man who, with his overgrown hair, thick mustache, and gold-rimmed aviator glasses, looked rather like he stepped right out of 1975.

"I'll have the daily brew, Doug, with just a pinch of sugar and..." putting her hand on his hairy forearm, asked, "What did you say the specials were today?"

Sara and Mattie exchanged amused glances while Aubrey just rolled her eyes.

Still, Nancy's touch seemed to spellbind Doug. "Lemon poppy seed scones and asparagus Swiss cheese quiche."

"Oh, the quiche sounds delicious," Nancy gasped. "I'll have that."

With a wink, he said, "You got it."

Turning his attention to Aubrey, she said, "Hot green tea and a lemon scone, please."

Mattie said, "The same," and Sara, pointing to Nancy, said, "I'll have what she's having."

"Thanks, ladies."

As soon as he was out of earshot, Sara leaned across the table to Nancy and said, "There goes your wedding date."

Watching as the not-unattractive coffee shop owner made his way to the kitchen, the food editor shrugged. "We'll see."

Aubrey spread her white cloth napkin across her lap and whispered, "You're terrible. It's so obvious he likes you. You have to ask him to your mom's wedding."

"I will if you ask Malcolm to Mattie's," Nancy teased, being sure to overenunciate the name of her friend's crush.

When the young widow fell silent, Sara was reminded of one of the many reasons why Claire did not think highly of Nancy. Noticing her absence, she asked, "Where's Claire?"

Just then, Doug appeared with a large tray that he set on the adjacent table. Moving her silverware to make room for her scone, Mattie whispered, "Ultrasound."

A spark of alarm prompted to Sara to whisper back, "Is everything OK?"

With a nod, Mattie assured her. "Oh, yeah. At least I think so. It's just routine, given her age and everything."

Addressing Doug, she asked, "Hey, I've been meaning to ask, do you do wedding cakes or sweet tables?"

On their way to the office, Mattie deliberately hung back with Sara while the other two rushed off to meetings. Just as they were about to enter the Gazette Building, Mattie asked, "OK, so what's going on?"

Sara turned on her before pushing through the lobby's revolving door. "What do you mean?"

When they emerged from the other side, Mattie gave her a knowing look. "You're really going to make me pull it out of you? OK, first of all, you hate Monday mornings more than anything on the planet, yet here you are, bright and early, oozing sunshine and butterflies."

"I am not," the music critic whispered as her eyes darted around the lobby, hoping no one she knew heard Mattie's sunshine and butterflies remark.

"You are too," Mattie pressed with a smile. "Who is he?"

Sara pressed the Up button. "OK, let's say, hypothetically, I do seem uncharacteristically happy for a Monday morning. Why does it have to involve a guy?"

Mattie held up her hand and gave her a disparaging look. "Don't insult me. Come on, dish."

Turning away from the elevator that had just arrived for them, the pair walked over to an empty bench against a far wall of the lobby and sat down.

"Well, for starters," Sara confessed under her breath as her eyes scanned the lobby, "Jer ditched me and moved back to the UK while I was on the road."

Hearing Mattie gasp, she continued, "So the owner of the building sublet our apartment."

She felt the blush rise in her cheeks and her mouth pull into a smirk as she concluded, "And I have a new roommate."

Several seconds passed as she let the announcement sink in.

"And..." Mattie prodded with a face-splitting grin.

Looking into her face, it dawned on Sara that Andrew's place of employment and the venue for Mattie's wedding ceremony were one and the same. Out of an abundance of caution, she was careful not to divulge too many details.

"And what?" Sara hedged.

"What's he like?" Mattie gasped.

"Why are you assuming it's a he?"

"Because you're blushing, and your eyes are all sparkly. In all the time I've known you, I've never seen you like this. What's he like? Is he cute? What does he do?"

With that morning's stained-towel incident still very fresh in her mind, she blurted, "He's another musician, and, so far, he's a pain the ass."

Then she pictured him bundling her up in the afghan the night before when she was frozen to the core and imagined him carrying her sleeping self to bed and tucking her in, two nights in a row.

After a heavy sigh, she admitted, "And I could definitely fall for him."

Ten minutes later, her investigative reporter pal had extracted the full scoop behind Sara's sunshine and butterflies.

With a wink, Mattie nudged her shoulder into her much-taller friend's arm. "Well, whether he's gay or not, it sounds like you've got yourself a wedding date."

Sara pictured herself dancing cheek-to-cheek with Andrew on the dance floor during the reception at their publisher's swanky country club.

Without any further prodding from Mattie, she was prone to agree.

* * *

Across town, Claire gasped as the ultrasound technician squirted cold gel onto her warm belly. "Can't you guys warm that up first?"

Ignoring her, the technician asked if they wanted to know the sex of the baby.

"You can tell this early?"

"We should be able to, depending on the baby's position."

Claire and her husband, Paul, exchanged glances in the dark of the diagnostic imaging room at Chicago General. After a minute of reading each other's minds like long-married couples do, they both made a face and shook their heads, "Nah."

"It'll give us something to look forward to," Paul explained.

"Exactly," Claire echoed.

The technician nodded and then began moving the sensor over Claire's skin like she was using a game controller on some exciting new prenatal video game. She half expected to see a score pop up on the monitor.

Instead, as the technician continued to take image after image, Claire saw what looked to be a teeny tiny foot appear on the screen. Tears springing to her eyes, she squeezed Paul's hand. "Oh my God."

Through a broad grin, Paul sighed at the emerging image of his fifth child. "Never gets old."

A quick knock sounded on the door, and a nurse popped her head in. "Excuse me, Denise, you've got a call. It's your husband. He said it's an emergency." With a sigh, the technician set the sensor down. "I'm so sorry. I'll be right back."

"Oh, sure thing," Paul said, watching as she left them alone in the dark room. Then, leaning over his wife with a dangerous grin, he kissed her and whispered, "Wanna make out?"

With a laugh, Claire pushed him away. "That's what got us here in the first place." Looking toward the door, she flung an arm under her head and added, "I hope everything's OK."

A few minutes later, another knock sounded.

"Hello, Claire," Dr. Weber said as he walked into the room. "Janet's got to run home, so I'll finish up here."

Propping up on her elbows, she asked, "Nothing serious, I hope?"

"Oh no. Her husband locked his keys in the car, and she needs to run home and get the extra set."

Claire eased back down on the table, unable to shake the feeling of impending doom. "Oh, good. Glad it wasn't anything serious."

Reaching his hand across to Paul, the doctor said, "Good to see you again."

"How are ya?" Paul asked as he shook the hand of the man who delivered their first four children.

"OK, so what do we have here?" the doctor murmured, staring at the screen as he pressed the sensor over Claire's lower abdomen while punching a bunch of buttons on the console in front of him. "Looking good..."

The unmistakable image of a hand appeared to wave at them. "Aw, hi, sweetie," she cried.

"Would ya look at that," Paul whispered. "I don't remember the older guys' scans being so clear."

The doctor didn't seem to hear him. Instead, his attention was locked on the screen. "What do we have here?" Clenching Paul's hand, she asked, "What's the matter? Is something wrong?"

The doctor, looking a little stunned, turned to look at them. "In all my years...well, it's really quite rare."

Feeling her heart thud to a stop in her chest, Claire squeaked, "Tell us."

"In all my years," he started again before breaking into a smile. "I've never delivered five boys to the same family."

Claire fell back against the pillow. *And you never will.*

Flopping an arm over her face, she moaned. "We didn't want to know."

"Oh. I'm so sorry. I thought I saw a note in your file that you wanted to know," said the man who had referred to her as being "of advanced maternal age" not one month before.

"Hey, well, as long as he's healthy, right?" Paul grinned as he watched Clare wipe the gel off of her belly with a paper towel the doctor had given her.

"Right," she growled back.

"OK. I'll see you in another month. Have a good one," said the worst OB ever before exiting with his stethoscope between his legs.

As soon as she was upright, Paul held Claire's face in his warm hands and looked in her eyes, nearly blinding her with the gleam in his. "It's a boy. And he's healthy. How lucky are we, huh?"

Wrapping her arms around him, she smushed her face against the lapel of his black suit coat and mumbled, "Very, very."

He planted a kiss on her head and gave her a quick squeeze. "Come on. We've got to get to work."

A short cab ride later, the two were at the Gazette Building. Before Paul ascended to his job on the 24th floor, he kissed Claire good-bye on the 7th. On her way to her cube, she stopped by her editor's office to inform Dianne that she had a better idea for that week's column and would get it to her within the hour. Forty-five minutes later, she read the new submission, entitled "Looking on the Blue Side," before sending it:

It's official. This Plate Spinner has just learned that her fifth little saucer, due to arrive later this summer, is decidedly blue. And I'm just not sure how I feel about that.

Maybe it's the way I found out. During a recent routine ultrasound, the technician had to step away. Her replacement? None other than my well-degreed (former) obstetrician who made the erroneous assumption that my husband and I wanted to learn the sex of our child.

Seeing that I'm on the cusp of entering my second trimester—otherwise known as that blissful phase when morning sickness ceases and unbridled use of the "but-I'm eating-for-two" card commences, my immediate reaction was anger.

"I thought you wanted to know," was his hapless defense.

How dare he rob me of the daydreams I had been counting on to get me through the next six months? The ones in which it was still possible that our impending arrival might indeed be of the female persuasion. Not likely after already bringing four boys into the world, I know, but come on.

The star of my daydreams was, of course, my potential baby girl. Immediately upon her arrival, I would dress her in every shade of pink on the planet. Bonding instantly, we would become fast friends—besties even, enjoying tea parties, Disney chick flicks, and, as soon as she was old enough, mani-pedis.

It was everything I could do to not strangle him with his stethoscope while demanding, "But who's going to wear my wedding dress?"

Instead, I gave my (did I mention former) OB the death glare that works so well on my sons when they have the misfortune of reaching for the last piece of pizza (or cake). Lucky for him, the familiar swoosh-swoosh of a tiny heartbeat filled the darkened room, and I was faced with the stark realization that I have another human being growing inside of me.

How could I be angry in the presence of a miracle?

Well played, doctor. Well played indeed.

Then I saw my son's teeny little hand wave at me. That simple, exquisite gesture was all it took to remind me that I don't even like tea, am not a fan of Disney's princess propaganda campaign, and have not gotten a mani-pedi since my wedding day.

I glanced teary-eyed at my husband who evidently had not gotten a ticket on the same emotional rollercoaster I did. If he was harboring any dashed daddy-daughter fantasies, he hid them well. In fact, by all appearances, he was nothing short of ebullient, spouting things like, "Yes! We have a basketball team" and, crazier still, "two more and we've got a cross-country team."

Uh, no.

Still, his euphoria was contagious, prompting me to ponder the blessings of boys. If I really concentrate, I can almost see beyond the left-up toilet seats, the smelly clothes, the ever-present sophomoric humor at the dinner table, and all manner of sports equipment cluttering my house like it's a big-box athletic store. I see instead their sweet smiles, remember the warmth of their hugs, and cherish the thought that, no matter what, boys will always love their mothers.

It's no small responsibility transforming boys into bright, caring, responsible young men who will, one day, bring me the daughters (in-law) for which I long. I just hope my boys know that at least one of their fiancées had better be willing and able to wear my wedding dress. Perhaps I should write them a note.

Dianne responded with her trademark brevity via their interoffice instant messaging system: *Brilliant.*

Claire noted this with no small degree of satisfaction.

But when Diane IM'd again not a moment later with: *Next week: ltr to future DILs. Thx,* she closed her eyes and smiled, certain that she had to be the happiest working mom in the Windy City, if not the entire Midwest.

* * *

Sitting in the chair facing her editor's desk, Sara wished that Mike Teegan preferred instant messaging to in-person meetings.

"So what did you want to see me about?" she asked, biting the inside of her cheek as she watched him get up from and close the door to his office behind her.

After the weekend she'd had, she had a whole new appreciation for the fact that her job was the only stabilizing factor in her life. Once she was given an assignment, she was all over it. Knew exactly what to do and how to make it work. When she was on the job, she felt in control. When she wasn't, not so much. Especially lately.

"I read your Krypto Blight piece."

"Yeah?" She gripped the arms of the chair she was sitting in, thinking of all she had given up for the feature—her boyfriend, seventy-five percent of her wardrobe, her passive agnostic lifestyle. He'd better as hell like it. 'Cause if he didn't— well, she had no idea what she'd do if he didn't, but it wouldn't be pretty.

Images of overturned office furniture filled her head as did the subject line of an email emblazoned with the words, *Letter of Resignation.*

The former Woodstock attendee turned successful editorial executive smiled at her.

"You've really outdone yourself. It'll post Friday as part of the Grammy preview feature."

Oh, thank God.

Through an uncharacteristic gush of a grin, she replied, "I'm so glad you liked it."

Mike did a double take at her smiling face. "You feeling ok?"

"Yeah, why?"

After assessing her for several long seconds, he ventured, "I don't know. Your makeup is different. And you seem...cheerful."

Must stop smiling at people.

Unable to force a frown, she waved him off. "What about my write up on Ellie Klein? What did you think?"

He sat back in his chair, "Yeah, about that."

Sara felt her grin disappear faster than Ellie's fanbase after she declared her move from country to pop.

Edging forward in her seat, she started, "I know you didn't ask for it, Mike, and let me assure you, I worked on it on my own time, but I really feel like it had to be said, ya know? And I thought if we could get it out there before, say, *Rolling Stone*, it might go a long way toward bolstering the paper's credibility."

At this, his face slowly morphed into a scowl. "You think the *Gazette* has credibility issues?"

"What? No! That's not what I meant."

As she tried yanking her foot from her big mouth, she started having an out-of-body experience. Even though she felt like a big bad gainfully employed music critic, looking down on herself, she saw an insecure kid from Wisconsin whose lack of a college degree, a mother, and a clean conscience made her come off like a blithering idiot in the eyes of her editor.

Me replace Daryl Swerl. Right.

Her mouth finally stopped moving, and she looked down at her hands. "You know what? I'm just gonna stop talking."

Mike's confused expression broke into a smile. With a chuckle, he replied, "Good, 'cause I wanted to let you know that it's posting tomorrow." Leaning forwarded, he added, "I wanted to tell you in person."

Sara, having a hard time getting her cool back on, gave him a quick nod. "That's great. Thanks."

Patting the top of his desk with his hand, her editor surprised her again. "Listen. Why don't you take the rest of the day off, huh?"

Expecting to be given her next assignment, not be sent home, she blurted, "Excuse me?"

"You heard me. Take a day off. It's what people do when they've been on the road for almost two weeks and, I see," he said, pointing to his laptop screen, "working on the weekend again. You need a break."

He got up and shooed her toward the office door. "Go on now. Take the day. Enjoy it."

Doing what?

Sara closed Mike's office door behind her as she left and was wondering what to do next when her phone chirped in her pocket. Pulling it out, she saw she had just received a text from a number she didn't recognize. She tapped the screen.

Andrew here.

Doing her best to quash another excited little zing that zipped through her, she started typing, *How the hell did you get my number?*

About to hit Send, Sara paused when another text came through.

Have mtg in Joliet. If u get home before me, put dish in fridge in oven—45m @ 350, pls.

With his use of the word *home* scraping against her sensibilities, she muttered, "He made dinner for us?"

On the way back to her desk, she deleted her previous unsent text and replaced it with *No prob*, noting yet another thing Jer never did for her.

With no particular urge to go back to the apartment, she shut her laptop down and tried thinking of what she could do with her newfound freedom. Taking a cue from Claire, by all rights a professional plate spinner, Sara drafted a list.

After writing, "Get a haircut," she promptly crossed it off.

Need an appointment.

Next, she wrote, "Go grocery shopping," only to cross that off as well.

Would I get stuff just for me or for both of us?

She started chewing on her thumbnail.

I could just stay here and work.

With half a mind to do just that, she was about to turn her laptop back on when she overheard two women chatting as they passed by. Something about catching an end-of-the-season clearance sale at Macy's.

What a fine idea.

Sara slipped her laptop in her bag and made her way to Water Tower Place intent on replacing at least some of her depleted wardrobe at the famed department store and perhaps some of the other shops peppered throughout the multileveled mall as well.

Three hours later, she was back at the apartment. In the bedroom actually. A half-dozen shopping bags littered the bed. That it was made up better than she had left it that morning did not escape her attention.

She flung open the closet doors. A good three-quarters of it was filled with Andrew's things. And the remaining quarter would hardly suffice.

First things first.

She hoisted the box of her personal things on top of a bin on the shelf above the clothing rod, careful not to hit the light bulb poking out of the socket on the ceiling.

Then, with a shrug, she shoved all of his hung garments to one side, smushing dress shirts against dress pants and suit coats. While she was sure Andrew would be mortified, she had no qualms using the same line of reasoning he had given her for enduring the whole church choir thing.

It's only for six weeks.

After hanging up her new skirts, dresses, and blouses, she turned to the dresser. When it was hers, she always put her underwear in the top drawer, then jammies and comfy clothes, then shirts, then jeans and tights. She slowly pulled open the top drawer to find it about half-filled with a limited variety of carefully folded solid and plaid-print boxers.

Figures.

Moving them to one side, she dumped her lacy bikini briefs and bras on the other. She did the same with the remaining drawers. When she was finished, she felt accomplished and settled.

The lovely aroma of rosemary chicken invaded her nostrils. Gathering up the shopping bags, she made her way to the kitchen where she folded them all back up and shoved them against some paper grocery bags already folded in the pantry.

Noting that it was only four o'clock, she turned on the stereo and ran her index finger along the row of Jer's abandoned CDs, looking for one that would strike her fancy, pausing on some before resuming her quest. She was about to give up when her finger landed on Sam Phillips' *Martinis and Bikinis*.

Perfect.

Singing along to her favorite track, aptly titled, "I Need Love," she poured herself a glass of Pinot Grigio that she had picked up on the way home along with a small loaf of sourdough from an artisan bakery and a bouquet of daisies and danced alone in middle of the kitchen, waiting for the timer on the casserole to ding. When it did, she set it on top of the oven and set the temperature dial to Warm, wrapped the bread in foil, and placed both back in the oven. Spying an already-tossed salad big enough for two already made in the fridge, she pulled out the brandy-snifter-slash-swear-jar and filled it with water before cutting the daisy stems short enough for them to pop out at just the right height.

Setting it on the kitchen counter, she took in the vision of domestic bliss.

Something's missing.

To complete the scene, she located two rough-woven place mats that were tucked in a drawer under the oven mitts and set them on the kitchen counter. Next, she topped them with two place settings, just as Andrew had before serving her Chinese food on Saturday night.

How very Barbie of me...

She checked the time, wondering when he would be home.

Home.

Taking a big swig of her wine, another thought crossed her mind, and it scared the crap out of her.

I could get used to this.

Before she could take another sip, she heard a key slide in the lock. Not wanting to look too eager (or too Barbie-esque), she ducked into the bathroom, emerging a short time later to greet Andrew.

And the man he had brought home with him.

"Oh."

Andrew, who she couldn't help but notice looked quite dashing in his suit, tie, and overcoat, was smiling at her. "Sara, hi."

Holding his hand toward his ~~companion~~ ~~friend~~ fellow Ken doll, he said, "This is David Fahey. He's the head of music ministry at Saint—"

I'm such an idiot.

She didn't hear the rest of what he said. Feeling her insides start to cave in, she reached for her jacket that she had abandoned on the couch earlier and nodded at him. "Nice to meet you."

Andrew narrowed his eyes at her then glanced at his friend. "David, this is Sara."

With a rather dazzling grin, the blond GQ-model wannabe stuck his hand out toward her. "Nice to meet you."

Before she had a chance to shake it, Andrew slipped between them, gripped her shoulders, and looked her in the eye. "Don't go."

To David, he said, "I'll be right back" and disappeared into the bedroom.

The blond Ken doll leaned toward her. "Andrew and I go way back." Then he leaned even closer and whispered, "He's told me all about you."

Blurting the first thing that popped into her head, as she often did after a sip or two of wine, she scoffed, "But we've only just met."

By way of a reply, he tilted his head toward the place settings on the counter. "I hope I'm not interrupting anything."

"Oh no," she started as she plunged her hands in her coat pockets. "It's nothing."

Probably should've popped a breath mint.

Feeling her cheeks warm, she felt compelled to explain. "Just dinner. I'm not normally here. This early. Got time off for good behavior."

Stop talking.

While David gave her a polite grin, he did a poor job masking the fact that he was rather disturbed by that last comment.

"Huh. Well, I'm, uh, just here to get some music I need from Andrew. I don't know how he got his hands on it, but last I looked, it was out of print."

Sara nodded, and the two stood looking at each other for a long awkward moment before Andrew came sweeping back, waving some sheet music sans overcoat and tie.

"Sorry, the bin I had it in was..." with a quick glance at Sara, he finished, "a little hard to get to."

With that, David bid her adieu, and Andrew showed him to the door.

She had just started looking through the CDs again when she heard him come up behind her and say her name.

Lowering the volume ever so slightly, she turned. Mustering her cool, detached voice out of some far corner of her otherwise-flustered self, she raised an eyebrow and said, "What's up?"

Go me.

OK, so maybe it had more to do with the glass of Pinot she had almost polished off before he walked through the door with his blond buddy.

"I just want to let you to know—"

Oh God, here it comes...

Doing her best to remain poker-faced, she held his gaze while her insides braced herself for what he was about to tell her.

"I'm not—"

She leaned a little closer to him. "What? You're not what?"

Interested in me?

Interested in girls?

Ready for a relationship?

In favor of legalized marijuana?

He leveled her with one of his smoldering looks that had her wishing she had changed into some of her new lacy undergarments, just in case.

"What?" Her mouth formed the word, but no sound came out.

Biting his bottom lip, he nodded back toward the kitchen and said, "Sure that Pinot Grigio goes with what I made for dinner."

CHAPTER SEVEN

———

"In any moment of decision, the best thing you can do is the right thing, the next best thing is the wrong thing, and the worst thing you can do is nothing."
—*Theodore Roosevelt*

Dear Plate Spinner—
I've got three kids, ages four to eleven, and I work full time as does my husband. The problem is our daughter. She's the only girl, and while I'm trying to teach by example that she should be a strong independent woman, reliant on no one and able to blaze her own trail, she's turning into a spoiled rotten little prima donna girly girl right before my very eyes.
Do you think it's a phase, or should we seek professional help?
Signed "At Wit's End"
P.S. I forgot to mention, she's the four-year-old.

Using her index fingers, Claire pecked out, "Sorry, can't relate" and was about to hit Send when Mattie burst into her cube with enough energy to punch a hole in the ozone layer.

"Hey, ya busy?"

"No. Just uninspired. What's up?"

"Nick was just offered a contract to teach PE at Knollwood next year. He's so excited."

"Hey, that's great news."

Mattie's happiness was boundless. And contagious. So much so that Claire felt the urge to divulge her own bit of news that wouldn't be made public until later that week. Leaning forward, she whispered, "Paul and I got some good news of our own."

"Tell me," Mattie demanded through a dimple-baring grin.

"It's a boy." Hearing the words come out of her own mouth was cathartic. She felt a tsunami of excitement well up inside of her. Either that or it was the giant burrito she scarfed down for lunch just an hour before.

As Mattie wrapped her arms around her and moved her right and left, she exclaimed, "Five boys. That's so fantastic! Paul must be crazy excited."

With a chuckle, Claire conceded, "Oh, he is. He's already looking into getting a new jogging stroller for the two of them."

"Of course." Mattie laughed. Then, sweeping a glance over the rest of the cubes on the floor, she sank back down and asked, "Have you seen Sara lately?"

Claire had. Several times since running into her after Mass as a matter of fact, but not wanting to betray her pal's request for confidentiality, she just nodded.

"As much as I hate to say it, I'm so glad Jer left. He wasn't right for her. And she never would've dumped him on her own. But this new guy, he sounds like he'd be a perfect fit."

Claire frowned.

This new guy?

Fairly sure Mattie and Nick would have met with Andrew while planning their wedding ceremony at St. Matthias, she asked, "Did she tell you his name?"

This seemed to confuse her. "No. You?"

"Ya know, I don't recall. You're right though. It is good news."

"Yeah," Mattie agreed, but was quick to add, "I just expected her to be a whole lot happier about it, though, ya know?"

On this the Plate Spinners, both past and present, agreed.

* * *

On the morning of her first official choir practice, Sara, having overslept by a good half hour, bounded out of bed wearing nothing more than a skimpy tank top and panties, grabbed fresh underwear out of the drawer, and yanked a sweater and a pair of leggings out of the closet. Hoping to get in the shower first, she was not pleased to find the bathroom already occupied.

After listening for a moment, she knocked on the door. "Andrew? You gonna be much longer? I have to get ready for work."

The sound of something hard tapping against the sink came through the door.

"Uh, yeah. Just give me a couple of minutes."

She hung her head back and glared at the ceiling.

Can't he finish shaving in the kitchen?

With nothing but the thought of being on time to her 8:00 am planning meeting with Mike and Daryl, she announced, "Sorry. I gotta get in the shower. Hope you're decent."

She grasped the handle, turned it, and pushed. But it only went a few inches before Andrew blocked it with his foot. From what Sara could see in the mirror, it looked like she had caught him mid-scrape. Locking his astonished eyes on hers, he stopped and exclaimed, "I'm *shaving*."

Throwing her head back a second time, she pleaded, "Yeah, and I'm really late. Come on. It's just me."

Nothing.

"Can't you just close your eyes for a second so I can jump in the shower?"

At that, the door swung open.

"Thanks."

Making sure his eyes were indeed shut, she slipped into the men's-body-wash-scented steam and paused to give him a quick once-over, zoning in on where he insinuated his tattoo was allegedly located as he stood in front of the sink wearing nothing but a towel cinched at hip level.

I knew he was bluffing about having a tattoo.

Turning her back to him, she tucked her clean clothes into the towel rod, stepped into the shower, and yanked the not nearly opaque enough shower curtain behind her.

How am I just noticing this now?

Before turning on the water, she slipped off her panties and tank top and dropped them in a lacy little heap on the floor.

"OK, you can open your eyes," she announced.

With a hard tap of the razor against the sink, she heard him respond, "You said I only had to keep 'em closed for a second."

Sara made a mental note to go online after her meeting and check apartment listings.

Ever since Monday night, when she'd made those three progressively foolish mistakes, starting with getting all dreamy-eyed and domestic over a stupid casserole he had made for them, assuming his professional colleague was, well, more than that, and the highly egregious rosemary-chicken-Pinot-Grigio pairing, she tried avoiding him at all costs so as to prevent a repeat performance—until that morning, when she found herself standing buck naked in the shower while he finished shaving.

After a lightning-fast soap down, shampoo, and rinse, she turned off the water. Tucking the edge of the shower curtain around her, she reached for the towel draped on the rod next to her clean clothes. It was just out of her reach.

She then watched in horror as Andrew turned and used it to dry his just-rinsed face and draped it over his shoulders when he was finished.

"Hey, I was gonna use that." She made no effort to hide her irritation.

Without saying another word, he walked toward her, and she tightened her grip on the shower curtain.

What he did next prompted her to want to take a second shower, this time a cold one, if only she had the time.

With his eyes fixed on hers, he gripped the towel that was tied around his hips and pulled the right side dangerously low to reveal a small, elegantly scripted tattoo. *McGuigan.*

Then, after reaching over to grab a hand towel, he tossed it to her and said, "All you had to do was ask."

I'm really beginning to hate this apartment.

Twelve hours later, she found herself sitting stone-faced in the midst of the chattering alto section at St. Matthias. Granted, the atmosphere seemed much more relaxed than it had on Sunday, and she had to admit everyone was being so friendly and seemed genuinely glad to see she had returned. Except Andrew, who didn't even seem to notice that she had arrived not five minutes after he did.

Whatever. Let's get this over with.

"Here, dear." Glynnis, her alto neighbor, handed her a little slip of paper. "Better get your music in order. He's kind of a stickler about starting on time."

Why am I not surprised?

Sara looked over at him, standing there in Levi's (her favorites, yes, but still) and a plain gray crew neck sweater. He was talking to Marge with one eye on her and one on the clock affixed to the wall behind her.

"Thanks, Glynnis."

She examined the list of over a dozen pieces of music. Some in the hymnal, some in her music binder. Thankful that Marge had placed the music in her binder alphabetically, she had barely gotten herself organized when she heard him say, "OK, we've got a lot to go over tonight, and we don't have a lot of time because cantor practice starts in an hour."

Thank God.

"Lorelei, Daphne, and Sara, I'll need you to stay for that."

While Sara was looking around wondering who the other Sara in the choir might be, she heard him say, "All right, let's get started. Everybody up."

After plowing through the majority of the list in the allotted time, she felt like someone had taken a blowtorch to her vocal cords. Granted, when she sang karaoke, she only had to do one, maybe two songs, but Andrew had demanded that each section repeat their part, measure by measure, until perfected.

Looking with envy at the others around her who were smart enough to have brought water bottles, the beautiful harmonies they produced when he had them all sing together echoed in her head like a choir of angels. She still couldn't get over how much she missed hearing it.

"OK, thanks everybody. See you Sunday. 9:30 sharp."

He turned and started chatting with all of the soloists who sang at Sunday Masses as they congregated by the Steinway.

When she slipped one arm in her jacket sleeve, he left them and walked right up to her. "Where are you going?"

Arching an eyebrow, she said, "Home."

Edging closer to her, he whispered, "I told you. I need you at cantor practice."

Realizing he was referring to her when he was ticking off names before practice, Sara shook her head. "Oh no. No way. That wasn't part of the deal."

She had been a cantor before, back at St. Xavier's, and loved it—probably because her desire to live at a particular address wasn't hanging in the balance.

Raising an eyebrow of his own, he scraped, "Well, that was before Irene Pavlik fell and broke her hip. I need you to fill in Easter weekend."

Sara looked over his shoulder at the group that had stayed, mostly women, a few men, all looking like they belonged at a senior citizen's bridge tournament.

With a quick shake of her head, she mouthed, "No."

He lowered his chin. With the hint of a smile playing at the corner of his eyes, he mouthed, "Please?"

When all she did in response was narrow her eyes, he added, "OK. You can have the bedroom this week *and* next."

Before he could get the last word out, she said, "Deal."

Approaching the small group, she said, "Hi, I'm Sara."

Two hours later, she burst into the apartment right behind him, more revved up than she ever remembered being after karaoke night—and she hadn't even been drinking.

"Ya know, that was actually kind of fun. You should let us do duets. Or quartets. Or, hey—have you ever thought of doing like a flash mob kind of thing where members of the choir could be peppered throughout the congregation, and then, one by one, they each stand up and start singing?"

Andrew turned to her after he hung his coat up in the foyer closet. He looked beat but amused all the same. "This is Mass we're talking about. Not an episode of *Glee*. I'm glad you enjoyed it though," he managed while stifling a yawn. "Sorry for putting you on the spot like that. You were a trouper."

Feeling a warmth spread over her face, she didn't bother suppressing a grin. "Thanks."

After hanging up her coat, she followed him down the hall into the kitchen area like an excited puppy who wanted to play as soon as its master returned. "Listen, I'm sorry about this morning. I shouldn't have barged into the bathroom while you were shaving."

He plopped on the couch and stretched his long legs on the trunk in front of him before failing to suppress another yawn. "Forget about it. Why is it so cold in here? Aren't you cold?"

She didn't catch the surprise in his eyes when she plopped right next to him.

Ignoring his questions, she tucked her feet under her and turned to him before blurting, "And you. You're *so* good. I had no idea."

He stared at her for a long couple of seconds with a grin breaking across his shocked face. "I can't believe you just said that. I mean, I'm not surprised. I just can't believe you said it out loud."

Sara was quiet. Then, after replaying what she had just said, laughed harder and louder than she had for a very long time. Feeling lighter than air, she gave him a not-so-light shove in the shoulder. "Now whose mind is in the gutter?"

Giving her a look that would have prompted Sister Marcus to chase after him with a cattle prod if she'd seen it, he titled his head and said in a barely audible voice, "I'm not the one who said it."

And all of the sudden, Sara couldn't seem to focus on anything other than his warm sparking eyes. Like cobalt-blue magnets, they reeled her in. As she leaned closer, she felt him raise his arm that would otherwise have gotten smushed between them and drape it across her back. His hand pressed against her with just enough pressure to be encouraging.

He's so gonna kiss me back this time.

Feeling her heart race, her eyes dropped to his mouth.

The things she wanted to do to it.

The things she wanted him to do to her with it.

She started to feel sensations in her body that had been dormant for so long—too long. On reactivation, though, they managed to trip an alarm in her brain.

Whoop, whoop. Ken doll alert. Commence evasive action. Repeat. A Ken doll has been spotted in the immediate area. Commence evasive action.

With a feather soft brush of her lips against his parted ones, she pulled back and whispered, "Good night, Andrew."

She waited for his eyes to meet hers. While the sparkles were gone, they were still generating enough smolder to cause significant burns on her already-scorched heart.

Feeling his hand run up and down the length of her back, he whispered. "Good night."

Sara went to bed. Alone. And, having not fallen asleep for a very, very long time, she did not have a good night. Not. At. All.

* * *

"Stand still, sweetheart."

Sara watched as Lucy DeRosa, Mattie's future mother-in-law, hovered behind her with pins sticking out of her mouth. "I don't want to snag the silk."

"Sorry Mrs. De—"

Feeling a hard tug on her wedding dress bodice, Mattie looked over her shoulder at the woman taking it in. "Stop with the Mrs."

Glancing at Sara, her sister Claudia, Claire, and Aubrey all sitting on the bed in Nick's old room that was now Lucy's sewing room, she replied through a dimpled grin, "Sorry, *Mom.*"

Lucy squeezed her shoulder from behind, "That's more like it."

Then, looking at Mattie's bridal party, she asked, "So what did you girls have in mind for your dresses?" Before they could answer, she started rattling off ideas, pulling pins from the corner of her mouth as she spoke.

"Something similar to Mattie's, but with straps or maybe cap sleeves, or did you want to go with something completely different? I was at a wedding last year, Lina Guirerri's daughter. The bridesmaids all wore these very ruffly gowns. Now I don't have anything against ruffles, and I can manage them just fine, but they were just too different from the bride's. Know what I mean? Made it look like they didn't belong together." When she finally stopped talking, she looked at the women perched on her son's old bed and repeated, "Know what I mean?"

They nodded in unison.

"To tell you the truth, Mom, we've already decided. Claud, did you bring the picture?"

As her sister and matron of honor handed Mrs. DeRosa a picture of the one dress they had all agreed would compliment their disparate sizes, including Claire's ever-expanding girth, she continued, "And we all like the color daffodil."

Lucy glanced at her over her reading glasses, "Yellow?" Looking directly at Sara, she shook her head and said, "Bad color. It'll make Sara here look jaundiced, Aubrey will look like a ghost and you, Mattie, with your gorgeous red hair?" She just shook her head again. "No way."

Sara glanced around the room. Mrs. DeRosa made a good point. She hated the thought of wearing a yellow gown but didn't want to hurt Mattie's feelings. She seemed so set on it.

"Oh, OK," Mattie started. "Any recommendations?"

Clearly pleased that her opinion was requested, Lucy shot out, "Red."

Claudia pointed her finger at her sister. "Told ya."

Sara chimed in. "Works for me."

Everyone looked at Aubrey. "I though June weddings were supposed to be pastel-colored?"

Lucy shrugged. "Gee, I never heard that before. I suppose if you were planning an outdoor wedding, pastels would be pretty, but even roses are red. Am I right?"

Turning to Mattie balancing on a stepladder before her, she placed her hands on her hips. "What do you think, hon? It's your wedding."

Mattie looked down at her, then over at her bridal party, three-quarters of which were nodding at her.

"Think you could swing red, Aubs?"

Realizing she was the only hold out, her soft-spoken friend waved. "Oh. Yeah. Count me in."

Mattie clapped her hands together. "Excellent. Red it is." Leaning over, she hugged Lucy. "Thanks, Mom."

Sara, who couldn't be happier for Mattie, felt a tiny little something inside of her die. Again.

* * *

When Andrew got up that morning, he knew something was wrong. He could feel it coming on during choir practice the night before. That heavy, wet blanket of fatigue, the pressure in his head, the achiness. He was hoping a good night sleep would do the trick, but after what Sara did—well, OK, it wasn't all her fault.

Truth be told, if he were feeling better, he wouldn't have let it end when it did. Yeah, there was so much about her he didn't know, but there was so much about her that he already liked. A lot. The smell of her perfume, the faint traces of which stuck to his clothes all day long, her infectious laugh, the way she would sing a hymn she just learned while she was cooking or working on her laptop, the way she packed him a lunch when she made one for herself, and that she would stop whatever she was doing and camp out on the couch whenever she heard him play the piano.

He marveled, too, at how, after only two encounters, she had already managed to defrost several of the more stalwart members of choir.

And then there's the way she looked in her underwear the morning before.

He knew he shouldn't have peeked, but come on. He was, above all else, a guy, and she was—well, she was nothing short of gorgeous.

Maybe it was for the best that she said good night when she did.

Wouldn't want to get her sick.

At least that's what he told himself as he drifted off to a very fitful night's sleep.

By 6:00 am, he'd had enough with the tossing and turning. He had to get up and out, away to think. Certain some fresh air would help, he snuck into the bedroom where Sara had buried herself under the blankets.

It was everything he could do to not crawl in there with her.

After changing into his sweats, he headed out. First, he went to his office to check his schedule. Relieved to see that he didn't have any appointments, he sent texts to his back-up musicians, asking them to take over his Masses for the weekend and sent a note to Marge asking that she notify the choir that they wouldn't be singing the next morning.

She responded almost immediately. "Will do. I knew you were coming down with something. Push liquids, and stay in bed until you feel better."

He was just getting back in his Jeep to head home and do just that when his phone rang.

Sam.

"Hey, stranger. How come I haven't heard from you all week?"

His little brother, just getting off the night shift, sounded apologetic. "Work's been pretty crazy. I didn't wake you up, did I?"

"No, I've been up for awhile. What's up?"

"Not much. You up for some coffee?"

Not really.

"Yeah. Sure. Of course. Where?"

"The usual?"

"I'll be there in 15."

"See ya then."

Geddes was an old coffee house that predated all of the chain-store replicas. Not one coffee cup in the place matched, you couldn't get it *to go,* and you couldn't leave without sinking your teeth into one of their ginormous muffins. Only, on that particular morning, all Andrew wanted to do was go home and go to bed.

With Sara.

To sleep.

Arriving before his brother, he waved at the manager who was tending to a customer at the far end of the shop and slid into a booth that gave him a good vantage point of the entrance. While he waited, he stared out at the gray skies and dirty snow piled against the curb that wasn't going anywhere as long as the temperature remained below freezing.

"Good morning. What can I get for you?" It was Sally, the part savvy businesswoman/part new age gypsy manager, always ready with a smile and a story if you were up for it. But today, he was definitely not up for it.

Hoping to intercept what might otherwise be a long conversation, he managed a smile and said, "Hey, Sal. My brother'll be here any minute, so two black coffees and two muffins."

With a wink, she said, "You got it." Pausing before she left him alone, she asked, "You feelin' OK?"

Reassuring her with a quick nod, he sank a little lower in the booth and stared at the cars going by, wondering what he had gotten himself into with Sara—and what he should do about it. Ever since he opened the door on Sunday night and saw her on the other side, he felt like something had switched on inside of him. Life had suddenly become exciting and purposeful. Her coming back that night, because she wanted to, was all the validation he needed that she was indeed the answer to his prayers.

Just don't blow it.

He could see it in her eyes whenever he nitpicked about stupid things like hand towels and making the bed before she left for work in the morning. But he also saw the way she looked at him at practice, like her soul had been asleep for a very long time and was just now starting to come alive again.

Kinda like when she was about to kiss him the night before.

"Just let it ride," his father would say. His mother always preferred the biblical version. "Leave it in God's hands."

No problem.

He covered his face in his own hands, trying to do just that when he heard Sam's voice.

"Jesus, you look like hell."

Andrew opened his eyes and saw his little brother, a fully armed and uniformed Chicago policeman sitting across from him.

"Nice to see you too."

The frown on his face deepening, Sam continued, "I'm serious, man. You look like you haven't slept in days. New neighbors keeping you up at night?"

I wish.

"Here you go." Sally deposited their coffee and muffins and with a jangle of her bracelets was off again to check on other customers.

"What's the matter?" Sam asked as he tore into his muffin.

Seeing as he was the one who set Andrew up with Leanne, the older sister of his best friend back in Minnesota, he had been wrestling all week with telling Sam about Sara. Feeling a blast of warmth blow down on him from a vent in the ceiling, he hunkered down over his coffee cup.

"Is this about Leanne?" Sam asked, taking a sip of his coffee. "'Cause I'm telling you, man, I still don't know how you get over a shock like that. Never saw it coming. She seemed so perfect for you."

Covering his face again with his hands, Andrew let out a low groan. "No. This is not about Leanne." He glanced up at the ceiling and then pushed his full coffee cup away from him. "I think we both knew she wasn't perfect for me."

Sam nodded and shrugged one shoulder.

"OK. So, tell me. What's goin' on?"

Raising his eyebrow and staring at the center of the table, he vocalized the one thought on the forefront of his mind. "I think I might've met someone who is."

* * *

After Mrs. DeRosa got each of their measurements, the five female members of the bridal party piled into Lucy's big old Buick sedan and headed to Parnell's Fabrics. Following her up and down the aisles, they examined bolt after bolt of every shade of red taffeta available.

Stumbling on one labeled, "Firecracker Fusion," Sara called out, "Found it."

Claudia got to her first. "Ooh, I like it."

Aubrey appeared to be a tad shocked at the brash shade but got over it quickly when Sara showed her the label. "It's perfect."

By the time Claire and Mattie found them, the bride-to-be was looking rather disheartened. When her eyes fell on the fabric, she looked less than enthused but said, "Sure. Why not?"

"Matt," Sara urged. "Check the label."

Just as Sara had hoped, she was rewarded with a broad grin. On seeing that the fabric had almost the same name as the Firecracker Half Marathon that turned the tide of her and Nick's romance, she exclaimed, "It's perfect."

"Well, all right then," Mrs. DeRosa laughed after she finally caught up with them. "Bring every bolt you can find with that same label over to the cutting table while I go look for some tulle."

Two hours later, Sara was heading back to the apartment not sure what she'd find. While it was a Saturday, by the time she had gotten up that morning, it looked like Andrew was already long gone. The couch looked untouched, and the coffee pot wasn't even turned on. Hoping she hadn't crossed another line the night before when she gave him an almost-kiss, she pulled into Bell's Market.

I suppose I could call him. See if we need anything.

Checking the time, she saw it was 4:30.

What if he's already at church?

Taking her chances, she headed into the store for some bare essentials: ice cream and ramen noodles.

"Hello," she called into the shadow-filled apartment as she closed the door behind her. "Anybody home?"

Guess not.

Feeling her lack of sleep from the night before catch up to her, she slipped her ice cream in the freezer and set the box of ramen on the counter. When she turned toward the living room to turn on the floor lamp, she let out a gasp when she saw Andrew lying on the couch, apparently fast asleep.

Even though he looked to be wearing sweats and a hoodie, he was curled into a fetal position—like he was cold but too tired to do anything about it. Grabbing the afghan from the back of the couch, she unfolded it and spread it over him. Taking a step away, she paused and looked back down at him. His hair was all messed up, and he clearly hadn't shaved.

What's going on?

In the soft light coming from the kitchen, his face looked red. As in flushed.

Crouching down, she touched the back of her hand against his cheek and pulled it back almost instantly.

He didn't feel warm. He felt hot.

Getting up, she went into the bathroom. She used to keep a big bottle of Tylenol on the bottom shelf of the medicine cabinet.

Weird that I haven't had to use it once since he got here.

She opened it slowly and found a different bottle but the same brand.

Great minds...

Shaking two into her hand, she went to the kitchen and filled a glass with water.

She set the glass on the trunk and crouched before him again. Giving his shoulder a jiggle, she whispered his name.

No response.

Next, she smoothed some thick soft hair off his forehead and stroked her fingers through it a couple of times.

I could do this all night long.

Speaking a little more loudly, she called him by name and added, "Wake up. You need some medicine."

At this, his eyes squinted open. With a wince and a groan, he turned on his back. "What time is it?"

"5:30. Come on now. Can you sit up?"

When it was clear he couldn't manage it on his own, Sara pushed him vertical just enough to wedge herself between his back and the arm of the couch against which his head had just been lying.

Propping him up in a sitting position, sort of, she shifted around so his back was leaning against her chest. That way she was able to reach over and grab the glass of water waiting on the trunk. Working from behind him, she raised the two tablets to his mouth with her right hand as his head rested against her shoulder.

God, you smell good.

"OK, here. Take these. They'll get your fever down."

When she felt his mouth open, she pushed them in and raised the glass of water to his lips. Holding his head upright with her left hand, she held the glass in her right, watching over his shoulder so she wouldn't spill it all over him. "Come on now, babe. Drink up."

Oops.

At that, he raised his left hand, tilted the glass up and swallowed.

"Good job."

Switching the glass to her left hand meant letting go of his head, but since she had to return the glass to the trunk, it was a risk she was willing to take. As she leaned forward and did just that, he turned his body toward her as if aggravated with the interruption, forcing her back against the couch as he snuggled into her like she was a pillow. His pillow.

At least the glass was where it belonged.

Sara looked around her. The apartment was dark save for the glow coming from the street well below the bay window and the oven light in the kitchen. After she stretched one leg down the length of the couch on one side of him and propped the other up on the far edge of the trunk, she was actually quite comfortable.

And there was a Ken doll asleep in her arms.

Doing her best to drape the afghan around them both, she pressed her hand against Andrew's still hot cheek, knowing it would take a while for the meds to kick in. In the stillness of the moment, she looked down at what she could see of his face as she gently combed her fingers through his hair. Then, in a low soft voice, she started singing the song that was forever present on her shoulders and in her heart.

When she had finished, there was nothing left for her to do except exactly what the chorus instructed—close her eyes. So that's exactly what she did.

CHAPTER EIGHT

———

*"You know you're in love when you can't fall asleep because
reality
is finally better than your dreams."*
—Dr. Seuss

Hours later, Sara awoke to the sound of her phone, tucked in her purse way over on the kitchen counter, chirping text after text. She couldn't feel her one arm below the elbow and her chest felt damp.

What the...?

She tried to sit up but felt something heavy pressing against her.

Oh, right. A gorgeous man.

Her movement seemed to stir him. Lifting his head from her, well, *bosom*, he blinked a few times before looking up at her.

"How ya feeling?" she whispered.

In a surprisingly swift move, he sat up looking confused and more than a little embarrassed. "I'm so sorry."

Of course. It was after all *her,* and she was so not the top choice of Ken dolls the world over.

"Don't worry about it," she mumbled.

The apartment was darker than it had been, the only light now coming from under the oven hood. She sat up and pulled her one leg out from behind him.

Wondering what time it was, she tried pushing back the deflated feeling that threatened to drag her down with it.

She picked up the glass of water still sitting on the trunk, handed it to Andrew, and instructed, "Finish this, and I'll get you some more. Or would you prefer tea?"

She retrieved her phone and checked her messages. Five texts. All from Nancy.

Gah. Karaoke.

It was after eleven. She had missed it.

After shooting off a quick text of apology, she shut her phone off and took the empty glass from the patient.

"Water's fine. Thanks."

She filled it and returned to the couch where he had moved to the opposite end and was facing her with the blanket still wrapped around him. "I don't know what happened. Last thing I remember was coming home to take a nap."

Sara filled him in on her adventures in nursing, sticking with the facts, excluding all else, especially her use of the word *babe* and his own private performance of her favorite James Taylor song.

Pulling his mouth into sort of a smile, he whispered, "Sorry if I spoiled your evening."

At this, Sara let out a chuckle. "No worries." She thought of the guys from the Sports section lording over their apparent victory at the bar. What's a little friendly competition if the other team didn't get to win every once in a while?

"How ya feeling?" she asked again, resisting the urge to reach over and feel his forehead.

Andrew ran his hand through his sweat-damp hair and looked at it with disgust. "Like I need a shower."

Nodding toward the bathroom, she urged, "Go for it. A nice steamy shower might do you some good."

While he was doing that, she took the afghan and stuffed it in the washing machine with some detergent and softener. Lifting the lid of the trunk-slash-coffee-table, she pulled out a big thick fleece blanket and set it where he had been sitting and then changed into her snowflake-patterned pajama bottoms and an old, gray, long-sleeved T-shirt emblazoned with the Green Bay Packers logo.

So sexy.

She was looking out the bay window, focusing on nothing in particular when she saw Andrew return and sit back down on the couch as far away as possible from where she had been sitting.

Plopping down again, she noticed that he had changed into different sweatpants and a T-shirt that had *MPD* in big block letters on the front. Pointing to it with a frown, she asked, "More pudding, dammit?"

With a hearty laugh, he said, "No. Minneapolis Police Department."

When he didn't offer an explanation, she asked, "And you're wearing that why?"

"Oh, well, my dad gave it to me. He's on the force."

Ah, two cops in the family.

"How 'bout your mom?"

"Same as me. Up in a suburban Minneapolis parish. Where I grew up."

"Huh."

He pointed to her T-shirt. "I wouldn't wear that outside here if I were you."

Sara looked down at the logo. "Oh, no worries. I'm not big into football. In fact, I'm not big into any sport."

Andrew pressed his lips together. "Yeah. Me neither."

Gah. Enough with the small talk.

She looked down at her un-manicured nails, trying to think of something to say that would break the ice.

"So, 'Close Your Eyes'?"

He said it so softly, she barely heard him.

Whipping her head up, she narrowed her eyes and asked, "What did you say?"

"That's the name of it?"

"What?"

He reached back and patted his shoulder.

So he had heard her singing to him. Great. Her secret was out. Well, one of them anyway.

Ice. Broken.

As long as he didn't catch the *babe* slip too.

Feeling her flight-or-fight instinct kick in, she shifted around and picked up her phone.

I wonder what Nancy's doing now?

Andrew edged a bit closer to her. "I don't think I ever heard it before. It's really lovely."

Blinking back the moisture welling up in her eyes that she was too tired to cry out, she explained, "It's pretty old. The official title is, 'You Can Close Your Eyes.' James Taylor. *Mud Slide Slim and the Blue Horizon*."

She reached for a tissue from a box on the chest, not noticing that he moved to the cushion right next to hers.

Oh.

"Tell me."

Bristling, she turned to him and asked, "Tell you what?"

With the softest of touches, he brushed the bangs from her eyes and stroked her cheek with his thumb, looking at her like he had just unearthed a piece of rare china.

"Why it makes you cry."

Sara took in a ragged breath.

Tell him everything, and he'll be outta here by morning.

She looked into his eyes, so kind and warm.

Don't tell him, and stay an emotional train wreck.

While neither option appealed to her, in that split second, she made the decision to compromise.

"My mom," she started before clearing her throat. "She used to sing it to me at bedtime."

Andrew said nothing, so she continued. "She, um, left when I was eight." She stared off into some distant memory. "Didn't even say good-bye."

Feeling his hand knead her shoulder, she tilted her head toward it and said, "So there you have it."

"I'm sorry."

"Not your fault."

"No, but I know how it feels to lose a parent. Both of mine died when I was six."

Horrified, she turned to him. "Oh, how awful. What happened, if you don't mind me asking?"

He raised both eyebrows and said, "Plane crash. In the middle of a cornfield. A friend of my dad's had just gotten his pilot's license and offered to take them up for a ride. All I know is the plane took off from some little rural airstrip, and had just started its ascent when it nosedived."

With his eyes locked on hers, he added, "No survivors."

Sara covered her mouth with both hands before exhaling. "That's awful. I'm so sorry."

Two dead parents trump a woman with a bad case of wanderlust who abandons her kids any day.

He just shrugged and looked away.

"I seem to recall you mentioning a brother?"

At this, his face lit up. "Yeah. Sam. He's the one here in Chicago with me. Then I've got three other brothers and two sisters back in Minneapolis."

Sara didn't know what to say except, "Wow."

"Well, yeah, it started out with just me and my brother, but we ended up with the Benets who eventually adopted the two of us. It was a blessing really. Still is."

"Can I ask you something else?"

"Sure."

"Your tattoo."

He gave her a devilish smile. "Yeah?"

Feeling her cheeks flame, Sara grimaced. "I really didn't get a good look at it."

At this, he moved a hand to the waistband of his sweats and asked, "Wanna see it again?"

Through an embarrassed smile, she spoke softly. "Maybe later. Just tell me. What does it say?"

"McGuigan. It's my birth surname."

"Ah. When did you get it?"

"On my eighteenth birthday."

"Were your adoptive parents all right with that?"

Andrew nodded. "My dad went with me. Had mine and my brother's names tattooed on his arm under the rest of the kids' names."

With a grin pulling at one side of her mouth, Sara whispered, "Your dad sounds like a pretty cool guy."

"Yeah, he's pretty great."

Feeling better now that the conversation was not about her and her tales of woe, Sara stood up. "I'm gonna get a glass of wine. Can I get you anything? You must be starving."

"Nah, I'm good."

She returned with a glass half full of Shiraz, intent on keeping the focus off of her. "So, it must be great having such a big family."

"Oh, yeah. It is. How about you? Any siblings?"

Crap.

"Uh, yeah. One. "

When she didn't say any more, he prodded. "Brother, sister?"

"Brother." Before she could stop herself, she blurted, "And I miss him more than words can say."

Andrew just sat watching her, waiting for more.

Taking a long pull of her wine, she explained, "We, uh, had a bit of a falling out. A couple of years back."

"That's too bad."

She stared into her glass, mesmerized by the way the light from the kitchen illuminated the liquid within. "It was my fault," she heard herself say. "I just can't bring myself to go back."

"Sorry if I'm crossing a line here, but does this have anything to do with the nickname you won't tell me about?"

Sara took a deep breath, wondering how it was that she was sharing more with Andrew in the space of one hour than she ever shared with Jer in their time together.

Must be the wine-induced Tourette's.

She looked into his eyes that were boring into her with both patience and concern.

"Trouble."

He frowned. "Trouble?"

"My nickname. Pop called me that for as long as I can remember." With a rueful laugh, she looked back down at her glass. "When I was little, I actually thought my real name was Trouble Cleff. Well, until one of the nuns at my grade school caught me introducing myself to the other kids that way." She looked back at Andrew with a weak smile. "She set me straight, but the name stuck."

The two sat there quietly for a few minutes before Andrew pulled the blanket up around his shoulders as he yawned. "Well, I don't know about you, but I feel like I could sleep for another twelve hours."

"Oh. Sure."

Sara set her glass down and pressed the back of her hand against his cheek. "Yeah, your fever's coming back. Let me get you some more Tylenol."

When she got back, she stood in front of him, watching him pop the pills. "Tell you what. You take the bed tonight. You'll be more comfortable there and, well, I'm gonna be up for a while."

Drowning myself in the rest of that wine and a little Ray LaMontagne.

The patient looked up at her. "Ya sure?"

Nodding, she replied, "Absolutely." She started stepping away. "Just let me go in and change the sheets first."

"Oh, don't worry about it. You've done enough."

She turned and watched as he started to stand up, still clutching the blanket around him. "Man, you really must be sick if you don't care about—"

Sara would've finished what she was saying if the ailing Ken doll hadn't grasped her hand and cut her off with a most unexpected request.

"Come with me?"

It launched a heated debate in her warring subconscious, on one side of which her inner wild child was shouting, "Go for it!" while the parochial-school-girl side growled, "Do. Not. Go. There."

She sucked in a breath, trying to conjure images of Sister Marcus smacking her ruler against her open palm or twirling her rosary over her head like a bolo. When those images failed to quell the side of her that wanted to raise his temperature more than any fever could, she tried stating the obvious.

"But you're sick."

With a gentle squeeze of his hand on hers, he asked, "Is that the only reason?"

Knowing this was not a question to be taken lightly, she cursed the wine for stealing any and all coherent thoughts from her brain.

Arching an eyebrow, she quipped, "Well, maybe you should try inviting me again when you're feeling better." And then cringed.

Can't believe I just said that.

Apparently, the wine had swapped out her coherent thoughts with a newfound ability to talk like a saucy bitch.

Tugging the blanket tighter around him, he stepped closer to her and whispered, "Good idea."

Go me.

"But tonight," he continued with his eyes growing glassier by the second, "I just want to sleep with you. Really sleep. No fooling around."

Well, damn.

Sara just stared at him a minute. "Well when you put it that way..."

* * *

"So what did you do?" Mattie gasped at Ferndell's the next morning before shooting off her breakfast order like she was a bidder on the floor of the Chicago Mercantile Exchange. "Veggie omelet, egg whites only, fruit on the side, whole wheat toast, unbuttered."

The waitress looked at Sara who absently said, "The same." Then, remembering that she skipped dinner the night before, put her hand on the waitress's forearm and continued, "But regular eggs, hash browns *and* fruit on the side, and slather the toast with butter. Oh, and can I have a jumbo blueberry muffin to go, please?"

After Aubrey ordered a bowl of baked cinnamon-apple oatmeal, the waitress left them alone and Sara finally replied, "I did it. I slept with him. All night long."

"But, Sara," Aubrey scolded, "you hardly know this guy. And he was *sick*."

Ignoring her phobic friend, Sara looked into the distance over her head and added, "Yeah, but it was so...*intimate*. I've never done that before."

Mattie's face spread into a devilish grin. "Oh *really*? Care to share?"

Her question kicked Sara off the cloud she was riding on. "What?"

"What have you never done before?"

"Oh," after blinking a few times, she propped her elbow on the table and rested the side of her face in her hand. "Slept with a guy without having sex first."

Mattie smiled and nodded. "It's pretty great, isn't it?"

When Sara raised her eyebrow at her, she bit down on her lip. With a hushed voice, she explained, "Nick and I agreed to wait until after we're married." Then she quickly added, "Please don't tell Nancy."

Overshare.

Sara jutted her chin out. "Wow, Matt. That's great. I—wow. I didn't know couples actually did that anymore."

"I think that's awesome, Mattie," Aubrey said as she tucked her butter blonde hair behind her ears. "If I ever find anybody again, that's what I'd do, and if he didn't want to then I'd know that he's not the right guy for me."

Hugging them with her eyes, Mattie reached out and patted both of their hands. "You guys are the best."

"That being said," Sara laughed, "if it were me, I would've dragged his ass to City Hall the minute he proposed."

"Tell me about it," Mattie chuckled. "But, we've waited this long. What's a couple more months?"

Sara indulged herself in the memory of her and Andrew's torrid night of snuggling, remembering how lovely it was to wake up with his arms wrapped around her.

There's no way in hell I'm waiting months.

After their food arrived and they'd started eating, Mattie asked her, "So who is this guy anyway?"

Sara set her fork down on her plate and hunched her shoulders up. "Actually, Matt, I think you two have already met."

Mattie stopped mid-chew. "What do you mean?" she mumbled.

Pulling both eyebrows up under her bangs, she announced, "He's the music director at St. Matthias. I believe he'll be playing at your wedding?"

As Mattie and Aubrey started peppering her with questions, Sara heard herself clipping out one-word replies, telling them as little as possible because she knew full well that a relationship with a Ken doll—especially one who worked in a church for God's sake—was doomed from the very start. Still, she was having a hard time not getting sucked into the excited swirl her pals were generating—not unlike the girls she'd see congregating at each other's lockers in high school, talking about the boys they had crushes on. She wouldn't have been surprised to find that her face was spotted with zits and her teeth were once again covered in braces by the time they were through with her.

Not that she ever congregated around lockers in high school because A) she didn't have any *besties*, and B) the only guy she ever had a crush on was the vile Jimmy Mabry, the scumbag in Ken-doll's clothing whose father owned the local car repair shop. Not exactly the type of news she wanted to spread like wildfire through the halls of St. Xavier's.

Andrew, on the other hand—well, there was a time she would've blasted over the loudspeaker in the principal's office that she was falling for a guy like him. But that was a long, long time ago.

Now, more than ever, she wished some Silicon Valley whiz kid would come up with an Undo button that could correct lives, not just words, that were badly in need of an edit—or in her case, a complete rewrite.

On her drive home, a call from Mike Teegan brought her back to reality. Apparently, Daryl Swerl was out sick and needed someone to cover for him that night. The assignment? Interviewing the legendary guitarist Jeffrey Tinsdale before his concert at the House of Blues.

"So, ya interested?" She could actually hear Mike grinning through the phone.

Her response, while not especially professional was clear and direct. "*Hell* yeah."

A few minutes later, she was about to slide her key in the lock of the apartment when she heard Andrew at the piano, sounding out the opening bars of a song he had only just heard for the first time the night before. Not wanting to interrupt, she pressed her ear against the door and listened as her heart thudded loudly in her chest.

Mesmerized, she closed her eyes. She could just picture him sitting there, both hands floating over the keys as he deciphered the melody already stamped on his memory, creating an arrangement all his own.

She opened the door very slowly, but there was no getting around the loud click that would sound when it shut. As soon as it did, she heard him seamlessly transpose what he was playing into something much more secular.

God, he's good.

"Hey," she called out as she came down the hallway.

When she reached him sitting at the piano, she resisted the urge to slide onto the bench next to him and curl herself around him as she had the night before. Because if she did that, she might suggest that they take a nap, which would be a really bad idea because A) there would be no napping involved, and B) despite what her breakfast buddies might think, he wasn't the one for her, and she knew it.

Besides, she had work to do.

So, instead, she stood casually next to the cabinet and asked, "How're you feeling?"

By the looks of it, he had showered and shaved but still looked exhausted.

Leveling her with a sweet smile, he said, "Thanks for last night." Then he picked up a slip of paper that was sitting on the music stand in front of him. "And for the note."

Wanting to spare him the pain of waking up alone and dejected like she had on more occasions than she cared to remember, she wrote a little note and taped it to the medicine cabinet mirror where she was sure he'd see it.

"Meeting friends for breakfast. Be back in a bit. Hope you're feeling better. xo"

She shook the small brown paper bag she was holding. "I didn't know what you like for breakfast, so I brought you a muffin. Are you hungry?"

"Yeah, I probably should eat."

Motioning him over to the kitchen counter, she asked, "How about some coffee to go with it? Or tea?" She had to bite down on her lip to refrain from asking, "Or me?"

He pointed to the teapot that was starting to spout steam. "I'll get it. Do you want some?"

Caffeine already racing through her veins, she declined before dropping onto a barstool.

"So my editor called with an assignment while I was driving home from the restaurant," Sara announced, unable to keep the excitement from her voice. "I get to interview Jeffrey Freakin' Tinsdale before his concert at the House of Blues tonight."

Andrew looked at her with a blank expression. "And he is...?"

Eyes still bright, she laughed. "You're kidding, right?"

When he still looked dumbfounded, she started tossing him clues. "Jeffrey Tinsdale, the greatest guitarist to emerge on the music scene since Eric Clapton, Jimmy Page, and Eddie Van Halen combined?"

Nothing.

"Jeffrey Tinsdale, front man for The Rockaways, well, before they disbanded?"

Andrew pressed his lips together and slowly shook his head.

Oh, this could be a problem.

Giving it one last shot, she lowered her voice while raising both eyebrows. "Jeffrey Tinsdale, who wrote the rock classic, 'Pithy Love'?"

At this he gave her a clenched-teeth grin and mouthed, "Sorry."

"Oh my *God*. How can you not know who Jeffrey Tinsdale is?" When all he did in reply was shrug, Sara put both hands palms down on the counter. "All right, that does it."

With his now-troubled eyes wide, he asked, "What?"

Pointing at him, she said, "You're coming with me."

Taking a step away from her as he dunked a tea bag in a mug of hot water, he chuckled. "I don't think so."

Sara moved to the couch where she pulled out her laptop and plugged it in. "We should leave here by two."

He came and sat right beside her on the otherwise very empty couch. "I'm still not feeling that great."

Without looking at him, she reached a hand over and pressed the back of it, as clinically as possible, to his forehead.

Cool as a cucumber.

Hunched over her laptop, with a heavy faux sigh she looked at him sideways. "Faker."

* * *

Still fever-free, but still not feeling a hundred percent yet, Andrew took his time getting ready for work on Monday morning after Sara had left in an excited rush to see what her editor thought of the interview she had submitted the night before.

To think, just three days before, when she barged into the bathroom nearly naked while he was shaving, he was seriously considering releasing her from the deal they had struck.

With yet another sigh, he stopped what he was doing, again, and thought about her—the way her dimples only popped out when she smiled, the richness of her laugh, the way she sang to him when he was half asleep, the feel of her fingers combing tenderly through his hair.

Then there was the way she felt lying next to him in bed.

And the look on her face when she was sound asleep.

So perfect.

The ringtone on his phone pulled him out of his daydream.

"Hey, Mom. What's up?"

"How are you feeling?" She asked breathlessly. "I just got off the phone with Sam, and he said you didn't seem quite yourself when he saw you on Saturday."

He hung his head back for a second before responding, thinking of all the times he told his brother to not tell her things that might worry her especially given the distance now separating them from her.

"I'm fine. Just a bug. I stayed in and slept all weekend."

"Well be sure to stay hydrated, and rest when you need to, all right?"

With a chuckle, he replied, "I promise."

Just when he was about to say his good-bye, her heard her ask, "Now what's this I hear about a new girlfriend?"

I'm gonna kill Sam.

Before he could reply, she practically reached through the phone, grabbed him by the neck, and asked, "Who is she, and when can we meet her?"

"Easy, Mom. It's really not as serious as all that."

Not yet anyway.

Not easily appeased, she lowered her voice and asked, "So where'd you meet her? What can you tell me about her?"

"What's with all the questions? You sound like dad interrogating a suspect."

The phone was quiet on the other end before he heard a muffled voice, like she was holding it against her hand while she was talking to somebody nearby. After a few seconds, her voice came through loud and clear. "Listen, honey. There's somebody here who would like to talk to you. Do you have a few minutes?"

He pulled his phone away from his ear and looked at it. Who could possibly need his mother to get permission to talk to him instead of contacting him directly?

A cold chill ran down his spine.

Leanne.

"Actually, Mom." He spoke loudly into the phone so whoever was there with her would be able to hear. "I've got to get to work. I'll catch up with you later. Love you. Bye."

Lost in thought as to what Leanne could possibly want to talk to him about, he wasn't ready for another interrogation as soon as he came through the office door at St. Matthias.

"Andy, you look awful, dear. How are you feeling? Are you sure you should be here today?"

Stopping in front of the receptionist's desk, he looked down at the frail Mrs. Gibbons. "I feel better than I look. How are you?"

She motioned for him to come closer. "You forgot to RSVP to the Spring Fling Gala, so I put you down for two, just in case."

Gala?

Sure he heard her wrong, he asked, "I'm sorry. What gala?"

She opened the top drawer of her desk and pulled out a creamy white post card stamped with the parish emblem and handed it to him. As his eyes scanned the details of the black tie

Spring Fling fundraiser being held at the Union League of Chicago in three weeks, he remembered.

Since the thought of attending alone didn't appeal to him, he hadn't planned on going, even though Father Steve had asked that he make it a priority to attend.

But that was before Sara entered his life. The idea of slow dancing with her filled his head as he handed the invitation back to Mrs. Gibbons. "No, I didn't RSVP, did I?"

In a move that seemed to take her quite by surprise, he leaned down and pecked her wrinkled cheek. "Thanks for thinking of me, Mrs. G."

Sauntering down the hall to his office, he called over his shoulder, "Plan on saving a dance for me."

When Andrew got settled in his office, he pulled out his phone and texted Sara. *R u free on the night of the 29th?*

CHAPTER NINE

———

"If you can't get rid of the skeleton in your closet, you'd best teach it to dance."
—George Bernard Shaw

Sitting at her desk on Monday morning, Sara could hardly believe all that had happened to her since she arrived at Mike's planning meeting the previous Friday morning with just seconds to spare. Friday night's choir and cantor practice, the kiss she almost gave Andrew afterward, going to Mrs. DeRosa's to get measured and go fabric shopping, then coming home and finding Andrew passed out on the couch with a fever.

Here, she paused, wanting to replay every single detail of what happened next.

When she caught her reflection in the black screen of her blank monitor, she gave her head a quick shake.

Stop obsessing. Get your ass in gear, and find another apartment because Easter is just a month away.

Given the overwhelmingly positive things happening to her at work, she figured a raise, if not a promotion, was imminent. First, there was all that praise she received on her Krypto Blight piece, especially since, as she predicted, the band didn't win squat at the Grammy's the night before. *Congratulations, you totally called it,* Daryl Swerl himself texted on her way into work. Second, her editor couldn't say enough about her interview with the a-m-a-z-i-n-g Jeffrey Tinsdale—the most talented and humble music legend she had ever met in her life.

Points for not gushing once during the entire interview.

She was just about to dive into her reader emails when she heard her phone chirp.

It was Andrew, asking what she was doing on the 29th.

She checked her calendar and saw that it was completely wide open. Still, she could think of any number of things to do on a Saturday night.

For starters, karaoke. *There is, after all, a trophy to win back.*

Any number of concerts in area clubs. *I just haven't been able to find any good ones yet.*

Oh, and giving herself a pedicure. *After all, sandal season is right around the corner.*

But to him, she texted, *Nothing. Why?*

He answered immediately. *I need a date.*

That little zing zipped through her again. With an uncharacteristic smile creeping over her lips, she texted back, *For what?*

Dinner dance. Union League Club. Black Tie.

Her mind became filled with images of old people in formal wear sitting like statues at big round tables in a stuffy, cigar-smoke-filled, men-only club, the walls of which were probably covered in dark paneling, pearl necklaces and black cummerbunds as far as the eye could see.

She started texting, *Pass* when another text came through.

Open bar.

Deleting her earlier response, she texted *I'm in* and then sat staring at the words on her phone, wondering just what it was exactly that she was in for.

The next week and a half went by in a blur. Both busy with work, Sara saw little of Andrew but discovered that sneaking a peek at him sleeping each morning before she snuck out was just as addictive as her daily dose of caffeine.

Floating down Michigan Avenue on her way to work, she enjoyed the added bonus of warmth and sunshine that a sudden but brief burst of spring had afforded her, brightening the otherwise dreary March. While flowers planted up and down the Magnificent Mile had yet to pop, there was an invigorating freshness in the air that made everything feel new. This, coupled with the fact that she had an actual formal date with Andrew a week from Saturday to look forward to, made everything in Sara's life seem almost perfect.

Almost.

There was just that one little thing, that one little mistake that she could never undo, lurking deep in her subconscious, ready to pounce whenever she started to feel a glimmer of happiness. So, the closer the date got, the busier she made herself, doing her best to block it from her mind altogether.

Everything was humming along just fine until she got a text from Mattie on her way into the office that Friday morning, informing her that their dress fittings with Mrs. DeRosa the next day had to be postponed because she had to finish a rush job on a neighbor's premature and gravely ill grandchild's christening gown.

She was still working hard to erase certain sad images from her mind when she was practically accosted by Claire, who wanted her opinion on her latest column.

"I didn't get any feedback from Dianne on it. Not a peep all week." Thrusting the Lifestyle section at Sara, she demanded, "Read it and tell me what you think."

"Calm down," Sara advised as she took the paper from her. "Dianne wouldn't run it if she didn't think it was worthy. You know that."

Claire gave her head a quick shake, "But she's been in meetings all week. What if it slipped through, and it wasn't supposed to?"

Narrowing her eyes, Sara asked, "Do you always get this paranoid when you're pregnant?"

"Yes," the normally put together Plate Spinner moaned. "And I hate it." Pointing to the paper, she added, "The only cure is to get lots of reassurance from the people I love and trust, so come on. Read it and tell me if it's awful."

Sara tried not to gape at her friend. "Uh, all right. Sure."

She sat in her chair and silently scanned the following:

Dear Future Daughter-in-Laws,

I know I haven't met you yet, but when I do, please don't be frightened if I come running at you waving a tape measure.

If you find that last bit alarming, please, hear me out.

As the mother of all boys, I just realized I have no one to whom I can endow my wedding dress. My mother's before me, it's a lovely ball gown embellished with Chantilly lace and yards of tulle, complete with a matching bolero jacket and pillbox hat. It would be a shame to let it go to waste (insert heavy, prolonged sigh here).

But, I digress.

As I was preparing my youngest son's breakfast the other day—a kitschy dish we like to call "Egg-in-Bread"—and I arranged it on his plate just so, it occurred to me that you may someday curse the ground I walk on, accusing me of not only pampering your future husband but, worse, creating a needy man who demands that his spouse match, or even exceed, his mom's level of doting.

For shame.

I handed my youngest his food, and he thanked me. But when he pushed the envelope and asked for some milk, I nearly snarled, "Get it yourself."

Then I set out his clothes for him (after I made his bed, of course).

Far be it from me to raise a high-maintenance hubby. However, since he is my youngest, I fear the damage may have already been done with my older sons. Please accept my sincerest apologies.

I didn't intentionally set out to create narcissistic oafs, incapable of independent living. I blame working-mother guilt.

I'll admit it. I put my career first. After dumping them in day care, I would rush to my job as if the Earth itself would stop spinning on its axis if I was but a minute late.

By the time I'd pick them up at the end of a long day, I invariably felt compelled to demonstrate my affection by doing irrational things like shoving my beloved Eric Clapton CDs—

Here Sara paused and arched an eyebrow at her friend. "You like Clapton?"

Eyes wide, Claire nodded.

"I have an even greater level of respect for you than I did five minutes ago."

"Keep reading," the columnist laughed.

Sara refocused on the page, finding where she had left off.

Like shoving my beloved Eric Clapton CDs into the glove compartment so we could instead sing along with the likes of Raffi, Ariel, and Belle. I mean, really, who wants their little cherub humming "I Shot the Sheriff" during circle time?

At this, Sara laughed. "Good one."

Then, exhausted to the point of insanity, I didn't think twice about putting my boys' needs before my own—even if it meant storing extra clothes for them in their diaper bag while I rushed to work with oatmeal-stained shoulders, or cutting their meat for them so I could enjoy my own meal in peace. (I swear I won't do this at your wedding reception.)

As they got older, I kept their schedules so jam-packed with Scouts, sports, and school, that again, I felt too guilty to make them do chores. I know, I know—bad move. Is it any wonder they avoid eye contact with me as I read off my to-do list on Saturday mornings?

Please believe me when I tell you, I did it all out of love. Perhaps you'll understand better once you have children of your own.

I. Can't. Wait.

Well, anyway. Sorry to be so long-winded. I'm sure I'll be thrilled to finally meet you when the time comes!

Hugs,

Your Future Mother-in-Law

P.S. It's a size 6. Just sayin'...

Sara handed the paper back to Claire. "Stellar. One of your best."

"Honest?"

After Sara nodded, Claire stood as she blew out a sigh of relief. Then, all of the sudden, the smile left her face, and she sucked in a breath.

"What's wrong?" Sara stood and put a hand on Claire's elbow. "You OK?"

With a smile slowly creeping back over her mouth, Claire took Sara's hand and placed it on her belly.

Unable to pull it away, Sara was astounded by how firm it was. Almost as if Claire really did have a basketball under her shirt.

Then she felt something move under her palm.

One gasp and her eyes flooded as they met Claire's.

"Wow," she said, though the word itself never made it out of her mouth.

Grinning at her friend, Claire squeezed Sara's hand before releasing it and said, "Thanks for the feedback. I'll let you get back to work."

Before she left, Claire turned and asked, "Hey, did you get Mattie's message? No fittings tomorrow."

All Sara could do was nod. And try for the bazillionth time to beat her regret back into submission. She had almost done it too. By the time choir practice rolled around, she was feeling mighty fine about the weekend sprawling eventless in front of her—that is, until practice ended.

Andrew had just said, "See you Sunday, everybody," when Glynnis gushed, "Sara, this is my grandson, Jamison. Isn't he darling? My daughter is driving me home tonight and brought him in for a visit."

Before Sara could react, Glynnis thrust the bundled-up infant into her arms.

She awkwardly held the baby away from her, doing all she could to avoid looking into the little cherub's face.

Oh. My. God.

While the other mothers and grandmothers in the choir busied themselves with putting their music away and getting their coats on, Sara was looking for someone to hand the baby off to when Andrew of all people swept him out of her arms.

Holding him like a pro, he looked into the angelic little face and asked, "Hey, who do we have here, huh?"

She watched in stunned silence as he tickled under the infant's chubby cheek with his finger, eliciting a smile from the baby and coos from the women now surrounding him. When he made eye contact with Sara and smiled, she felt as if she had taken a bullet to the chest.

I gotta get outta here.

Leaving her music on her chair, she slipped out of the nearest exit and headed for Lake Shore Drive. At each stoplight along the way, she texted a different friend, groping for a way to distract herself from the wave of baby-induced anxiety she felt building up inside of her.

Given the hour, she didn't even try Claire.

She tried Nancy instead. *Whatcha doing?*

Interviewing hot chef. Ttyl, Nancy replied.

Mattie, too, was apparently busy. *@ track meet with Nick.*

Of course.

Even Aubrey wasn't available. *Visiting my nana. U OK?*

Out of options, she took Foster Avenue to the southbound Lake Shore Drive entrance ramp. Somewhere between Irving Park Road and North Avenue, she realized she had nowhere to go but home.

By the time she heard Andrew slide his key into the lock, she was already in her snowflake pajama bottoms and long-sleeved Green Bay Packers T-shirt, wrapped tightly within the blankets of the opened sleeper sofa, staring out at the snow falling in front of the bay window of the darkened apartment.

She didn't turn to greet him. Not when she heard him open and close the foyer closet to put his coat away and not when she heard him set his keys onto the kitchen counter. Not even when she sensed him stop on his way down the hall and whisper her name.

She didn't move. Not until she heard the bedroom door click closed behind him.

* * *

There was no denying Andrew loved kids. Close to all of his nieces and nephews, he cherished any time he could spend with them from the time they were newborns on, which might explain why working with the children's choir was, hands down, his favorite part of the job. And it was one of the things he had loved about Leanne. She had such a way with them. It was just too bad she didn't want to make any with him. Or anyone else for that matter, apparently.

It might also explain why he confiscated Glynnis's grandson from Sara's arms when it looked like she didn't want any part of it.

In the few weeks they had been living together, he wasn't surprised that the topic of kids hadn't come up. Given what he did know about her, he also wouldn't be surprised to learn that she wasn't interested in having a family of her own. Still, he had never seen her look at him the way she did before leaving the church. Like he had broken her heart.

He got out of there as quickly as he could, not that he expected to find her at home, but he hoped that she'd be there. There was so much he wanted to ask her. So much he was hoping she'd share with him. If only she'd let him in.

Disappointed to come home to an empty apartment, he debated waiting up for her as he made his way down the hall into the kitchen area.

The last thing he expected was to find her already asleep. And on the sofa sleeper when it was her turn to take the bedroom. Still, with a wedding scheduled for the next morning, perhaps it was best if he turned in early. So, after checking to see if she might still be awake, that's exactly what he did.

Three hours later, though, he woke up with a start and looked around his dark room, his heart pounding in his chest.

What in the world?

He thought he heard a sound coming from the other side of the door. Or did he dream it? Deciding to investigate, Andrew slipped his pajama bottoms on and slowly opened the door.

The first thing he noticed was a faint glow coming from the living room. As he got closer, he saw it was coming from the TV in the corner. An old black and white movie was playing. In it, a guy in black tie and tails was talking to a pretty blonde woman in a feathery white dress. Or maybe he was singing to her. Andrew couldn't tell because the volume was so low.

The room felt cold, and he wished he had pulled a T-shirt on.

He glanced at Sara. By all appearances, she seemed to be asleep. She was in the same position as when he came home earlier, but this time there was a small mountain of used tissues next to her pillow, and the remote was in her hand. He carefully tugged it from her grasp and pushed the power button.

"Oh, don't turn it off," she mumbled. "This is my favorite part."

Andrew turned it back on and then watched as she pushed herself to a sitting position.

Without looking at him, she threw back the blankets covering the spot next to her and patted the mattress.

He climbed in next to her and pulled the blankets high around him to ward off the cold.

Before he could say anything, she took the remote from him and turned up the volume. After a few minutes of watching the couple dance while the guy sang a song about being in heaven and dancing cheek-to-cheek, he stole a glance at her. The wistful look on her face tugged at him. He looked back at the screen and saw the pair break into a tap dance then leap through the air across a lofty dance floor.

"Think we should try that next Saturday night? I bet we could pull it off."

At this, Sara let out a shadow of laugh that was loaded with regret.

When the on-screen pair finished dancing, she clicked off the TV. Even in the dim light coming through the bay window at that late hour, he could see that she looked like she might cry.

"I was just kidding about the dancing," he offered, hoping to get a smile out of her.

If anything, it had the opposite effect.

She took a deep breath and with chin starting to wobble, exhaled, "Andrew."

"Yeah?"

As tired as he was, he had a feeling whatever he could get out of her would be worth the exhaustion he'd feel tomorrow.

But she just gave her head a quick shake and whispered, "Never mind."

"Are you sure? Did I happen to mention that I'm a great listener?"

When she didn't respond, he nudged her shoulder with his.

Nothing.

So he waited.

After a few quiet minutes, she took his hand and looked into his face. "Stay with me?"

Andrew reached over and cupped her cheek with his other hand. "Are you OK?"

She leaned into his touch. "I just want to sleep with you. Really sleep. No fooling around, I promise."

He felt a smile tug at his mouth. "Well, when you put it that way."

And with that, they both sank back under the blankets.

The next morning, Sara woke up with a smile on her face in the first time since…well, since the weekend before when she slept with Andrew the first time. Both times, she slept like a rock. Today, though, she was surprised to find it was already 11:45.

And that she was alone.

Oh.

She floated to the bathroom. Once she flipped the light on, she saw a note taped to the mirror written in what looked to be hurried handwriting. *Have a wedding at 10:30 and a funeral at 2:00. Catch you later.*

That was it. No greeting. No x's and o's.

Well, at least he left a note.

She took a deep breath, set it on the counter, and stepped into the shower, enjoying the pleasant buzz of excitement she couldn't shake even if she wanted to. Best of all, any guilty feelings from the day before had vanished entirely.

* * *

Playing Pachelbel's "Canon in D" as he had for countless weddings before, Andrew saw bridesmaid after bridesmaid make their way up the long aisle in the middle of the flower-festooned church out of the corner of his eye. When the bride and her father followed, all in attendance stood, and Father Steve started the Mass.

But Andrew's mind was miles away. Eight to be exact. He wondered if Sara was still sleeping and wished above all else that he had been able to stay with her. He didn't have the heart to wake her up before he left.

At least I left a note.

"Do you take this woman to be your lawful wife...?" The words drifted to where Andrew was sitting. Lifting his eyes from the music in front of him, he watched as the mother of the bride dabbed at hers while her husband sat beaming beside her.

How easy it was for him to picture his own parents sitting there. Well, across the aisle since he'd be the groom. He caught himself wondering who would be sitting on Sara's side besides, maybe, friends from work.

Snap out of it.

Just because they had slept together again, it didn't mean they were destined for the altar. Still, it was a hell of a lot more than he had ever done with Leanne, and look what that had gotten him.

As soon as the Mass ended, the happy couple made their way down the aisle.

As soon as Andrew finished playing Charles Callahan's "The Rejoicing" from *Suite in G*, he slipped off of the organ bench and texted one of his backup musicians, asking if she could fill in for the rest of the day.

* * *

Engrossed in concert listings, Sara stood at the kitchen counter, staring at her open laptop and singing along to an old Stevie Nicks hit. If she didn't have the volume cranked as high as she did perhaps she would've heard the apartment door open and wouldn't have let out a shriek as soon as she felt someone hug her from behind.

"Sorry," the devilishly handsome man chuckled as she spun around in his arms.

"What are you doing here?" she gasped while her heart knocked against her chest. "I thought you had a funeral this afternoon."

With a shrug, he released her. "I'd rather hang with you, if that's all right. You seemed kind of down yesterday."

"Well, how nice is that? What did you have in mind?"

He shrugged. "Anything. Just let me get comfortable first."

Anything? So tempting...

While he changed, Sara thought of the one thing she tried to get Jer to do with her but with zero success. Pulling up the site on her laptop, she had the answer she needed by the time Andrew came ambling out of the bedroom in jeans and a sweater.

"So what's the game plan?"

"How 'bout we grab some lunch and then go," she took a deep breath and chirped, "ice skating at Millennium Park."

"Heh, no."

"Oh, come on. They're keeping it open this weekend because of the snow."

He gave his head a quick shake. "Sorry. No."

"Seriously? Why not?"

"Never been," he clipped, easing onto a barstool.

She looked incredulous. "You're from the land of a thousand lakes. How did you manage to slip across the border without ever strapping on a pair of skates?"

He held up his hands. "Mom didn't want me injuring these. No sledding or skiing either."

Sara nodded. After a few seconds, though, she gave him a disapproving look. "I'm sorry, but that's no excuse for not learning how to skate. I have half a mind to report you to the Minnesota State authorities."

At this he let out a hearty laugh. "All right. I surrender."

Sara's right eyebrow flew north, her mouth pulled into a smirk, and her mind, well, that went directly to the place Sister Marcus warned her never to tread.

They didn't call me "Trouble" for nothing.

As if reading her mind, Andrew continued, "You'll have to show me what to do."

Uh...

"To skate," he said pointedly.

Dang.

Looking as flip as possible, she shrugged. "Sure. But it'll cost you."

He kept his eyes on her and lowered his chin. "What did you have in mind?'

If you only knew.

She pressed her lips together. "Come to karaoke with me tonight." Then she plastered on a cheesy grin. "Come on. You'll love it. I've heard you sing. I bet you can belt out Barry Manilow with the best of them."

After another loud laugh he declined, citing that, as an employee of the Chicago Archdiocese, he had a reputation to uphold.

Sara nodded. "OK, fine. Skating lessons on the house. Let's go."

* * *

A few hours later, Andrew sat on a bench while Sara knelt before him, lacing up his skates.

After threading the laces through the openings that straddled his ankles, she looked up at him. "How does that feel?"

"Fine?"

She tugged again.

"Ow. That's kinda tight."

"Good," she grunted. "These really have to support your ankles, especially when you're not used to it."

After she finished, she held out her hand and pulled him to a standing position with a smile spreading across her face. She put her gloves back on. "Follow me."

He gripped the railing for dear life as he watched her effortlessly float along. The long skirt she had on over her tights floated behind her as she gracefully glided by.

"You go ahead," he called after her. "I'll be fine."

With eyes bright and cheeks pink, she circled back around to him and held out both hands. "Come on. You can do it."

There was something about letting go of the railing that set off all sorts of alarms in his head. He could hear his mother's voice as clearly as if she were standing right beside him.

What if you break your wrist?

God forbid it doesn't heal right. You'll be maimed for life.

You'll never play again.

That last one echoed in his head as he held his hand up in a wave at Sara. "I'll just stay here and watch you."

The blades of her skates cut against the ice as she came to a stop right in front of him.

"Now where's the fun in that?"

She gripped him around the waist and held onto him while he attempted to stand upright on the ice.

"If you feel like you're gonna fall, just throw your hands up in the air and drop on your ass—sorry, *bottom*. It has the most cushion, and chances are, you won't break anything."

Looking around the rink, she pointed to a little boy who had done just that.

"See?"

All he could do was nod.

Sara let go of him, and he started to flail.

Where's the fun in this?

After steadying him again, she took his hand in hers. "Come on. You've got this. Nice and slow. Just pretend like you're walking."

Standing between her and the railing, which was just out of his reach, he started shuffling along.

"That's it," she exclaimed. "Keep your ankles straight."

After an excruciatingly long time, they made it all the way around the rink once.

"You did great." She grinned as she pulled in front of him, taking both of his hands in hers. "Thank you for doing this." Tugging him closer, she gripped him tightly around the waist. "Thanks for—" Her voice dropped to a raspy whisper, "*Every*thing."

Looking into her sparkling eyes, he forgot for a split second that the only thing between him and instant pain was her grip on him. "Anytime."

Her cheeks were as red as her lips. As she panted, little wisps of her breath floated on the air in front of him like tiny clouds. And she was still smiling.

With Chicago's skyline starting to illuminate all around them, Andrew laughed, exhilarated over surviving something so risky and new. Taking her face in his gloved hands, he pressed his lips against hers and didn't stop until a juvenile speed demon brushed by, causing him to wobble and flail.

"I've got you," Sara breathed as she pulled him smack up against her and kissed him just as she had the night when she had locked herself out of the apartment.

Only this time, he kissed her back.

Lost in the moment, he barely heard his name being called. Not until he was almost completely surrounded by 7th grade girls from the St. Matthias.

Unlocking his mouth from Sara's, he looked longingly into her woozy eyes and did his best to maneuver next to her without falling on his ass—er, *bottom*.

"Hi, Mr. Benet," several of them sang out. The others just gawked and giggled.

"Girls. What a surprise."

He looked around at the half-dozen faces that were grinning at him expectantly. "You didn't come all the way down here by yourselves, did you?"

"No," Molly Evans, the ringleader, replied. Pointing in the direction of a woman aiming a cell phone in his direction, she exclaimed, "My mom brought us."

When the woman lowered the camera and waved, he held up his hand and gave a quick nod to Sherry Evans, head of the PTA.

Great...

"Well, it was nice bumping into you, girls. See you in church tomorrow."

"Bye, Mr. Benet," they chimed in unison as they raced away.

Shuffling back to the safety of the railing, he leaned against it.

Sara swooshed to his side. "I'm so sorry. This is the last place I thought we'd run into anybody from the parish."

He frowned at her. "Don't be sorry. I'm not sorry."

Looking truly troubled, she looked in the direction the girls had gone. "I don't want you to lose your job on account of me."

He brushed her overgrown bangs from her eyes. "It's not a big deal. Really." With another laugh, he added, "There's nothing in my contract that prohibits dating."

"Yeah, but I'm in choir."

"So?"

"And we're living together."

He lifted his shoulders in a shrug. "We're roommates. And that's nobody's business but ours."

The look on her face told him she wasn't convinced. He wasn't sure he was either, but after that kiss, he so didn't care.

Turning to face her, he lifted her chin until her eyes met his. "I bet the last place we'd run into anybody from church is at a karaoke bar. Know any good ones?"

At that, her face lit up like fireworks on the fourth of July.

CHAPTER TEN

———

"I had a perfectly lovely evening, but this wasn't it."
—Groucho Marx

Thawed out and ready to sing her fool head off at Kildare's, Sara led Andrew to the table normally filled with members of the Lifestyle section.

"This is gonna be so much fun," she assured him. "You're gonna love it."

The bar was no more crowded than usual, and it looked like the competition had already started. Felicity Carlisle, a fashion editor, was on stage doing her impersonation of the late great Whitney Houston, powering her way through "I Will Always Love You."

As he walked behind her, the karaoke virgin asked, "So how does this work?"

Sara stopped and turned. To be heard over the noise, she instinctively clutched Andrew by his jacket with both hands and pulled him close before relaying into his ear, "This is live band karaoke which means anybody can hop up on stage, the band starts playing something, the words appear on that screen over there, and you just go for it."

She looked into his face to see if she had made herself clear. That he seemed rather petrified did not escape her attention. That her mouth was oh so close to his didn't either.

"It's about time you got here," she heard Nancy bellow. Tugging at Sara's coat sleeve, she pointed to two chairs she had been guarding with her life.

Damn. It.

As they took their seats, Sara announced to the familiar faces at the table, "Everyone, this is Andrew. Andrew, everyone."

Introductions over, Nancy leaned over and said a little too loudly, "Sure, he's cute, but can he sing?"

Sara watched as the color left Andrew's face.

"Get him a beer," Nancy hollered at a waitress who had just passed by their table.

Addressing Andrew, she asked, "Bottle or draft, sweetie?"

When he didn't respond, Sara turned to him. "Bottle or draft?" Breaking into a grin, she added, "Sweetie."

His smile returning, he replied with his voice low. "Draft."

"Draft," Nancy hollered back.

"Got it," the waitress yelled when she skirted behind the bar.

Sara felt her entire body blush when Andrew squeezed her hand under the table and give her a wink.

The assistant food editor addressed him again. "So, do you sing or what?"

"Uh…a little, but I won't know any of the songs they play here."

"No worries," Sara interjected. "You can cheer us on."

After an intern from Sports did a not-bad job on Green Day's "Boulevard of Broken Dreams," it was her turn.

"Wish me luck," she breathed before handing him her coat and hopping up onstage, where she heard several faceless members of the audience yell her name.

But when the band started playing, "You Oughta Know," by Alanis Morrisette, she turned around to face the band members. Catching the lead guitarist's eye, she shook her head and said, "No. No way. Not tonight."

He nodded her over and silenced the rest of the band. Ignoring the boos and hisses coming from the audience, Sara finally turned and pulled the microphone from its stand just as the opening notes of Adele's "Rolling in the Deep" started thumping loudly behind her. A few bars in, the entire bar was clapping along.

As she poured her soul into the heart-wrenching song, she made a point of not looking at Andrew.

Because he was very much on her mind as she sang it.

When she finished, she put the microphone back on the stand. The crowd was on their feet, including the Ken doll who kissed her in broad daylight just a few hours earlier.

As Sara stepped down from the stage, she saw him put his fingers in his mouth to deliver a piercing wolf whistle, and, in a flash, she was a little girl again, playing in the woods behind her house in Wisconsin, knowing she was in trouble again for staying out after dark.

The effect was sobering. If she let it, the memory had the potential to transform her into the same insecure mess of girl she used to be and in many ways, still was.

Not tonight.

Forcing a smile, she made her way directly to Andrew who appeared to be completely gobsmacked by her performance. "That was outstanding."

No longer having to force her grin, she melded into his open embrace.

I could stay here forever.

After just a minute though, he gave her shoulders a squeeze. "We should probably get going," he started apologetically. "It's getting late."

"But it's so early," Nancy protested.

Sara regally addressed everyone at the table as Andrew helped her on with her coat. "I believe my work here is done. Carry on."

Settling into a seat on the nearly empty train on the Brown line, Andrew draped his arm across her shoulder. Snuggling into him, she observed, "This was the best day ever" and thanked him again before kissing him on the cheek.

Only, he didn't exactly look like he agreed. He looked like he was a hundred miles away.

Not sure she wanted to hear the answer to the question she was about to ask, she asked it anyway. "What are you thinking?"

He removed his arm from her shoulder and gave her a penetrating look—not the kind that would have Sister Marcus reeling. It was the kind that had her guard go up faster than her Aunt Ruby's hand at bingo night. When he finally spoke, his question surprised her. "Were you thinking of Jer when you were singing back there?"

To herself, she thought, *No, actually, I was thinking of us.*

But to him, she said, "No. I wasn't thinking about Jer."

Andrew gazed out the window at the dark walls of the train tunnel.

Knowing she shouldn't ask yet another question to which she didn't want to hear the answer, she asked it anyway. "Who were you thinking of when I was up there."

Before he could answer, their train slowed and then jerked to a stop, and they got out.

He didn't reply until they emerged onto Chicago Avenue and headed north on Franklin.

"Leanne Thorsteinson."

"I'm sorry?"

"That's who that song made me think of."

When he looked at her, she could see a world of hurt swirling behind his baby blues.

She walked beside him in silence, dread clenching her insides while she waited for him to say more, but he didn't.

Taking her hand in his, he gave it a reassuring squeeze.

Only she didn't feel reassured. She felt like this best day ever was about to become one of the worst.

After they had hung up their coats in the foyer closet, he walked into the hallway and flipped the switch that illuminated all of the framed photos she had passed by every single day since he moved in but never once gave a second look.

Pointing to the first one of a smiling couple holding a baby boy, he said, "That's me with my parents. My mom was pregnant with Sam in this one." The one next to it was of the four of them. Andrew couldn't have been more than three or four years old. Cute as a button.

"That's the last one they took of us as a family before they died."

She glanced at his face. He looked stoic but was gripping her hand harder than he had for their entire walk from the train.

Her heart broke for him.

"I'm so sorry," she breathed, but it seemed ridiculously inadequate.

He stared at the photo for a few seconds longer.

"To tell you the truth, I don't really remember much about them."

Giving her hand a tug, they moved down the hall a bit.

In the next one, he and Sam were both much older. High school, maybe, and both looked crazy happy. Andrew was in a cap and gown. Sam, a bit shorter and stockier, looked just like him.

"Nice. You guys are definitely brothers."

Sara studied it while he moved on to the next photograph. As he stood looking at it, he released her hand and straightened the frame.

Stepping to his side, she saw it was a group shot. Andrew stood right in the middle and had both arms around a pretty, petite blonde who was baring her perfectly straight teeth in a blinding smile as she stood in front of him.

Barbie.

Sara looked at him, waiting for the story behind it. When he didn't deliver, she offered, "I take it that isn't one of your sisters?"

Her question seemed to jolt him back to the present. "Oh, uh, no." Pointing to the Barbie doll, he explained, "That's her. That's Leanne. Thorsteinson."

We could've had it all.

Sara lifted her chin. "Girlfriend?"

"Back then, yeah," he explained. "This was taken at my parents' anniversary party."

She looked at it again. In it, Andrew was wearing the same blue Henley sweater he had on the night they met. "When was it taken?"

"About a year ago."

Oh, boy.

Summoning her thick-skinned armor, she took a deep breath, raised both eyebrows, and asked, "And when did you say you moved to Chicago?"

When he turned to look at her, his eyes were dark, his expression unreadable.

"Let's sit."

Sara glanced at the clock. It was after midnight. "I take it you're not playing at seven o'clock Mass?"

He shook his head.

She took a seat at one end of the couch, watching as he grabbed a beer from the fridge before positioning himself at the opposite end.

Sara waited, pretty damn sure she didn't want to hear what he was about to tell her.

"Back in high school," he started, "my senior year, the older sister of Sam's best friend was asked to homecoming by this guy, one of the football players on the team. She didn't know him really well, but he was, ya know, a football player, so she was pretty excited about it."

Sara nodded.

"So she gets all ready for the dance, and the guy doesn't show. Doesn't call. Nothing. Stands her up."

"I hate jocks."

Did I just say that out loud?

"I know, right?"

Guess so.

"Anyway, Sam is over there playing video games with his buddy and sees this happening, feels sorry for her, tells me all about it the next day, and goes on and on about how I should ask her out."

Andrew stopped and took a swig of his beer. "I knew Leanne from school, and we were in choir together at church, but I never hung out with her or anything."

He kicked his shoes off and stretched his legs out on the coffee table. "Anyway, I waited a couple of weeks before I asked her to the movies. And she said yes."

He stopped and stared at Sara for a minute.

She narrowed her eyes and resisted the urge to ask him if there was a point to his story.

"So, yeah, we dated for—" He blew out a breath before continuing. "Years. All through college and then, what, almost five years after that. Her idea, not mine."

Sara opened her mouth to speak, but all that came out was, "Huh."

Andrew raised both eyebrows and chuckled. "Yeah." Then he gave his head a shake and put his beer down. "So, last summer. In June, I forced her hand and proposed."

Sara held her breath.

Andrew grabbed his bottle back. "She said 'no.'"

Oh, thank God.

"And," he continued while working on a corner of the beer bottle label, "she took the opportunity to inform me that she wanted to become a nun. Just didn't know how to tell me."

He stared at his shoes for a few seconds and mumbled, "After all that time."

Again, Sara was speechless. Almost.

"I don't know what to say."

He looked at her and let out another chuckle. "That's exactly what I said."

Great minds...

He started peeling the label off of his bottle. "I didn't see it coming. After all that time, I just didn't see it coming."

Quietly, Sara prodded, "So you moved to Chicago...?"

At this, he lifted his head. "Yeah. I heard a position had suddenly opened up at St. Matthias. It was right about the same time Sam was due to graduate from the police academy here, so it was perfect timing."

"And you haven't been home since?"

"Well, we both went home for the holidays."

Sara nodded. And waited.

"That's when I heard she was a candidate with the Sisters of St. Joseph of Carondelet. It's a convent up near where we lived."

She nodded again. "Have you talked to her since...?"

Don't make me say it.

"Since she dumped me?"

Bingo.

"Yeah."

"Nope. But my Mom does apparently."

Narrowing her eyes at him, she came right out and asked, "Are you still in love with her?"

Before she could finish her question, he looked directly at her and said, "No. Not at all."

Taking a deep breath, he exhaled and said, "Clearly, it was a blessing. Can you imagine marrying someone who didn't trust you enough to confide in you?"

Sara's chest tightened. She wasn't sure she'd ever be able to confide in him. At least not now. Maybe not ever.

After a few quiet moments, she got up and moved much closer to him. Feeling him wrap his arm around her, she brushed some hair off of his forehead and ran her finger down the bridge of his nose. "For what it's worth, I'm glad she said 'no.'"

At this he smiled. "That makes two of us."

For the remainder of that week, Sara trolled department stores and resale shops trying to find a gown for the dinner dance. Normally relishing her height, the inability to borrow clothes from friends was definitely a drawback.

Before she knew it, the week was almost over, and she found herself sitting next to Glynnis at choir practice, listening to Andrew read the tenors the riot act about using the rhythm the composer intended, not making their own up on the fly.

Glad she wasn't in the hot seat, Sara sat back and took a big swig from the water bottle she had tucked under her seat. When it was the alto section's turn to go over their part, she was more than ready and started singing loud and proud.

Not two measures in, Andrew stopped playing the piano. Looking toward the section, but not focusing on any one of them in particular, he announced loudly, "This isn't American Idol. If you can't hear the person singing next to you, you're singing too loudly."

Cocking an eyebrow, she fixed her death gaze on him, but he didn't give her the satisfaction of making eye contact.

"Again," he announced before counting them in.

As they started singing, he called out, "Much better."

Damn straight.

But not four measures later, he shot out, "Come on, ladies. I didn't say to sing slower, did I?"

Holy hell.

When practice was over, she made her way to the choir room to return her binder to its designated slot and grab her coat, thinking of the best way to tell him that if he stopped with the insults during practice, he'd probably stop bleeding choir members.

She was just coming back out again when she heard Marge ask Andrew, "So if you still need a date for the gala, I checked with my niece, and she is available."

Sara seemed unable to move all of the sudden.

The gala he invited her to is a church function?

Why she would've thought otherwise, she wasn't sure, but that he neglected to mention that little nugget gave her pause.

Free drinks, though.

But, then again, with everyone in choir apparently going, why did he ask me?

She was pondering that very thought when she heard him say, "No thanks, Marge. I'm good."

The old lady who took the fine art of interrogation to a whole new level asked, "But you said you weren't going to go by yourself. Shirley told me she put you down for two."

Crap, she's good.

Wondering if Marge was a reporter in a previous life, Sara held her breath and watched as he waved to a few choir members as they said good night.

Pointing to the back of her neck, she heard Marge ask. "Is it her?"

What is she doing? No one's standing behind her.

Starting to think Marge was more delusional than nosey, Sara was further confused by her reaction when she saw Andrew give her an almost imperceptible nod.

With his back to her, she couldn't see his face, but she could tell by Marge's that what he must've done or said both shocked and surprised her. "Oh, really?" she grinned. "Well, good for you."

She watched as Marge patted his arm before turning to pack up her things. And it was right about then that he turned and saw Sara standing there.

Even with other choir members still milling about, chatting, he broke into the warmest of smiles. "Hey." While it could've been the lighting, or the late hour, his eyes looked...well, sparkly. Either that, or his fever was coming back.

Not sure whether to laugh or cry, Sara just lifted her chin toward him in acknowledgment and said, "Ciao."

Commence evasive maneuvers.

Wanting to get in her car, beat him home, and get into bed before he even walked through the door, she waved good night to the other choir members she rushed past on her way out. The cold, crisp night air was just what she needed. Walking through the parking lot, she tried clearing her head and telling herself that what she just witnessed wasn't about her.

Just one more week.

Then what?

Wishing she had prioritized a pedicure over going to some lame church gala, she brushed a layer of newly fallen snow off of her trusty little Honda's windshield.

There was only one person who could help her sort through what was going on in her head and heart. The only question was would she still be up at that hour.

As soon as she was buckled in and flipped her defroster on full blast, she heard the opening chords of Robert Palmer's "Bad Case of Lovin' You" coming from her purse.

Retrieving it before she pulled out of the parking lot, she checked to see who was calling.

Claire?

"Holy crap, it's like you're psychic or something. I was just about to call you."

With a laugh, Claire replied, "Hey you, is everything all right?"

"Yeah. Well, no. Can you talk?"

"I have a better idea. Can you come over? My sister is about your height and has a closet full of gowns. She dropped some off today, and I thought you might want to come take a look. I'll be up for a while yet. Somebody, and I'm not mentioning any names," she heard Claire call out into the distance, "forgot to tell me he volunteered me to bring cupcakes to the school's bake sale tomorrow."

"Oh. Do you want me to pick some up on the way over?"

"Awww, thanks, but I've already got them started. How soon can you get here?"

Ten minutes later, Sara sat in Claire's spacious but warm cupcake-scented kitchen, assuring her that all of her boys, husband included, were otherwise occupied upstairs.

"Here." Handing a stack of garment bags her sister had left hanging on a hook in their mudroom, Claire directed Sara to the powder room where she could try them on.

Getting Claire's opinion on the ones she really liked, Sara finally settled on a sleek silver satin strapless gown with tiny rhinestones embellishing the fitted bodice and the edging of the almost-sheer matching wrap.

"Please thank Kate for me."

"Absolutely."

"I'll be sure to send her flowers or a bottle of wine or *something*."

Pouring them both some tea, Claire sat at the head of the table, while Sara slipped into the chair just to her right. "No worries. She's got more dresses than your average bridal shop."

After a quiet moment, Sara felt her friend studying her over the rim of her mug. "You look different."

Brushing her bangs out of her eyes, Sara waved her off with a sigh. "Yeah, I'm overdue for a trim, and I've kind of cut back on the makeup. Time for a new look."

Claire continued to look at her like she was an abstract sculpture on display at the Museum of Contemporary Art. "No, that's not it."

Moving her mug out of the way, Sara planted both elbows on the table and covered her face with her hands.

"Claire," she moaned. "I'm in trouble."

Nearly knocking her own mug over, Claire asked. "What do you mean? Are you—oh hon." Dropping her voice an octave, she asked, "You're not *pregnant*, are you?"

At that, Sara dropped her hands from her face. With a stone-cold serious expression, her voice was flat as she replied, "No, I'm not pregnant."

With a hand to her chest, Claire exhaled, "Thank God."

A frown etched over Sara's forehead. "What would you do if I said I was?"

"Sweetie." Reaching over, Claire smoothed the back of her fingers against Sara's cheek and cupped it in the warm palm of her hand. "I'd make sure you knew that you weren't alone, and then I'd ask what I could do to help."

Not only did that simple little gesture make Sara sorry for challenging her, it triggered a longing for her mother that she hadn't felt in a very long time. Suddenly, all she wanted to do was unload everything her heavy heart was getting really tired of lugging around.

"Claire," Sara rasped as she felt the emotions already starting to surface.

Getting up, Claire moved her chair right next to Sara, put an arm around her, and squeezed.

"Come on," she urged as she tightened her grip. "What's this all about, huh?"

Sara turned to her friend, who was wearing yellow ducky pajama bottoms with a royal blue Knollwood High School sweatshirt pulled tight over her very conspicuous baby bump.

"I don't know where to start," she whispered.

Which was a lie. She knew exactly where she had to begin.

Massaging her forehead with her fingertips, troubling images she thought she had banished forever started escaping from the nether regions of her memory.

Two pink lines on the pregnancy test stick.

The awful one-story clinic on the outskirts of Madison.

The unimaginable pain.

The crushing guilt.

The soul-robbing shame.

Her face twisted into a sob. "Oh, Claire."

Burrowing her face in her friend's shoulder, Sara cried until there wasn't anything left. The whole time, Claire didn't budge, as uncomfortable as she must have been. She just stroked Sara's hair and kept repeating, "Everything's gonna be OK."

Two hours later, with a mountain of used tissues filling a paper grocery bag at her feet, Sara looked into her friend's tired eyes. "I should let you get to bed."

"Oh, don't worry about me," Claire replied as she squeezed Sara's hand. "In the morning, I get to sleep in."

Tilting Sara's chin up, she looked into her eyes and said, "I can't believe you've been keeping that inside for this long."

"Thanks for not judging me." She drew a deep breath. "I'll be honest. I never really thought twice about it until Andrew came along."

Her eyes started to fill again. "He's too good for me."

At this, Claire sat up. "Oh, like hell he is."

Ignoring Sara's shocked expression, she squeezed her hand and said, "Come on now. I'm getting a little tired of you telling me how you're not good enough, or you don't deserve this or that. It's time you put all of this behind you. You deserve to be happy as much as everyone else."

With a gasp, Sara hissed, "That's easy for you to say, Claire. You haven't done what I've done. There's no way to put that behind me. Life doesn't come with an undo button." Appalled that she found herself glaring into her tired friend's face, she softened her expression and mouthed, "It doesn't."

Still holding onto her hand, Claire broke into a gentle smile and said, "Oh yes, it does."

* * *

The first thing Sara saw when she woke on the morning of the gala was Kate's gown draped across the seats of all four barstools that had been turned around so they were facing her. The wrap lay neatly folded on top of it. Having gotten in so late the night before, she was fairly sure that's not the way she had left it before collapsing on the sleeper sofa that Andrew had open and ready for her. What she was sure of was that she knew what she had to do and wasn't looking forward to it. Not one bit.

Assuming she had the place to herself, she got out of bed. With nothing on save a skimpy tank top over her snowflake pajama bottoms, she made up the bed and folded it back into place. According to the oven clock, it was already 11:30.

Good God.

Given the amount of light coming through the bay window, she knew it was late, but she was surprised to see that half the day was almost over. And relieved that her sleep was deep, not interrupted with bad dreams or insomnia.

So glad it's Saturday.

Stripping down, she checked herself in the mirror before she ducked into a steamy shower. Her eyes still looked swollen and bloodshot from all of the crying the night before. And her hair. Now that she had lightened up on the makeup, the flat black color just wasn't doing it for her anymore.

Reaching behind the shower curtain, she turned off the water. After wrapping a towel around her torso, she opened the bathroom door and peeked out, just in case. Not seeing or hearing Andrew, she made her way to the kitchen, where she had left her phone.

Pulling up her contact list, she selected a number and waited for someone on the other end to pick up. When they did, she said way more cheerfully than she intended, "Hey Chelsea. It's Sara Cleff. Have any openings this afternoon for a cut and color?"

"Uh, yep. Sure do. How's one o'clock?"

"I'll take it."

Step one in her undo process: Return hair to natural color. A cosmetic change, sure, but as Claire said the night before, "Baby steps."

After a shower and a bite to eat, she made her way downtown for some ("Come on, say it with me," Claire had urged) *pampering.* Use of this word in regard to herself still brought a look of distaste to Sara's face.

Plopping into Chelsea's chair she stared at her reflection as the stylist raked her fingers through her dull black strands, asking, "So what are we doing today?"

Sara knew exactly what she wanted. "Same style, an inch off all around, and this color has to go."

Ready with a picture somebody had taken of her and Kerry after he had helped her win a pie-eating contest by holding her hair out of her face while she dug in, Sara held it up for Chelsea to examine.

As the stylist peered at it, she instructed, "As close to that color as you can get, OK?"

"You got it," Chelsea promised before asking, "What's that white stuff on your face?"

"Whipped cream."

"And who's the guy?"

With dry-eyed resolve, Sara said, "My brother."

"He's pretty cute." With a quick squeeze on her shoulders, Chelsea winked. "Looks just like you."

Two hours later, Sara walked out already feeling a little undone, sporting a fresh cut and her God-given hair color.

Next stop, Nordstrom for some shoes to go with Kate's gown. Knowing she needed just a little bit of a heel to keep the hem off the floor, she didn't want so much heel that she'd be taller than Andrew. With no expectation of how that evening would roll, her only hope was to get in one slow dance with him, cheek-to-cheek.

And he has to initiate it. Otherwise, it won't mean anything.

While she was trying on a pretty pair of low-heeled silver sling backs, the opening riff from Prince's "When Doves Cry" sounded from the depths of her purse. Snatching it before too many eyes turned her way, she answered without seeing who it was.

"Hey there." The sound of Andrew's voice filled her with a bittersweet mix of excitement and sadness.

"Hey. I'm shoe shopping for tonight. What are you up to?"

With a warm chuckle, he replied, "I'm still at church. Looks like I'll be playing at the five o'clock. My backup seems to have caught the bug I had last weekend."

"OK. Do you want me to just meet you at the gala?" she asked, crouching over on the little step stool she was on to try to tune out some of the store noise.

"That's what I was thinking. Is that all right with you?"

"Yeah, sure."

"But I need you to do me a favor."

At this, she put the shoes down, stood up, and poked a finger in her free ear to hear him better. "I'm sorry. What?"

"Can you bring my tux to the church for me? It's in a black garment bag in the closet. The shirt and shoes that go with it should be in there, too, at the bottom."

"Sure, yeah."

"OK, see you in a bit."

Before she hung up, she said, "Hey. Wait a minute. I can't go walking into church carrying your stuff. What will people think?"

But he had hung up already.

Checking the time, she made her way to the nearest register with the sling backs and then headed back to the apartment where she deposited them before gathering Andrew's tux. Twenty minutes later, she was walking through the narthex, realizing she didn't have the slightest idea where his office was.

She spotted a kindly looking older gentleman standing near the room where the ushers stored the collection baskets. "Hi, I'm looking for Andrew Benet. Can you tell me where I can find his office?"

He smiled and pointed to a door on the other end of the building. "That's the church office. His office is through those doors."

"OK, great. Thanks."

With the crowd starting to gather for Mass, she wanted to hurry up and get out of there so she could get home and get ready, sight unseen. Bursting through the office door, she found that the lights were off, and it appeared to be empty. Walking up and down the corridor that led to the staff offices, she found that each door was locked.

Who locks doors in a church?

Back in the main office, she decided the best thing to do would be to leave his tux there with his name on it.

With her back to the door, she lay the garment bag carefully across the desk and pulled a large sticky note off of a pad that was sitting near the phone. Clicking a pen, she started writing his name, but nothing appeared on the paper. She shook the pen. Still nothing.

"Dammit."

"Can I help you?"

Swirling around, Sara found herself face-to-face with Andrew. With a slow smile creeping over her mouth, she raised her eyebrows as recognition registered on his face.

With a low, sultry voice, she asked, "Did someone here order a tuxedo?"

But he didn't smile back. Coming through the door right behind him was Marge, a few of the sopranos whose names she still didn't know, and the kindly looking older gentleman from the narthex. All dressed in formalwear.

C-r-a-p.

"Uh, Sara. I believe you know Marge."

She nodded at the diminutive librarian with a scowl that could take down a rabid grizzly.

"Marge."

"Sara?"

"And these," Andrew continued, "Are the members of the parish council."

One of the women came forward with a smile and extended her hand. "Hi Sara. Lorelei. We met at cantor practice last week? I love what you've done with your hair."

Sara touched her fingertips to her bangs. "Oh, thanks. I'm sorry. I didn't recognize you." Waving her hand toward the soprano's rhinestone-studded aqua cocktail dress, she said with as much sincerity as possible, "You look lovely."

Her eyes darted to Andrew who had sidled up next to her to get the garment bag while Lorelei explained. "We just need to pick up the silent auction items that Andrew here was kind enough to store in his office for us."

"Uh, did you all need a hand?"

While some of the men paused to consider her offer, the rest of the women kindly declined as they nudged their spouses down the hallway.

Digging his keys out of his pocket, Andrew handed them to Lorelei. "You guys go ahead, and start loading everything up. I'll be right there."

When they were alone, he turned to Sara. "Sorry about that."

She shrugged. "No worries. I don't embarrass easy. Hope I didn't get you in trouble though."

With a smile, he moved a little closer. "Everything OK? I'm guessing you got home pretty late last night."

As brightly as possible, she thanked him for having the bed ready. Then, pressing her lips together, she nodded. "I'm good." Tilting her chin lower, she added, "I'm very good, actually."

Although smiling, he looked confused.

"Never mind."

No minds in the gutter tonight.

Turning to leave, she was halfway through the door when he called after her, "Sara. Take a cab tonight. That way we can drive home together."

As she saw members of the parish council fill in behind him, their arms full of boxes and their face registering no small amount of surprise, she just nodded—

And told her dashboard the entire way home all about Step Two in her undo process: Tell Andrew everything.

"Maybe Claire's right. If he loves me, *which* I'm not even sure he does, what I did won't matter. It happened way before we met."

"But what if she's wrong? If I'm upfront with him and he turns me out of the apartment and his life?"

A shudder ran through her. "I'm not sure I can bounce back from that."

Pulling to a stop at an intersection, she looked in the rearview mirror. "Because you went ahead and fell in love with him, didn't you? Even after I told you not to."

She gripped the steering wheel with both hands and shouted, "Shit!" at the top of her lungs.

Out of the corner of her eye, she saw a guy driving a delivery truck the next lane over laughing at her.

After flipping him off, she pressed her foot to the accelerator as the light turned green and resumed her dashboard-speak. "Let's just see how tonight goes. Just play it cool. Let it ride."

Sounds like a plan.

When she got home, the first thing she did was crank a little Pat Benatar and sang "Heartbreaker" as loud as she could while she got ready, thankful as ever that she lived in a soundproofed unit, even if it was just temporary.

About to walk through the door to grab the cab she had ordered, she realized she didn't have a coat to wear over her gown. Flinging open the foyer closet, she raked through its contents and pulled out Andrew's black overcoat, the one he was wearing when he came home on casserole night.

"This will have to do," she muttered to herself as she pulled it on, slipping her clutch in the pocket and carefully draping the folded wrap over her arm. Picking up the hem of the gown, she made her way to the taxi waiting at the curb. All she did the entire way to the Jackson Boulevard address was close her eyes and inhale the hint of Andrew's scent coming off the coat collar, trying to brand it in her memory. Just in case.

"Union League Club of Chicago," the driver announced as they pulled up.

Handing him his fare plus tip, she felt the door open beside her as the doorman offered his hand to her.

"Good evening, Miss."

No one had ever called her "Miss" before, unless she counted her dear Aunt Ruby who would call her *Missy* every time she scolded her.

Sara stepped through the doorway he had opened for her and took in the luxurious lobby, the floors of which were covered in classically patterned carpets, and the walls were lined with dark wood trim and decorated with various works of art, all in gilded frames. Never having been to a formal event—not even prom in high school—a tingly little zip of excitement ran through her.

"May I take your coat, Miss?" The coat-check girl waved from behind her counter.

She slipped it off and handed it over. "Here you go. Thanks."

Taking the little ticket from her, the girl said, "Don't loose this. It will be a madhouse later."

Sara popped it in the sleek black clutch she had borrowed from Claire. "Got it. Thanks. Uh, can you tell me where the St. Matthias Spring Fling Gala is being held? My date has our invitation."

My date.

"Absolutely. It's in the Main Dining Room on the sixth floor. The elevators are right over there."

Turning to where she had just pointed, Sara said, "Thank you very much."

She unfolded her wrap as she made her way over and draped it across her shoulders. When the doors parted, she stepped in and pushed the button labeled 6. A moment later, she felt her phone that she had set to vibrate buzz to life in her clutch.

It was Andrew. *Where r u?*

Instead of responding right away, she made her way to the check-in table behind which a middle-aged woman with a pinched look on her face sat.

"May I see your invitation, please?"

"Oh, well, my date has it."

"And who would that be?"

"Uh..." Scanning the crowd around her, she hesitated.

"I'm sorry, but I can't let you in without it," said the woman, who looked so very pleased with herself for keeping a cunning gala-crasher from entering the event.

She was about to ask, "Well, can you just point me to the bar, please?" when she felt a hand at her waist and heard a familiar voice say, "She's with me, Denise."

The woman beamed. "Oh, hi, Andrew. I didn't see you there."

Sara turned, and there he was.

Wow.

There was just something about a guy with black hair wearing a black tux. She couldn't get over how good he looked.

As he ushered her through the crowd to the bar, she said, "You look really great."

"What can I get you folks?"

Turning to her, Andrew asked, "What would you like?"

Sara addressed the bartender, "Pinot Noir, please."

"Make that two."

While they waited, he whispered in her ear, "And you look breathtaking."

Feeling the entire side of her body that he was on blush, she mouthed, "Thank you."

"We should probably find our table. I think dinner starts soon."

With the wrap draped low across her back, they made their way to the dining room. Following him through the crowd, she couldn't help but notice the stares and hear the whispers.

"Look at her tattoo," someone actually had the balls to say out loud as she passed. If she were there alone, nothing would have stopped her from turning on whoever had said it.

It's just a frickin' tattoo, pal. Millions of people all over the world have them. Not a big deal. Got it?

But she wasn't alone, and tonight wasn't about her.

That didn't stop a wave of anxiety from threatening to wash over her and drag her down with it. Just as it began to surge inside her, she felt Andrew's hand slip into hers and give it a gentle squeeze.

"Come on. This way. There's someone I want you to meet."

Then he actually steered her in the direction from which the voice came.

"Father Steve, I'd like you to meet Sara Cleff."

Oh.

The priest looked pleased. Holding out his hand, he grinned, "Sara, so nice to meet you. You're in choir, yes?"

With her defenses still on high alert, she nodded while he kept talking.

"I was just telling everyone about my father when I saw you pass by."

"Uh-huh…"

"He was a tattoo artist back in the Philippines. Best in the country. Most of his customers came from the naval base there." Motioning to her upper back, he added, "Nothing as elegant as yours. Could you turn around, please?"

I'll be damned.

She faced Andrew who had been standing behind her and was now wearing a smirky *I-told-you-so* look on his face.

Turning back to the priest, she thanked him for the compliment.

"Have you two checked out the auction items yet?" one of the women standing next to the priest asked.

"Actually," Andrew piped up. "They've been sitting in my office all week, so I've seen way too much of them actually."

Almost on cue, a dinner chime sounded at the entrance to the dining room, signaling for the guests to take their seats.

Five excellent courses later, the waiters began whisking dirty dessert dishes away and started pouring coffee and providing after-dinner drinks. Sara's attention turned to the band that had been playing softly in the background throughout. As a singer and several more orchestral instruments joined them, it looked like they were about to crank it up a notch. She no sooner heard the beginning strains of an old standard (*"Tenderly"*?) when Andrew asked, "Care to dance?"

This is it.

Taking in his smile and the just-dimmed lights, she whispered, "I'd love to."

Joining a few other couples dotting the dance floor, she turned to him. He took one of her hands in his and placed the other at her waist.

He raised his eyebrow at her. "No leading."

"No problem," she laughed, feeling uncharacteristically nervous.

As other couples filled in around them, she felt him pull her closer.

I'm not in love. I'm not in love. I'm not in love.

Then it happened. He pressed his cheek against hers, and she closed her eyes.

I am so in love with this man.

Despite the song ending way too soon, she couldn't move, didn't want to. Until she heard him whisper, "Sara."

Eyes wide open, she pulled back just enough to look into his face as her heart started racing in her chest.

Don't say it.

His eyebrows pulled up as he opened his mouth to speak.

"I'm in love with you."

Damn it all to hell.

As the orchestra swelled into the chorus of the next song that had started while they stood there, he took her face in his hands and repeated, "I'm in love with you, Sara Cl—"

He would've finished what he was saying, too, if she hadn't pressed her lips against his to stop him from saying it again. And he kissed her back. Right there in front of everybody.

CHAPTER ELEVEN

———

"How can a woman be expected to be happy with a man who insists on
treating her as if she were a perfectly normal human being."
—Oscar Wilde

Andrew and Sara did not stay for the St. Matthias Spring Fling Fundraising Gala silent auction. In fact, they did not even stay for a third dance. While Sara retrieved his overcoat from the coat-check girl, Andrew gave his ticket to the valet. Once the Jeep arrived, they piled in and headed home, taking Dearborn Street because it was quicker at that time of night than Michigan Avenue.

The entire way home, she wrestled with when to tell him.

Before? *Ought to.*

During? *Definitely not.*

After? *Shouldn't.*

"Stay right there," he instructed after he pulled into his slush-filled parking space behind the apartment building. Opening the door on her side, as soon as she stood up, he leaned toward her and hoisted her over his shoulder.

"Andrew," she shrieked. "What are you doing?"

He didn't answer until he deposited her on the cleanly shoveled sidewalk in front of the building. "You would've ruined your shoes."

Under the streetlight glow, she could see how bright red his cheeks were from the exertion, or the cold, or both. As he panted, his breath fogged, and his eyes glistened brighter than the stars in the clear sky above them.

Before it is.

"Let's go inside," she whispered.

Only somewhere between the front door and the apartment door, she lost her resolve entirely.

Suddenly, she couldn't get his coat, and the scent of him that went along with it, off fast enough.

"Here, let me," he murmured. A quick glance at his smoldering eyes confirmed the sense of urgency she heard in his voice.

I can't do this to him.

With what little reason her rapidly intensifying flight-or-fight instinct hadn't robbed her of, she made up her mind to leave before things between them went any further.

It's for the best.

I never told him I loved him.

I'm doing him a favor, really.

I'm sure he'll thank me later.

She rushed down the hallway ahead of him, dropping her clutch on the kitchen counter before working the zipper down the back of her gown as she went, and closed the bedroom door behind her. After hanging it up in the closet, she pulled out her suitcase and filled it with as many clothes as she could before yanking on a pair of jeans, a turtleneck, and her short black boots.

Taking a deep breath, she braced herself.

Make it short and sweet.

Sara knew if she made eye contact with him, she'd never make it out of the apartment.

As soon as she stepped into the hallway, she heard his voice. Despite him standing just a few feet from her, it sounded like it was coming from very far away.

"What are you doing?"

Her heart thumping in her chest, she looked toward him but not at him. In a voice that sounded smaller and shakier than she intended, she said, "Thanks for everything, but I should be going."

"Go? Where? *Why?*"

Sara pulled her key chain out of her clutch, but working her apartment key off of the damn thing proved next to impossible with her hands shaking as much as they were. She was about to give up when Andrew covered them with his and pleaded, "Sara. What's happening?"

Shit.

She wanted to yell, "Just let me break your heart and get this over with, all right?"

Instead, she averted her eyes and issued a harsh warning. "Trust me. You don't want me."

"Yes, I do. More than anything." The tone in his voice harbored somewhere between confusion and anger.

She lashed out. "You don't even know me. You and me? It would never work."

"Why not?"

Don't look at him. Don't look at him.

With her eyes about to overflow, she started to sputter, "Because you're so...so...*holy*, and I'm not."

Feeling his hands at her elbows, he sat her down on a barstool, and demanded, "What the hell is that supposed to mean?"

She finally dragged her eyes to his. "I don't deserve you. I've done stuff, OK? Stuff that, if you knew about it, you wouldn't want me around anymore, so just trust me, all right? I'm doing you a favor."

She pulled her hands from his, grabbed her keys, put her leather coat on, and headed down the hall as she swiped at the tears streaming down her face with her fingers.

"But we made a deal."

His words followed her into the hallway as she closed the door behind her.

By the time Sara made it to her car, she was shaking like a leaf.

She started up her car and flicked through her contact list wondering whose place she could crash at for the night.

Claire? *I couldn't impose on her two nights in a row.*

Aubrey? She thought of her travel-writer pal's teeny tiny studio apartment in the Ukrainian Village. *No room.*

Mattie? *Getting busy with her fiancé, no doubt.*

That left Nancy. Given that it was a Saturday night, she knew just where to find her.

Kildare's. And that was the last place she felt like going. Out of options, she pulled out of her space and made her way there.

"What do you mean she's not here?" she asked Felicity Carlisle, a fashion writer who had, on more than one occasion, channeled Aretha Franklin in the Lifestyle section's bid for karaoke supremacy.

"She just isn't. Said something about staying home to binge watch Celebrity Chef."

"Seriously? OK, thanks," she shouted over some poor soul doing a sorry rendition of "Feelings" after one too many cheap shots.

Calling her at home which, in hindsight, would've been the smart thing to do if she were in the right frame of mind—which she wasn't—Nancy picked up on the second ring. "Hey, girlfriend. What's shakin'? I thought you had some big party thing tonight?"

"Uh, no. Listen, can I come over?"

Her question was met with dead silence.

"Nance?"

"Yeah, sorry—Bobbie Flay was just slathering a pork roast with mole sauce with his bare hands. He could slather me with mole sauce anytime."

Ewww...

Sara was seriously thinking of returning to the apartment and facing the music with Andrew when Nancy asked, "How soon can you get here? I'll whip us up some mango margaritas."

"Sounds perfect. I can be there in fifteen."

* * *

Andrew didn't go to sleep for a very long time that night. Instead he changed into his jeans and flopped on the couch feeling like his emotions had just been run over by a truck. He spent the next several hours vacillating between hoping she'd walk through the door again and wondering what the hell had happened. He woke up on the morning of Palm Sunday, still in his clothes and still on the couch, to a phone call from Marge asking if he would be playing at Mass that morning or not.

Not bothering to change, shave, or shower, he showed up with seconds to spare before the first service of the morning. When that let out a little earlier than normal, he ducked into his office to run an electric razor over his face and change into some dress clothes.

"Look what the cat dragged in," Marge droned as she passed him on the way into the choir room before the third service. "Where's your girlfriend?"

He ignored her, as well as anyone else who had anything to say to him that morning. Better that than to give them the reply he really wanted to which was, "None of your damn business."

When the last Mass ended, he tore through traffic to get back to the apartment, hoping against hope that he'd find Sara there.

Bursting through the door, he was disappointed to find it unoccupied. He was crushed, however, to find the rest of her things gone and her key on the counter. Next to a check made out to him for her half of the rent.

All he had left of her was her number in his contact list. Swiping down to the S's, he stared at it for a long time, wondering if he should call her or text her or do something. At a loss for what to do next, his eyes fell on the name right above Sara's.

Sam.

He pressed it and then pressed the green Call button.

"Hey, man. How're ya feeling?"

"Lousy. You off today?"

"You know it. Wanna hang out?"

"Yeah. That'd be great. I'm on my way."

Two hours and a couple of beers later, Sam was up-to-speed on everything there was to know about Sara.

"The thing is," Andrew concluded as he watched the late-March sunset from Sam's apartment window, "I can't imagine what she could've possibly done to think I'd shove her out the door when she told me about it."

Sam leaned forward. "You must really love this girl."

When Andrew didn't reply, he asked, "You got her license plate number?"

He tipped the last of his beer in his mouth and added, "I'd be happy to check it out for you."

Andrew shot him a look. "Is that legal? Can you do that?"

His brother shrugged. "It's a fine line. I could probably make a case for it though."

"What do you mean?"

"Unlawful entry, trespassing..."

With a grimace, Andrew exclaimed, "What? No. Absolutely not. I just want to know where she went and that she's all right."

Images of her crossing paths with another guy like Jer were one of the things that kept him up during the night, especially since she seemed to think that was all she was worthy of.

"You said you know where she works, right? Can't you just try to catch her there?"

Andrew rubbed his eyes. "Oh, yeah, right. Stalk her. Why didn't I think of that?"

With a laugh, Sam retorted, "Cause you were too busy asking your cop brother to do it for you."

Andrew took a deep breath and a long pull of his beer.

"Gimme her plate number, and I'll see what I can do."

Grabbing another two beers out of the fridge, he asked, "Do you know anything else about her? Where she lived before? Any relatives?"

Andrew shared what he knew which, admittedly, wasn't much. "She's from Wisconsin, some place named William's-something. She went to St. Xavier's parish, sang in the choir. Her mom ran off when she was young, and she's got a brother. An older brother."

Sam jotted everything down on a pad of paper. "Got it. I'll see what I can find out. In the meantime, wanna stay for dinner? I was gonna order some deep dish."

* * *

"Oh, it's gonna be so great having you for a roommate, Sara. I don't know why we never thought of doing this before."

Nancy set the box of things that Andrew had bought back for her on her kitchen table with a loud clank. "Why do you keep this junk anyway? Looks like it belongs at Goodwill."

"Careful, Nance. This 'junk' means a lot to me." Looking down at it, Sara whispered, "Now more than ever."

"Whatevs," Nancy replied using another one of her lame attempts to sound younger than she was. Talk in the newsroom was that she was pushing forty.

"Besides," Sara started, "Not all of us have doting, wealthy mothers. Hell, I'd settle for a poor, needy mother."

"Ugh, you can have mine." When Sara made a face, Nancy explained. "She's never really been a mother. In fact, I don't think she knows how. She just buys me stuff. In return, I have to stand up in her weddings." With a shrug, she concluded, "Which, I think, is fair."

"How many times has your mother been married, Nancy?"

The assistant food editor looked around her spacious West Loop loft. "Pffft, counting this new guy? Six?"

"Holy crap. Which one, if you don't mind me asking, was your dad?"

"Number two. And he was a real shit, so it's fitting, don't you think?"

Sara cringed while Nancy asked if she'd like another glass of wine to wash down the marinated shrimp kabobs and lemon-curry couscous she had made for dinner.

"No thanks, Nance. I'm good. Thanks so much for dinner. Let me clean up, and then I'm gonna hit the hay. I'm wiped."

"But it's only six o'clock. You feeling OK?"

"Yeah, I'm fine. There's just something I've got to do before heading in to work tomorrow."

The next morning, Sara called Mike Teegan to tell him she'd be getting in later than usual and made her way to St. Mathias to keep an appointment she had made with Father Steve. One that she hoped he would keep confidential as she'd requested.

Sanctity of the confessional and all that.

Parking a block away, she approached the building from the opposite end of where she knew Andrew's office to be and was relieved to find the narthex deserted and dimly lit.

She checked her watch.

Right on time.

Wanting to duck into the confessional without being seen, she was alarmed by the loud clank that sounded when she opened the door to the church itself.

So much for sneaking in.

Peering toward the front of the church where the choir sat, she was more than relieved to find it unoccupied. Especially by Andrew.

She took a deep breath and prepared herself for Step Three in her undo process: Go to confession, especially since she had baled completely on Step Number Two: Tell Andrew everything.

Seeing a light coming from under the door, she approached and knocked softly. A moment later, she heard Father Steve say, "Enter."

The setup was not what she remembered or expected at all. There was no divider of any kind between the priest and her. Just two comfy looking chairs facing each other.

Father Steve smiled and motioned for her to sit.

Sara did and then said the only bit of the sacrament that she could recall, "Bless me, Father, for I have sinned."

When he looked expectantly at her, she said, "I'm sorry, that's all I've got."

"How long since your last confession?"

At this, she blew out a breath then cringed. "Six years?"

He nodded. After a moment, he held both hands out and said, "Confess your sins."

I should've thought this through first.

Looking away, she tried to visualize the Ten Commandments she had learned as a kid. "Well, I take the Lord's name in vain. A lot. Um, I work on Sundays pretty frequently. Before meeting Andrew—" at the sound of his name, her face fell. Softening her voice, she continued, "Before I met him, I hadn't gone to Mass in a really long time."

Glancing over Father Steve's shoulder at a crucifix hanging on the wall, she continued, "I do not honor my mother because she abandoned me as a kid..."

Stop stalling.

She hung her head.

After a quiet moment, he asked, "Is there anything else?"

Sara nodded. When she raised her eyes to meet his, she started, "About three or four years ago, I got pregnant. Out of wedlock."

She said nothing more but kept her eyes on Father Steve. When they started filling with tears, he asked, "Did you give the child up for adoption?"

Biting down on her upper lip, she shook her head.

Pressing his lips together, the priest asked, "Miscarriage?"

Again, she shook her head. Wrapping her arms around herself, she rocked slowly back and forth in her chair, staring at her lap. After a few moments, she looked up and sobbed louder than she intended, "I terminated the pregnancy."

Father Steve reached over, covered her hands with his, and soothed, "My child. Neither height nor depth, nor anything else in all creation, will be able to separate us from the love of God. Not even this."

He handed her tissue after tissue until it was out of her system. When she was ready, he placed his hand on her bent head, delivered her penance, and said, "Your sins are now absolved. They are no more."

Undone.

Before she left, Father Steve cautioned, "Know this, Sara. The slate has been wiped clean by God himself. If you continue to live in shame for what you have done, you will be committing a sin against Him because you will be showing that you do not believe in His forgiveness. Do you understand?"

With a nod, Sara opened the door. "Yes, Father. Thank you."

She left the confessional and slipped into a pew at the back of the church to say her penance. When she was done, the priest's words echoed in her ears. "The slate has been wiped clean."

The first thing she did when she got back to the office was bring Kate's gown to Claire's cube. When she got there, Claire's hands were flying over the keyboard. Hearing the dress hanger knock against the plastic hook jutting out of her cube wall, she shot up an index finger and said, "One second."

Sara waited.

When she had finished, Claire spun around. "Hey, how was it? Oh, I love your hair. The color brings out your freckles."

Handing her a small envelope, Sara said, "This is for you. For the other night."
Claire tore it open and found the gift card to a north side spa on the inside. "Aw, you didn't have to do that."

"Yes, I did."

Handing her a second envelope, she said, "This one's for Kate. Maybe you two can go together."

"Sweet. Thanks very much." After tucking them in her backpack, she turned and asked with a chuckle, "So what's going on?"

"Can you stand up a second?"

"Sure."

She no sooner hoisted herself into a standing position when Sara enveloped her in a bear hug. "Claire, you were right."

Laughing, she patted Sara's back and said, "Tell my boys that, would ya?"

After they both sat back down, Claire looked expectantly at her transformed friend. "Why do I have a feeling this has something to with your visit the other night?"

With a nod, Sara replied, "It does." She pointed to her head. "I changed my hair."

"Love it."

"I did not tell Andrew."

"Oh. How come?"

"I chickened out, but I just went to confession this morning." At this, her eyes began to fill again, and Claire smiled broadly.

"I'm so proud of you. I know how hard that must've been." Taking her by the shoulders, Claire asked, "Don't you feel amazing now?"

Sara nodded, but the smile left her face. "No, that's a lie. I still have to tell Andrew."

"So what are you waiting for?"

"I can't do it. At the gala, on the dance floor, he told me..." Lowering her voice, she said, "He told me he loved me. I panicked and left."

Claire's eyes popped open. "Oh no! Where are you staying?"

"I'm afraid to tell you."

Giving her a droll look, Claire asked, "Nancy's?"

Sara nodded.

With a shrug, Claire said, "Well then she must not be so bad after all."

A quiet moment passed between the two before she said, "But she's not Andrew, is she?"

Again, Sara nodded.

"Don't wait too long, hon. He's a good one. I wouldn't let him get away if I were you."

* * *

Staring down an appointment-free Monday, Andrew knew he ought to check out some issues he noticed with the organ pipes at the back of the church before the Bishop's visit over Easter weekend. After the school students and parishioners cleared out following 8:00 am Mass, he changed back into his jeans and a T-shirt and ascended the steps for the messy job. He was only up there a few minutes, when he heard the door directly below him open and clang shut.

Must be one of the janitors.

After a moment, he heard another door close.

Assessing the pipes, trying to locate any potential trouble spots, Andrew froze when he heard a chilling admission rise up from the room below.

The confessional.

He never would have gone up there if he knew Father was doing confessions. They normally only made themselves available to do that before and after Mass on Sundays. But then again, it was Holy Week.

After he heard the door open below, he held his breath, not wanting to make a sound.

"Yes, Father. Thank you."

Sara?

As Andrew stood there stunned, everything fell into place like tumblers in a lock—her reaction the other night, what she told him about her past, what he now knew she did. It all made sense.

When he got home that night, Andrew did something he had never done in his own apartment before. He turned on the stereo.

Running his finger along the album cover spines, it took him only a second to find the one he was looking for—especially since he had alphabetized them shortly after moving in. He carefully pulled out *Mudslide Slim and the Blue Horizon,* set it on the turntable with side two up, and dropped the needle softly on the smooth band between the first and second tracks. By the time the song finished, he had an idea. By the time he listened to it at least a dozen more times, and ran it by his brother, he had a plan.

* * *

For the remainder of the week, Sara buried herself in work. The spring concert season was heating up, and she was already starting to get notices about summer festivals in the area featuring big name artists, veteran artists, and breakthrough artists.

Before she knew it, Saturday arrived and Nancy started assaulting her with things to do as soon as she woke up. "There's a celebrity wine tasting at Eataly. You can help me review a new burger joint in Wicker Park, or we could check out that hot new chef at a tapas bar down the street. What sounds good to you?"

With a heavy sigh, Sara sipped her coffee. "To tell you the truth, Nance, all I really want to do is go home to Andrew, but I burned that bridge."

Pouring herself a third cup, Nancy retorted, "From what you told me, you took a blowtorch to it."

At that, Sara set her mug down with a sloshy thud. "Hey, I did him a *favor*." Sopping up the coffee she had sloshed on the counter with a paper towel, she explained for at least the twelfth time since moving in with her pal, "It's better that he not get in too deep with me only to be disappointed later."

Nancy smirked. "Yeah, you just keep telling yourself that, sweetie."

An ache welled up in her, and she buried her face in her hands. "You're right. I blew it."

Sara then folded her arms on the kitchen table, laid her head down, and groaned. "What am I gonna do?"

When Nancy didn't offer anything by way of advice, she lifted her head and tried to put words to the ache in her heart. "I miss him so much. I miss watching him sleep before I leave for work in the morning, the sound of his voice, the feel of him in my arms." She reached for another paper towel, pressed it to her eyes, and added, "Even the way he never let me get away with anything."

"Well, if you ask me, I'm glad to have you back and unattached."

Sara looked at her, dumbfounded. "I just poured my heart out to you, and that's all you have to say?"

Nancy shrugged, seemingly unaffected by her friend's heartache. "What can I say? You've raised the bar so high at karaoke, we can't win without you. Besides, we're due. So, like I said, I'm thrilled to have you back."

With a long sigh, Sara replied, "Glad to be back."
Not.

CHAPTER TWELVE

———

*"After silence, that which comes nearest to
expressing the inexpressible is music."*
—Aldous Huxley

As much as Sara was not in the mood for a karaoke
smack down, there was something about being back at Kildare's
that she found comforting. The whole familiarity of the place
made her feel good. It was crowded, but not too crowded—
noisy, but not too noisy. The bar was draped with colored Italian
lights. It smelled like greasy burgers, and it looked just like her
Aunt Ruby's rec room—only with lots more beers signs, pool
tables, and a live band.

"Oh no, she's back," Tom Newman from Sports roared
the minute he saw her approach.

She fist-bumped him on her way to join the Lifestyle
team. "Hey, Tom. Ready to lose?"

"Where's Nancy? She said to meet her here, and that was
over an hour ago."

Felicity shrugged. "Don't know what to tell you. She was
here a while ago. Bathroom, maybe?"

Whatever.

"Welcome back, Sara. What can I get you?"

Sara looked up at the waitress wearing a black T-shirt
with the bar's name blazoned across her chest.

She didn't really feel like drinking anything. Hadn't all
week. But still, she felt compelled to ask, "What are the
specials?"

Even after making her recite the entire list, nothing appealed to Sara. "Yeah, I'm good for now. Just ice water. Thanks."

She watched Tom saunter up to the stage as the band started playing the opening chords to "Waiting for a Girl Like You."

"All right, here we go," Nancy said as she slid into a chair next to Sara. "Old Tom there thinks he's gonna hang onto that trophy with an old Foreigner song?"

"I don't think so," she shouted up to the stage, laughing.

"Where've you been?" Sara asked her.

Giving her head a quick shake, Nancy said something about checking out the competition before she heckled Tom some more.

When he was done, the crowd leveled him with applause as he made his way back to his table, gloating every step of the way.

"Slob," Nancy hissed.

Then nudging Sara, she said, "OK, kid. You're up."

Sinking lower in her chair, she protested, "Sorry, I'm not really up to it tonight."

"Don't apologize to me. Get your ass up there and apologize to him."

"Who?"

Sara turned and looked toward the stage where it looked like someone was relieving the band's keyboard player.

Andrew?

She looked back at Nancy and gasped, "What's he doing here?"

With a devious grin, she nudged Sara. "There's only one way to find out."

Feeling like the blood was rushing to her toes, she made her way to the stage. Andrew, seated at the keyboard, didn't look at her. The rest of the band stayed on the stage grinning at her but didn't look like they were going to play.

OK...

Then, from behind her, she heard the opening strains of the song she had sung to him when he was sick, the tattoo of which Father Steve had liked so much, that she and Kerry used to sing together after their mom bolted, before which, she used to sing her to sleep with.

Her breath hitched, and a rush of tears caught in her throat.

The music stopped.

Then she heard Andrew's voice behind her, as calm and reassuring as it had always been. As if she hadn't walked out on him exactly one week before.

"You've got this."

Turning to look back at him, her heart swelled. She took a deep breath and listened as he counted her in, unable to pull her eyes away until he gave a hard nod.

Out of a sad, ridiculous habit, she scanned the crowd for her mother's face while she sang. As expected, her mother wasn't there.

She was halfway through the second chorus, though, when her eyes fell on a familiar figure leaning against the bar.

She stopped singing. Right there in the middle of the song.

Nancy told her later you could've heard a pin drop.

Sara whispered into the microphone. "Kerry?"

She watched as the man stood straight up. When his face broke into a smile and he held his arms out toward her, she gasped, "Oh my God."

Trembling, with tears filling her eyes, she barged through the crowd to get to him. Leaping into his embrace, he stumbled backward as he caught her.

According to Nancy, that's when the crowd went crazy.

By the look on her brother's face, he was as glad to see her as she was to see him, and she didn't let go for a very long time. When she finally did, she looked around, trying to spot Andrew.

"Oh, he left awhile ago, sweetie. Said something about having to get back to church," Nancy said, pulling a face. "Aren't you going to introduce me to your brother?"

Head smack, of course—the Easter Vigil service is tonight.

Quashing back her disappointment at not being able to see Andrew and introduce him, she said, "Of course. Where are my manners? Nancy, this is my big brother, Kerry Cleff. Kerry, my friend, Nancy, assistant food editor at the *Gazette*."

Introductions over, Nancy pulled Sara aside. "Listen, I'm gonna crash at my Mom's tonight so you two can catch up at my place." With a wink, she added, "*Mi casa es tu casa.*"

"Thanks, Nance. I didn't know your mom was in town."

"She's not. That's why I'm crashing at her place."

"Ah…"

Wondering how many people had a hand in arranging this most unexpected, but overwhelmingly wonderful, surprise, she looked at her brother. "Ready to go?"

"Ready." They headed for the door. Once outside, he handed a valet his ticket.

Sara stopped in her tracks. "Wait. How did you get here?"

Kerry looked at her sideways. "My truck…?"

"No, I mean here," she clarified, pointing to Kildare's.

"That, little sister, is a long story."

Once they were settled on Nancy's red leather sectional with a couple of cold Goose Island pale ales, she asked Kerry to tell it to her.

"Yeah, so I was working at the marina Wednesday, checking boats comin' out of dry dock, when these two guys come walking in, one claiming to be a Chicago cop. So, naturally, I figured it had something to do with you."

Nudging him with her foot, she grinned. "Shut up."

"But when they told me who they were and what they wanted, we headed over to the grill and talked about it over lunch."

Sara smiled at the thought of her two favorite men on the planet sitting across a booth from each other in the Bay Shore Bar and Grill looking out at the sun catching on the dark-blue water of the cove. She wished she had been there with them.

"He's a pretty nice guy."

Sara blinked. "Who?"

"Andrew. Who'd you think?"

"Sorry, I was just picturing you guys up there. I'm really glad you got a chance to meet him."

"Yeah. Like I said, he seems like a great guy."

Rolling her head back, she groaned. "He's amazing." Looking right at her brother, she asked, "And do you know what I did?"

Kerry shook his head.

"I walked out on him. Can you believe that? Well, I'm sure he told you."

Again, Kerry shook his head.

"He didn't?"

"Nope."

"Oh."

"But he did ask me something."

"What?"

"He told me not to tell you."

Incredulous, Sara exclaimed, "So why did you say anything?"

Kerry shrugged and with a wink said, "Just to torture you."

With eyes narrowed, Sara tilted her head and sighed, "And to think I missed you."

The siblings stayed up well past midnight catching up on everything, exchanging stories. It wasn't until she sensed that he was ready to call it a night that Sara grabbed his hand and said, "Hey, listen. I just want to say how sorry I am. For everything."

Kerry gave her hand a squeeze. "Me too."

With her eyes starting to fill, she pressed her lips together and tried to explain the unexplainable. "I made a really stupid mistake. I knew I should've told you, come to you for help. I just didn't want to disappoint you again. So I tried to fix it on my own."

She swatted at the tears coursing down her cheeks as she whispered, "Tried to make it go away. And that just made everything worse."

Again, Kerry held out his arms. "Come here."

"Everything's gonna be OK," he breathed as he rested his cheek against the top of her head.

Sara gave him a hard squeeze. "I love you so much."

"I love you, too, Trouble."

Getting up early the next morning so Kerry could get back up to the marina that was gearing up for its busy season, she hugged him tight, thanked him for making the trip, and promised to visit very soon.

Before pulling away, he rolled down his window and motioned her over.

"What?"

"He loves you, ya know?"

Sara took a deep breath and blew it out before looking her brother in the eye. With a dismissive shake of her head, she said, "He wouldn't if he knew what I did."

Kerry just smirked at her. "That, little sister, is where you're wrong."

Feeling a wave of hope wash over her, she gripped his flannel shirt-covered arm that was resting on the window opening. "How do you know? Did you tell him? Did he say something? Did you guys talk about me?"

Arching an eyebrow, he pulled his mouth into the patented Kerry Cleff shit-eating grin and said with a wink, "You're just gonna have to trust me on this one."

"No. Come on. Don't do this to me."

Leaning out the window, he gave her a peck on the cheek. "See ya, little sister."

As he pulled away, he called out, "You better invite me to the wedding."

* * *

With Mass not starting for over half an hour yet, Andrew looked out over the pews that were beginning to fill with parishioners and *creasters*— people who only went to Mass on Christmas and Easter, feeling fairly confident that his chances of being offered a full-time position at the parish were slim to none. Especially after news of him having a female roommate, who was clearly more than just a roommate, surfaced after their very public display of affection at the gala.

With nothing to show for it other than a broken heart and a vow to never again try to recruit choir members in the frozen food section of the grocery store, he took solace in knowing that he was at least able to help mend a bridge between Sara and her brother.

Seeing the Bishop's vicars milling around at the back of the church, he took a look at the choir, dressed in their finest, all warmed up and ready to go. He pressed his lips into the semblance of a smile for the few who were smiling at him until his eyes fell on the empty chair next to Glynnis.

Without Sara in his life, he wasn't sure he even wanted to stay at this parish, let alone in Chicago.

With a sigh, he started shuffling through his music to make sure, one more time, that he had everything in order.

Thumbing through it, he saw that he didn't. "Fanfare" by Nicolas Jacques Lemmens was missing. Panic welling up inside him, he looked at Marge who sprang up from her seat and rushed over to the organ bench where he was perched. "What's wrong?"

"I don't have the recessional music."

"I'll check the choir room."

The memory of him taking it out of his binder while sitting at his desk came rushing back. "Never mind, Marge. I know where it is. Be right back."

I don't have time for this.

Cutting through the crowded narthex, he had just closed the main office door behind him when it opened again, and he heard a familiar voice exclaim, "Happy Easter, Andrew."

* * *

Where did all these cars come from?

Sara couldn't find a parking space within a 4-block radius of St. Matthias until she happened on a little VW Bug pulling out of a space just down the street. Backing in with just centimeters to spare on either end, she hopped out and made her way to the church as quickly as she could.

On finding that the narthex was nearly as crowded as the Paul McCartney concert at Wrigley Field, she elbowed her way into the church itself, knowing that was the only place on the planet where she wanted to be. Where she belonged.

Finally squeezing her way through the door, she looked toward the front, hoping to see Andrew and catch his reaction, if any. But he wasn't there.

What the hell? Where is he?

Unable to comprehend him not being there on Easter of all days, she closed her eyes and hung her head back as she fought to keep her emotions in check.

Claire was right. I waited too long. I've lost him.

Not sure what to do next, she just stood there, panting like an idiot, watching a small contingent of liturgical dignitaries mill about. She stepped out of the way. Crestfallen, she decided to check his office on her way out.

Relishing the quiet and solitude of the main reception area, she closed the door behind her and started making her way down the corridor to his office, out of which Andrew had just stepped with music in hand.

"Sara. What are you doing here?"

He was wearing a crisp white button-down shirt—which she wanted to wrinkle terribly by gripping it with both hands and pulling him to her. And she would have, too, if he looked as happy to see her as she was to see him, but he didn't.

So she started talking. "I wanted to say I'm sorry. We had a deal, and I completely dropped my end of the bargain."

He lifted his chin and held her gaze while pulling his office door closed. "The deal ended today, so no worries. You're off the hook."

Ouch. Didn't see that coming.

"And I wanted to thank you for bringing Kerry back into my life."

For a split second, she noticed his eyes narrow. She kept going.

"That was the best gift anyone's ever given me."

Something was going on behind those baby blues, but she couldn't put her finger on it. So she kept going.

"But that doesn't even come close to the gift that you were—"

She took a step toward him. "*Are* to me."

Save for his jaw clenching, his face remained expressionless, waiting.

So she kept talking.

"Before we met, I was a hot mess, which I never really minded until you came along and screwed everything up."

Seeing his eyes soften, she kept going.

"That night? When I told you I had done things that made me believe I didn't deserve you. Well, I know better now. I've been to confession, and, thanks to you, I've reconciled with my brother. Because of you, I feel like I have a chance at a brand new life."

With just one more thing to say, she ignored the door that was opening behind him.

"But all that doesn't mean a thing if you're not in it."

Just as he opened his mouth to respond, a pretty blonde head popped out of his office doorway and flashed her an apologetic smile. "Sorry to interrupt." The petite body that went along with it came out and stood next to Andrew.

Leanne.

Feeling like she had just been punched in the gut, Sara couldn't help but stare as the Barbie doll reached up, gave Andrew a kiss on the cheek, and whispered, "Take care."

Coming to her senses, Sara turned and started for the main office door, barely able to see straight.

"Sara, don't go."

Leanne came up behind her. "It's not what you think. I just came to apologize. And to say good-bye." Nodding back to where Andrew was still standing, she smiled and said, "He's all yours."

Then, with a quick wave, she opened the door and went through it.

After that, Andrew couldn't talk even if he wanted to because Sara had given in to her urge to wrinkle him. Most terribly.

* * *

After the last chord of "Fanfare" finished reverberating throughout the church, Andrew noticed Marge waiting at his elbow.

"Weren't you wearing a white shirt earlier?"

He just smiled, thinking of the new reason he had to keep spare dress clothes in his office.

When Sara came out of the choir room after putting her music away, he slid off the bench and took her in his arms. Right there in front of everybody.

"Ready to go home?"

Through a blushing grin, she replied, "I thought you'd never ask."

When most everyone had gone, the two were walking arm-in-arm down the main aisle of the church when Father Steve came rushing up to him. "Andrew, wonderful news. The Bishop told the parish council members attending the reception that he's going to recommend you for a special commission to play at Holy Name Cathedral."

He stopped walking. "Is that right?"

The priest laughed. "Yes, and they've agreed to extend you a permanent position here. Isn't that wonderful?"

With that, he smiled at Sara and said, "This day just keeps getting better and better."

* * *

On a warm, humid Saturday in June, Claire had just slipped a firecracker-red, taffeta bridesmaid dress over her head in the bridal room at St. Matthias.

"Sara, can you zip me up, please?"

"Sure thing." She moved behind her to tug the zipper up as Claire tried yanking the bodice up higher over her enviable cleavage.

"Thank God they have the air-conditioning cranked. I can't believe Paul and I got here late. Tomás and Marc took off for Boy Scout camp this morning, so when I went to remind Luke that he'd be watching Jonah, he reminded me that he'd been invited to his buddy's lake house starting today, so then I had to track down our neighbor Jacquie to see if she could take Jonah. Then, on the way here I realized that I completely forgot to get panty hose."

After checking her reflection, she continued, "OK. It's official. Lucy DeRosa is a miracle worker. If you look at me straight on, you can't even tell I'm seven months pregnant."

Sara glanced at her standing there in a strapless floor length gown that, while not fitted like the rest of the dresses, looked lovely on her.

"I know, I'm boring you to death, right?" Claire asked.

Sara just smiled and checked her lipstick in the mirror next to her. "No worries. Hey, did you get my letter?"

"No. When did you send it?"

"About ten minutes ago."

Claire picked up her phone to check her inbox and read:

Dear Plate Spinner—

My boyfriend and I only have three things in common: our address, the fact that he's a musician and I write about musicians, and that we both agree James Taylor is, hands down, one of the best acoustic performers ever. Otherwise, we're total opposites. He's reserved. I'm bold. He's neat as a pin. I'm not. He comes from a big family. I don't. He wants to get married and have kids, and I so do too.

Signed,
Deliriously Happy

"And it shows," the advice columnist exclaimed. "Look at you. You're beaming. Almost more than the bride."

Sara lifted her shoulders in a happy little squirm as Aubrey joined them and announced, "I think they want us in the narthex."

Just then, the door to the adjoining bathroom flung open and Mattie stepped into the room with her sister, Claudia, following as she cinched the last button on her bodice. "There. All set, hon."

"How do I look?" the bride-to-be asked.

After the others had finished gushing over her, Sara just shook her head with a disapproving look on her face. "Poor Nick."

Mattie's eyes grew wide. "What do you mean?"

With a laugh, Sara explained. "He's waited so long for this day, and you're going to go out there looking like this? Torture. Sheer torture to make him stand up there with you in front of a priest and not be able to lay a hand on you for what—an hour?"

After Mattie let out a guttural laugh, she leaned over and kissed Sara on the cheek. "Thanks. I needed some comic relief."

As soon as they stepped into the narthex, Sara's mouth pulled into a smug little smile when she heard the organ music start to play.

While Andrew had seen her gown, he had yet to actually see her in it.

"All right," said Mrs. Trotter, the effervescent church-appointed wedding coordinator. "Does everybody remember the order from last night?"

Being the tallest, Sara would go first, followed by Aubrey, and then Claire, after which Claudia would follow, and then Mattie on the arm of Lester Crenshaw.

They each stood obediently still as the coordinator checked to make sure their red tulle wraps covered their shoulders before handing them their bouquets.

"Oh, you girls look so pretty," she grinned.

Sara turned and looked at Aubrey, noting that she was paler than usual. "Here's a trick, Aubs. Just focus on my back. Don't look at anything else, OK?"

Aubrey gave her a nervous smile and whispered, "Thanks."

After a moment, Mrs. Trotter swung open the door to the church and put Sara in position. Looking straight ahead, she could see Tom, Mattie's brother-in-law, waiting for her by the front row wearing a traditional black tuxedo. Behind him stood John, a running buddy of Nick's, then Claire's husband Paul, followed by Nick's best friend and best man, Scott who, at that moment, nudged the fidgety groom and nodded to the back of the church.

Then Sara switched her focus to the only man she had eyes for, but from where she stood, his face was hidden behind the music in front of him. In a well-coordinated move, she heard Mrs. Trotter whisper, "Go ahead" at the exact same moment Andrew hit the first note of Pachelbel's "Canon in D."

Here we go.

Sara took a deep breath and stepped onto the white runner covering the main aisle. It wasn't until she was halfway to the altar that she was finally able to make eye contact with Andrew.

Seeing him do a quick double-take, she shouldn't have been surprised when she heard him miss a note. Still, she waited until she was standing just a few feet away to turn and mouth, "Amateur," before she puckered her lips and delivered a quick air kiss which he promptly returned with a grin.

"You did great," she whispered to Aubrey as soon as she joined her in front of the altar.

They watched as Claire and then Claudia joined them.

Everyone in attendance stood as soon as they heard Andrew start Mendelssohn's "Wedding March." One glance at the groom and Sara knew with absolute certainty that Mattie would be loved to bits for the rest of her life—a sentiment made that much sweeter when both the bride and the groom's voices broke while saying their vows. It was everything she could do to not picture herself and Andrew standing in front of Father Steve, exchanging vows.

Someday...

"You may kiss the bride," she heard the priest say. While everyone else's attention was on the crazy happy couple, Sara couldn't keep her eyes from drifting to the man she had tried to ditch at Bell's Market just four months before. Seeing that he already had his eyes on her, she felt her cheeks warm, likely turning them as red as her dress.

"How about a round of applause for the new Mr. and Mrs. Nicoli DeRosa?"

Thankful for the diversion, Sara turned and before long, heard Andrew play the recessional music. After filing out in the reverse order, Sara lined up with the others to form a receiving line in the narthex and then head back into the church for pictures.

A short time later, she was riding shotgun in a dark-blue Jeep flying north on I-94, heading for the reception at the North Shore Club.

As part of her ongoing effort to educate him on the classics, Sara selected a CD for the drive.

"Today's lesson," she announced before shoving it in the slot in his dashboard, "is Led Zeppelin's *Houses of the Holy.*"

He glanced at it with his eyebrow arched. "Why do I have a feeling there aren't any hymns on it?"

"That is correct."

Along the way, Sara did her best to ignore the way he winced when Robert Plant let loose on "The Rain Song." And the way he managed to bounce his left knee whenever he wasn't breaking or shifting gears.

"Are you OK?"

Before he had a chance to answer, she took a sharp breath and exhaled, "Oh my," at the sight of the sprawling mansion that apparently served as a high-end clubhouse.

Ken doll central.

Andrew got out and walked around to her side after handing a valet his keys. "Are you nervous?"

She pulled a face as she adjusted her wrap around her shoulders. "Pfft...please. I've sung in front of crowds before. And it's just the one song."

"But it's their first dance as husband and wife," he countered as he lunged in front of her to open the door. "Talk about pressure."

She stopped and frowned at him. "What's with you? You're the one who seems nervous. Are you OK?"

He gave her a quick nod. "Yep. I'm fine."

Not convinced, she suggested that they find the rest of the bridal party who were, not surprisingly, congregated by the bar.

After a glass of wine, Andrew seemed back to himself, and, when they started serving dinner, he gladly took his place at a table with Father Steve, a couple of Nick's aunts, and Mrs. Lester Crenshaw. Seated at the bridal table, Sara looked at him every time someone clinked their glass with a spoon to get the newlyweds to kiss, thinking of little more than what she would do to him when they got home later.

In the meantime, she took another swig of champagne and waited, as instructed, for the director of the band Lester had hired to call her over. At Mattie's special request, she would sing the one song she could always count on to snatch the karaoke trophy away from the Sports section.

That, along with a pair of his-and-her, matching, plaid, flannel pajamas, and she figured she was set in the wedding gift department.

The staff had no sooner cleared the last of the dinner dishes than they cleared the tables from the dance floor. Sara took her place in front of the band and watched as Mattie and Nick got in position.

Somewhere in the midst of singing "Because You Loved Me" to the newlyweds, she realized her focus had shifted to Andrew standing off to the side. She had never cared for the song. So overplayed, so schmaltzy, so...*sappy*. But on that day, in that moment, it brought tears to her eyes, and she had to fight to keep her voice from warbling.

By the time she had finished, Andrew was at the ready with a tissue.

After that, they danced until her feet hurt, but still, he seemed on edge. She figured it was because he wasn't drinking. They did, after all, have a long drive home.

"Come on, Sara," a tipsy Aubrey cried. "Mattie's gonna throw her bouquet off the terrace."

"Oh." She looked at Andrew, his cheeks red from exertion as he cracked open a water bottle.

"Go for it."

"Are ya sure? With my height, it's pretty much in the bag."

He nodded and waved her off.

She and Aubrey took their place on the manicured lawn beyond the stone terrace just outside of the ballroom. Sure enough, amid the slim field of single women in attendance, she nabbed Mattie's bouquet without a whole lot of effort. Granted, if Nancy had been there, it probably would've come to blows.

Next it was Andrew's turn. Amused, Sara stood nearby under the dark-blue velvet sky that was dotted with a million twinkling stars and watched as he positioned himself front and center, directly in the path of Nick's anticipated trajectory.

It seemed everyone was closing in around them, cheering while Nick teased the garter off of his giggling bride's thigh and then turned his back to the waiting bachelors. When he finally tossed it behind him, Sara watched it sail as if in slow motion through the air until one hand and one hand only reached up and grabbed it.

Before she knew what was happening, the crowd parted. With Mattie and Nick and the rest of the bridal party beaming behind him, she saw Andrew walk directly to her, garter in hand. And then, dropping to one knee, he proposed. Right there in front of everybody.

ABOUT THE AUTHOR

Barbara is an award-winning novelist and second-generation journalist. After spending a decade in maternity clothes, she has five boys to show for it and much fodder for her column, The Plate Spinner Chronicles, a long-running feature in the *Chicago Tribune*. A member of RWA's Windy City chapter, she still dreams of the day when her to-do list includes "Send NY Times book critic thank you note" and "Accept Godiva's request to be a taste-tester."

To learn more about Barbara, visit her online at
www.barbaravalentin.com

Enjoyed this book? Check out the other romantic comedy novels in the *Assignment: Romance* series! Now in print and all ebook formats from Gemma Halliday Publishing:

Mattie Ross is the *Chicago Gazette's* advice columnist, The Plate Spinner. But her latest assignment—training for the Chicago Marathon—has her paired up with the last man she'd ever want to train with...or fall for!

False Start
available now!

Claire is a burned out breadwinner ready to ditch her quest for happily-ever-after, and her husband, Paul, has traded his high-powered job for life as a stay-at-home dad. But when Claire drafts a letter to the Plate Spinner, both of their lives change forever...

Help Wanted
available now!